DNR:

Love's Final Gift

Teresa Little Smith

Dedication

For my husband Dan, an author in his own right who gave me the inspiration to sit down at my computer and write. Write what? Write what you know, advised Dan, and what better to write about than so very many patients who have inspired me to care harder, love more, and advocate for at the top of my lungs in order to meet their needs. Thank you, Dan. In case I don't say it enough, you are my world, and I love you.

For my beautiful children, Roze and Alex. I can't imagine this journey called life without both of you in it. God knows, you are my greatest blessings, and you prove to me every day that my world is Heaven, right here on earth. I love you both, MOST!

Acknowledgement

The number of nurses with whom I have worked over forty-plus years in nursing are too vast to mention by name. Your compassion, humanity and skill with patient care have helped me become the professional I am today and kept my focus on what truly matters: our patients. My gratitude, most especially, to the nursing staff of the SICU at Hospital of Saint Raphael, and to Georgianna Hull, our brilliant and the most compassionate Nurse Manager for whom I have ever worked: I am in awe of what you ladies and gentlemen accomplish on a daily basis despite insurance cuts, administrative overload, short staffing, and the frequent hostility and violence directed to our front line workers. I see you, and I honor you.

Great thanks to Marji Kellman MS, RN who knows every secret about me and is still my bestie! Vanessa Pomarico EdD, FNP-BC, APRN, FAANP who graced me with sisterhood and the benefit of her vast expertise to mentor me through my professional development and journey to Advanced Practice. And my first readers, Kathleen Surprenant and Marji, who convinced me my story was worth reading. Thank you all, so very much!

Contents

Prologue

Isaac was the luckiest man on earth. He was lying in bed next to the most beautiful woman in the world and she loved him in an almost surreal way, one he never could have imagined, not even in his wildest imagination. Even so, despite the perfection of her love, he knew, in his soul, he loved her more. Hovering in that dreamlike place somewhere between the liquid arousal of twilight sleep and the deep oblivion of slumber, he rolled over and pulled her against his chest as he had done so many nights before. Burying his face into the softness of her curls, he breathed in the familiar lavender scent of her shampoo and then sketched an imaginary line across silky skin where her nightgown dipped in front. Reaching underneath, ever so gently, he stroked the softness of her belly and then his fingers trailed downward, basking in the warmth and softness and love that were his wife.

Slowly she opened her eyes, lids still heavy with sleep. She caressed his face in a dream-like trance with soft hands that began to tingle with the heat from his body. She stroked cheeks that were coarse with several days' worth of stubble, customary compensation for a long weekend on-call, so commonplace in the life of a surgeon. As her knee slid between his legs and lifted gently against evidence of her husband's arousal, he pulled her more closely into his embrace, enchanted by the perfection of her body and the miracle of their life together.

She tipped her head back to kiss him gently and with a soft voice still husky from slumber, she whispered to him, "Wake up, Isaac, it's time to wake up."

Chapter 1

Isaac Goldman graduated tenth in his class from the prestigious Yale School of Medicine. With eight years of schooling behind him, he looked ahead to several years of internship/residency/fellowship, which would grant him the privilege of becoming a board-certified neurosurgeon. Well, if truth be told, he would not become just "A" neurosurgeon, but rather, "THE" neurosurgeon.

Academically, Isaac was brilliant. Like most interns beginning the first post-graduate year known as PGY-1, following four grueling years of the hell known as medical school, Isaac believed he knew everything there was to know about "saving lives and stamping out disease." Like most surgical interns, Isaac was a legend in his own mind. He had great expectations that an internship and neurosurgical residency would be a breeze. More aptly put, these years were merely a stepping stone to his illustrious career as a neurosurgeon. As well, like many surgical interns at the start of their post-graduate years, Isaac was about to fall flat on his face. He was twenty-six years old, still wet behind the ears, a starry-eyed neophyte on the brink of the rest of his professional life. He was also unbelievably naive to how to survive in this chaotic and foreign world known as the hospital.

Isaac shaved quickly to give himself extra time to grab a coffee on his way to the hospital and his very first day as a real, bona-fide surgeon. As he pulled the razor across his face, Isaac's mind wandered. He marveled at how differently a scalpel felt in his hand as living flesh gave way to the ice-cold steel of a surgical blade, in comparison to the cold, stiff flesh of the embalmed cadaver he had dissected so painstakingly in Gross Anatomy during the first semester of medical school. He envisioned the awe of a surgical team who stood by in wonder as his confident surgeon's hands removed a tumor, previously deemed inoperable by other, less skilled neurosurgeons. He envisioned dropping it triumphantly into a small steel basin held by a starry-eyed scrub technician, as other neurosurgeons observing in the gallery "oo-ed" and "ah-ed" at his meticulous technique and masterful expertise. He reveled in the glory of having saved another patient from a certain life of misery and debilitation as he basked, humbly, of course, in the praises of his colleagues.

Isaac imagined his long, confident strides to the Surgical Waiting room where he would brush off the accolades of a tearfully grateful family with rehearsed detachment and feigned humility in contrast to the arrogance he believed he was entitled to by sole virtue of his God-given talent. Then, as he mentally composed his acceptance speech for the most prestigious and coveted award bestowed upon very few in his chosen field, Isaac sliced right into his chin.

Unable to staunch the steady trickle of blood that welled up in the divot he had just created, Isaac cursed under his breath and hastily applied a sliver of toilet paper to the wound. It immediately flushed crimson. He glanced at his watch and cursed again, then promptly forgot his bloody chin as he flew out the door towards the start of his surgical career.

Saint Michael the Archangel Hospital was a small community hospital with a well-run surgical residency program, but its size belied its stellar reputation for producing top-notch surgeons. Isaac would leave St. Mike's capable and competent, with all necessary clinical proficiency and technical skill catalogued in his brain. Isaac had "matched" with this program from a list of top teaching hospitals in the country, and although he would have preferred either the hallowed grounds of Mass Gen or iconic Baylor, he was satisfied with his final placement. He couldn't complain. At least it was a surgical program, and not some boringly mundane medical residency. Like his mother, who had proudly sported a "My Son, The Doctor" tee shirt at his graduation party, Isaac was certain he would be recognized before long as the best intern ever to cross the threshold. Heck, he would be lauded as the best neurosurgeon ever to complete St. Mike's program, period.

On the first day of the first week that would prove to be the most chaotic of his life, Isaac showed up on the Surgical Unit at eight o'clock in the morning, stethoscope around his neck and a cup of coffee in hand. A pristinely starched and pressed lab coat covered his freshly ironed shirt and tie. The well-rehearsed aura of casual arrogance, which he had practiced in his bathroom mirror every morning since beginning medical school, adorned his face. Forgotten in his haste to get to the hospital was a bloody piece of toilet paper, firmly plastered to his chin. By now, it had become dark maroon, puckered, and adhered to what was, ironically, the first incision of his surgical career.

Isaac strode confidently onto the surgical unit which was to become his second home for the next three months, as well as for a good part of his residency. Although the patient population in this unit included the "overflow" of appendectomies, cholecystectomies, and any other -ectomies within the realm of General Surgery, its main focus was Surgical Oncology. Removal of cancerous growth was often the first step in the treatment of this dreaded disease, followed by chemotherapy and/or radiation. All treatment regimens were choreographed with the honed precision of a complicated, well-rehearsed waltz.

Ultimately, as with the approach to any disease or illness, cure is the goal. Cruelly, however, sometimes "cure" could be elusive. At that point, if the cancer became uncontrollable, the goal of treatment would become palliative. Surgery would not cure the cancer, but it would remove as much tumor as possible. Known as "de-bulking," the procedure was meant to alleviate horrible side effects of the invasive tumor monster: the dreaded pain and unbearable suffering that frequently accompany a terminal diagnosis.

Isaac looked around for his senior resident, expecting to see someone in a familiar white lab coat and scrubs with either a clipboard of test results or a large manila envelope of X-ray films tucked under his arm. Though his confident façade had dimmed somewhat, he tried to appear nonchalant as he stood amidst the bustle of the unit. Isaac sipped his coffee to hide his mounting panic as he racked his brain to remember what he had been told about the schedule for day number one. He heard a few snickers and fragmented whispers.

"…Must be the new intern…"

"… What time is it anyway…?"

"Aren't they already in the OR?"

Isaac's racing thoughts skidded to a halt, and he was seized by abject terror. He had committed the first gaff of his professional career, and it hadn't even started yet.

Out of the corner of his eye, Isaac noticed a solitary figure, with smudged eyes and the weary look of a night shift nurse coming off a long and hectic twelve-hour stretch. She sat at the nurses' station and scribbled furiously to document the goings on of her patients who had kept her busy and on her feet for much of the shift. Momentarily distracted, Isaac studied a small wrinkle in her brow that deepened as she struggled to remember in detail the sequence of events that had occurred during her twelve hour shift and then regurgitate it onto the pages of the chart with as much detail as her exhausted mind would allow.

The unit was short-staffed, as usual. Often, the nursing staff didn't have time to get basic nursing care done, let alone complete the overwhelming amount of paperwork that took up so much of their precious time. A hot cup of coffee was often a longed-for pipe dream, and visits to the restroom were complicated by the duress of finding a coworker who could monitor additional patients during the short time a trip to the bathroom entailed. By the end of a seemingly endless night shift, sleep-deprived minds focused on two things: reporting all life-saving information as quickly and as succinctly as possible to the oncoming shift and driving home as rapidly and as safely as possible to a soft, comfy bed and blissful sleep.

Isaac watched as she scanned the unit with the keen eyes of an experienced and seasoned nurse accustomed to detecting subtle changes in her patient's condition before they escalated into full-blown emergencies. He blanched as her eyes settled on him. Omniscience and arrogance gave way to confusion and guilt as Isaac said a silent prayer that she wouldn't laugh at him.

Isaac kept his voice cool and, he hoped, authoritative. "I'm looking for Dr. Simon. What time will he be rounding?"

At least she had the decency to bite her cheek and suppress the smirk Isaac knew he deserved, but then he groaned inwardly at her response.

"Well, 'he' is actually 'she,' and I'll page her for you. She's probably in the OR already- gall bladder, I think." As she reached for the phone, the nurse tossed over her shoulder, "You may as well take a seat. If she's scrubbed in, it could be a while."

To Isaac's chagrin, he had been dealt the triumvirate of intern embarrassment: mortification that he had been late for rounds, humiliation by a lowly nurse who mocked him with that poorly hidden smirk, and utter degradation by her comeuppance that Dr. Simons was, in reality, a woman. He walked into a small, glass-enclosed room located at the end of the desk, lovingly referred to as "the bubble" by staff members who relied on its seclusion for momentary escape and peace of mind. Isaac sat down at a table littered with plastic wrappers from the many packets of crackers which often substituted for dinner. Unused sugar packets were scattered in careless piles next to cold cups of gray, filmy coffee that staff had been too busy to finish. Picking up the only reading material available, Isaac put his head down and pretended to study a patient education pamphlet entitled, "Your Diagnosis Is Cancer-Now What?" He struggled to hold down what little bit of coffee he had drunk so that he wouldn't humiliate himself by puking in front of that nurse with her smug attitude, wrinkled scrubs, and those wilted curls which had long-since escaped her barrette.

"Bitch," he muttered to himself.

"The circulator wants to talk to you. You can use that phone there."

With difficulty, Isaac summoned what little bit of self-confidence he had left and strode to the desk. He picked up the phone and heard the circulating nurse in the OR say, "Simon's elbow deep in an open gut and can't break scrub, and her resident is holding retractors and can't come to the phone. I suspect the other interns are covering the floors. Why don't you find a medical student and help out?"

Humiliated now for more reasons than he could count, Isaac hid his shame at being relegated once again to scutwork - the mundane, behind-the-scenes tasks that kept patient care flowing on a busy surgical ward. Medical students comprised the bottom rung of the totem pole which ranked hospital hierarchy, so it stood to reason these tasks often fell on their lowly shoulders. Like most neophytes in the medical world, Isaac had pushed the thought of scutwork out of his head the minute the Dean of the Medical School had handed him his diploma and bequeathed upon him the title of "Doctor."

Another mistaken impression: medical students were the only ones stuck at the bottom of this political totem pole. As a select member of the elite country club of surgical interns, Isaac had assumed himself to be far above them and looked forward to delegating his own pile of scut to the medical students who were desperate for his approval. The realization that he was reduced once again to the status of a mere medical student brought a sudden rush of scarlet to his cheeks.

Isaac struggled to regain the air of self-importance he was sure he deserved by sole virtue of the alphabet soup after his name. He tried to keep his voice firm but nonetheless, it cracked. "I'll get right on it."

Isaac felt eyes burning into his back and he turned around to find that nurse intently staring at him. "Rounds start between six and six thirty. The interns generally get here pretty early to look up labs and get notes written. Med students usually start with dressing changes on the post-ops."

She subtly brushed her hand towards her chin and added final insult to injury with a parting shot. "Oh, by the way, looks like you need a sharper razor."

"Oh my God," ran through Isaac's mind over and over. Mentally slapping himself in the forehead, he quickly ripped the bloody paper off his chin and jammed it in his pocket. If he was lucky enough, he would find a sympathetic med student who might take pity on him and let him take over a dressing change. If he was lucky at all, maybe he would score a few blood draws. Heck, he'd settle for rectal exams, as long as he could hide behind closed curtains, out of sight.

Classes in medical school had begun no earlier than eight am. On clinical days, Isaac was expected to be at rounds by seven. For the interns, rounds on a surgical floor began at six am, before the operating room even began its first case, and, more importantly, before the attending physicians arrived. It was a general rule that the interns arrived earlier than their senior residents and would have all lab results and x-rays in hand, physical assessments complete, and notes already written in the charts.

Since this was the very first day, however, Isaac had fully expected his hospital orientation to begin at eight am. Surely, the chief surgical residents wouldn't expect the brand-new interns to jump in feet first on day number one. He assumed he would have time to meet his fellow interns and maybe rub elbows with the residents. He had looked forward to the opportunity to meet the many mentors after whom the interns hoped to model themselves, the attending surgeons at St. Mike's. What Isaac had not counted on was the fact that a hospital still had to run, and a surgical schedule still had to be followed. Time was not to be wasted. Least of all, it would not be wasted on a "Welcome to the Surgical Club" party. No one was available to greet him. In fact, he thought with a sudden rush of humility, no one probably cared.

Isaac would soon learn a very important lesson. Dr. Simon cared about three things and three things only. One: spending as much time as possible in the Operating Room, knife in hand, obtaining as much hands-on surgical experience as possible before her residency and fellowship ended and she was out on her own. That time was to remain uninterrupted by ridiculous minutia that any simpleton would know, let alone an intern who supposedly had advanced post-graduate education. Two: impressing the hell out of the Fellows- those surgeons who were approaching the end of the educational portion of their training, who expected the underlings to make sure their lives were kept really darned uncomplicated and their sleep uninterrupted. Three: looking really, incredibly, phenomenally brilliant in front of each and every one of her attending surgeons to ensure the best-written recommendation possible. These were critical to scoring a coveted position in the surgical practice of her choice. That meant her interns had better do their jobs not only effectively, but also efficiently. She expected her patients to get well and get out of the hospital in the least amount of time possible. That would keep costs down and would keep the insurance companies happy. If the insurance companies were happy and did not deny payment of any portion of patients' medical bills, then administration and the Attendings were happy. By the powers of deductive logic, if administration and the Attendings were happy, then Dr. Simon was ecstatic. That certainly did not happen today, and there would be hell to pay.

Knocked off his pedestal, ego deflated, and tail tucked tightly between his legs, Isaac began his day. He glanced over his shoulder as he walked down the hallway, scowled at the top of that nurse's head, and watched as her hand once again moved furiously across the pages of the chart on the desk in front of her. Isaac chalked her attitude up to that of the "MD Wannabe's," all of whom had the superiority complex he had been warned about by interns he, himself, had worked with during senior year of med school.

"Bitch," Isaac muttered to himself again, and he quickly dropped his eyes and quickened his pace down the hall.

As Isaac turned into a patient's room, his lab coat tails flapping in his wake, he didn't see the nurse glance up and smile at his retreating back. He didn't hear her mutter to herself, "Welcome to the start of your surgical career." He couldn't have known she wondered how long it would take him to realize that medical school had just barely prepared him for his career as a surgeon and that he, a mere mortal, was not quite the "God" he assumed himself to be. He had never heard of "M-Deity Syndrome," a term she used frequently to describe the arrogance of the interns when they first began working on Surgical Oncology. This was his first day as a real doctor, and Isaac pushed her completely out of his mind as he approached the bed of his very first patient.

Chapter 2

Faith was sitting in a cabana, a tropical drink in a hollowed-out coconut shell in hand. Her heavenly salvation, embellished by a toothpick skewered with pineapple and a cherry resting on the rim of the shell, allowed her to escape the chaos of the hospital world and gently eased her into a soothing and serene state of mind. Some might refer to this as simply a vacation, but to Faith, this was Heaven.

A beautiful breeze gently caressed her sunbaked skin, and Faith sighed with contentment as a total stud muffin in a gold satin thong fanned her with palm fronds. In a blissful state of relaxation, Faith gazed at the most beautiful sunset she had ever seen and tried to ignore an unpleasant, cold sensation seeping into her body. A gentle but chilly rain began to fall as papers that suspiciously looked like her meticulously written nurses' notes blew across the pristine white, sandy beach. She rushed to pick them up and tried desperately to gather all the documents that would keep her from being sued for negligence or, even worse, before they blew away and took her career with them.

A young man in a crisply ironed shirt with a cup of coffee in his hand, a stethoscope around his neck, and a small speck of bloodied toilet paper plastered to his chin, approached her. He frowned and assumed a haughty posture, held out an official-looking envelope, and arrogantly informed her, "My name is Isaac Goldman, I am God, and you are being served..."

Startled, Faith woke up freezing, naked, immersed in a bath now gone cold and devoid of all but a few straggly bubbles. The leaky faucet slowly dripped frigid water onto her feet. She was completely disoriented and startled to realize she wasn't snuggled under her down comforter. A brisk rub down with a thick, fluffy Turkish towel quickly restored warmth and sensation back into her numb body, and then she wrapped her hair in a turban and put on her soft, worn, favorite bathrobe.

Despite its shabbiness, Faith loved the warmth and security of this worn-out bathrobe that had once belonged to her mother. She had worn it while studying throughout nursing school, she had worn it nightly as she awaited the arrival of the results of her nursing boards, and she had worn it hanging out with her girlfriends as they sat around drinking cheap beer in her cheap apartment in celebration of becoming RN's, aka "Real Nurses."

Faith dried her hair on a low setting to protect the natural waves that a barrette was never quite able to contain and played out last night's shift in her mind. Did she remember to suction Mrs. Evan's tracheostomy before she left? Was there enough fluid left in Mr. Simmons' IV bag so the day nurse wouldn't have to rush to replace it? Did she remember to chart the five-beat run of ventricular tachycardia that occurred when she turned Mr. Sullivan onto his side?

Most importantly, had she remembered to chart her phone call to the on-call resident in the middle of the night? He was sound asleep at two o'clock in the morning when she had called him and Faith had asked him repeatedly to get out of bed and wake up; then she repeated back to him several times what the patient needed. The resident yelled at her for having the audacity to wake him up, and then hadn't even listened to any of the suggestions Faith had made to address the situation. Instead, he had snorted and then informed her that he was the doctor after all, and was capable of making his own decisions.

Faith had witnessed this phenomenon among the residents and interns time and again since she had become an RN and had started working in the trenches. At first, she was surprised at its pervasiveness and dumbfounded as well that nurses seemed to be the only ones who understood the concept of "team player." Over time, Faith had become accustomed to the "newbies" who assumed they were larger than life, who used their titles as justification to behave like pompous fools. Faith had jokingly referred to this phenomenon as the "M-Deity syndrome," respectfully, of course, and her co-workers had adopted this term as a sarcastic excuse for the interns who mistakenly assumed they were God-like and omnipotent. It seemed to be most prevalent in the summer months after the new interns began their careers in the hospital, before they learned the harsh reality of survival on the surgical floors. Faith was always amazed at the increase in the frequency of mistakes made during the summer months, many of which she and other nurses like her averted, not only by meticulous monitoring at the bedside, but also by virtue of years of experience that told them which interventions or medications might work, and which wouldn't. It wasn't about ego, it wasn't about competition, and it certainly wasn't about who was smarter. It was about patient care, patient safety, and first and foremost, doing no harm to anyone in their care.

Faith was the quintessential patient advocate. She prided herself on speaking up for any patient who was unable to speak for him or herself or for any family member who was intimidated by the perceived power or prestige that the physician might hold. She was respected not only by her peers but also by the attending physicians, and even by some senior residents who recognized that it was Faith who had saved them from unintentionally harming any of their patients, on any number of occasions. Rarely did anything escape Faith's attention, and the Attending physicians felt quite secure that their patients were well taken care of under her watchful eye.

Having slept only for a few hours, and in a cramped bathtub at that, Faith still felt mired in the thick, murky fatigue so familiar to anyone who worked the night shift. The crazy hours not only wreaked havoc with her body by throwing her internal clock askew, but they also left a subtle sense of fatigue that persisted into her days off, as if she could never sleep enough to recover those lost hours. The hectic shifts frequently left her with tension headaches that pounded at the base of her skull not only after particularly stressful nights, but also during extended hours beyond her shifts caused by the plethora of paperwork deemed necessary by the administrative "powers that be."

Faith pinched the bridge of her nose, willed the headache away, and grabbed some acetaminophen as she dressed, and then headed out the door. Days off were too precious to give in to a headache, and Faith planned on cramming as much into her waking hours as possible. She ran to the Laundromat and washed her two small loads of clothing: one load of day-to-day clothing and one load of scrubs and lab coats. She used the downtime during the wash and rinse cycles to catch up with current nursing journals, and after she threw the sopping clothes into the dryer, Faith mentally listed the things she had yet to do. Once her clothes were folded, she threw them into the basket and flew out the door to get the rest of her errands done.

After going to the grocery store to grab some easy-to-fix snacks and sandwich makings, the only food she ever ate at home since she hated to cook and rarely did it just for herself, she flew back to her apartment to vacuum the living room and straighten up her computer desk. Her kitchen and bathroom, like the kitchens and bathrooms of most germ-a-phobic nurses, were spotless and needed only some minor touch-ups. She put ingredients for grinders on a platter, some rolls in a basket, and set them out on the table along with condiments. Then, she threw some munchies in a bowl, placed them on the coffee table, and waited for her friend to arrive.

Shortly after 7 pm, the doorbell rang, and Faith rushed to open it. "Come on in! Munchies are in the living room. I'll grab us a couple of beers."

With two bottles of dark ale in hand, Faith followed her friend into the living room and laughed to see that she had already scarfed most of the cheese curls from the snack bowl. As she walked to the kitchen to refill the bowl with a fresh supply, she yelled over her shoulder, "Bad day?"

Becky laughed sarcastically and said, "First day with the new interns, 'nuff said."

Faith grinned. "I know. I met one of them before I left. Poor guy, he looked scared to death. I guess he didn't expect rounds to start so early. He's the one I paged you about." She just shook her head and chuckled. "I hope he clues in quickly, or he's going to worry himself right into a padded room."

"I don't think that'll even be an issue. He's so nervous now. I think he's ready to wash and wax my car. He's obviously teachable, he'll learn soon enough. These new interns are almost like a litter of puppies. They just want to be loved and scratched behind the ears once in a while. As smart as Isaac Goldman is, he's just a bit naïve. Give him time," Becky said with a shrug. She closed her eyes and took a huge gulp of beer, as if to wash away the stress of a typical day in the life of a surgeon, then rested the cool bottle against her forehead.

"Anyway, my simple laparoscopic gall bladder removal turned into an open belly case, and it shot the morning to hell. We fell behind schedule, and lunch went right out the window. I think I managed to fit in a lifesaver between cases. Then, the shit really hit the fan, and one of our post-ops coded. I just hope and pray Goldman can handle his first night on call without any major emergencies, because if my pager goes off before my alarm clock does, someone is going to pay dearly." Becky stopped to catch her breath and popped another cheese curl in her mouth. She held her now drained bottle out to Faith, "Hey, while you're up? I think I deserve it."

Faith laughed at her friend's not-so-subtle request, completely unfazed by her blunt manner and sharp banter. She brought two more ales into the living room and handed one to Becky. Their bottles clinked together as they drank a toast to the poor interns, and then they caught up on gossip over thick sandwiches that put most of the take-out places near the hospital to shame.

"That was great," Faith said as she sat back in her chair and wiped a smidgen of mustard from the corner of her mouth. She patted her now full belly. "Better than sex."

Becky rolled her eyes at her friend. "Ha! As if you would know! You need to get out more often, Faith. When's the last time you got laid, anyway?"

Faith grinned wistfully. "It's been so long; I think I've forgotten how. Lately, it seems like I'm at work more than I'm not, and on my rare nights off, I'm usually in bed by nine at the latest." As she noted the sarcastic grin on her friend's face, she winked and then added quickly, "Alone. And asleep!"

Becky laughed at her friend's attempt at humor. "How much are you working these days?" She took a huge bite of her second sandwich and without waiting for a response, she asked with her mouth full, "When was your last vacation?"

"Vacation? Are you kidding me? Until we get more staff, I won't be going on a vacation any time soon. And until the powers that be gets their collective heads out of their behinds and address our recruitment and retention issues, no nurse in his or her right mind would even apply for any of our open positions," Faith replied, with just a touch of annoyance in her voice. Before Becky could get a word in edgewise, she continued, "And as for when that last vacation was, hmmmm, let me think." Faith scratched her head and then held up a finger. "Oh, I remember now. It was the last time I got laid!"

Both women laughed hysterically, and Becky began to wrap the uneaten half of her sandwich in a napkin. "If you don't mind, I'm going to take this home with me and hopefully have a chance to eat lunch tomorrow. I think I better hit the road. If I stay up any longer, I'm going to fall face first into the bowel resection I have first thing in the morning," Becky said with a loud, drawn-out yawn.

"I'm trying not to get a visual on that, Beck. Far be it for me to contribute to you looking 'shit faced.'"

Becky groaned at the pun and slapped her friend playfully on the arm, then gave her a hug and kiss on the cheek. "You get some rest as well. That unit will fall apart if you get sick."

Faith shut the door behind her friend and, lacking the energy to wash the dirty dishes or to take out her trash, she padded down the hall to her bedroom. She shed her clothes into a heap on the floor and put her bathrobe back on, then flopped down on her bed to watch television. She thought wistfully about her next vacation, and even more wistfully about getting laid. Then, she considered the possibility of getting laid on her next vacation.

"Fat chance" was her last thought as she drifted off to sleep.

Chapter 3

Dr. Rebecca Simon was known for her incredibly flat demeanor and her intense, scowling face that rarely cracked a smile. Those who knew her well knew that a heart of absolute platinum lay under that gruff exterior. Those who knew her at all knew she was the finest chief resident St. Mike's had ever produced. She was one of only a handful of residents who learned very early on just how valuable the nurses could be to her success while at St. Mike's, and it had not one thing to do with them making her life easier or more pleasant.

As a first-year intern, Becky had established herself early on as an extremely bright, highly proficient, and incredibly skilled clinician. She had become so confident in her abilities that when one of her patients coded after a lengthy abdominal surgery meant to give him at least a few more months of quality time with his family, she was completely unprepared for his death. The efforts at resuscitation went on for what seemed like hours, and despite doing everything she had been taught to do for advanced life support, Becky felt totally responsible. She took it personally, and she took it hard.

Overwhelming guilt consumed her, and after the code was over, she sat down in the bubble and held her head in her hands. She ran the scenario over and over in her mind, reviewed every intervention she had performed, and considered every medication she had ordered. She had delivered shock after shock with the electric paddles in futile attempts to restore a heartbeat. Becky struggled with herself and desperately tried to figure out what she had missed, what she had forgotten to do, and what she could have done differently to save her patient's life.

Faith had been the nurse caring for this patient. After she had tended to her patient's body and cleaned up his room, after she had hugged and consoled a devastated family and walked them to the elevators, she arranged to have his body transported down to the morgue. Faith headed back to the nurses' lounge to grab a much-needed, quick cup of coffee, and as she walked past the bubble, she noticed the intern who had coordinated the code team's efforts.

Becky looked like hell, and it took Faith only a few seconds to realize she was crying. Faith hurried into the lounge and grabbed two cups of coffee, stuffed some creamers and a few sugar packets in her pockets, grabbed a roll of toilet paper, and headed back to the bubble.

Faith handed Becky a cup of steaming coffee and put some creamers and sugar packets on the table. "It's not the best coffee in the world, but at this time of night, I'd drink battery acid."

Nonchalantly, she handed Becky the roll of toilet paper. "Cost containment at its finest. God forbid they should waste money on real tissues."

Becky just looked at the paper blankly. Then she looked up at Faith. Then she began to laugh. She laughed so hard she snorted, and Faith laughed as well.

Faith sat down with Becky, and they drank their coffee in thoughtful silence. Becky took her last sip and stood up. "Listen, thanks for that."

"Hey, we've always got coffee on, couldn't survive a twelve-hour night shift without it. You're welcome to it anytime, really."

"Well, I appreciate that, but I meant thanks for, well, thanks. I just didn't expect him to die like that. I didn't see it coming. I honestly thought he would be going home to his family by the end of the week." Becky pulled in a deep breath, and her eyes began to fill again.

"This just sucks."

"You may not realize it, but you gave that patient the greatest gift anyone could have given him. You gave him a piece of yourself, and he knew you cared about more than just his tumor. That doesn't happen very often. I know his family appreciates it, and quite honestly, so do the nurses. It's always refreshing to feel like we're working together towards a common goal." With that said, a very tight friendship was born between Faith and Becky.

Word rapidly circulated that Becky Simon was not only an excellent surgeon, but wonder of wonders, despite her gruff exterior, she had a kind and compassionate heart. She quickly became part of the "team" of Surgical Oncology, and the nursing staff looked out for her as one of their own. If one of the Attendings showed up in a bad mood, they gave her a heads-up. They paged her to remind her of orders that had to be written or called her to clarify any order that looked suspicious.

They also invited Becky to join the spontaneous parties they threw for absolutely no reason at all or welcomed her into their homes for a real, home-cooked dinner amongst the chaos of family, rare treats for two reasons. One, she had no family on the East Coast, and two, she had very little time or energy to prepare decent meals for herself.

To Becky, the nurses were an extension of the family she had left behind on the West Coast. Hungry? They found her crackers and milk. Cramps? They located some ibuprofen. Bad day? They invited her to sit in the nurses' lounge for coffee and some lighthearted conversation.

Likewise, Becky never forgot to return the kindness. She brought coffee and donuts for the staff during the weekends she was on-call. She chipped in for the Sunshine Club every month to say thank you for the many cups of coffee she consumed in the nurses' lounge. Most importantly, though, she gave the staff a bit of herself. She got to know their names, their children's names, their dog's names, and then never forgot to ask about them. She counted on the staff as much for their friendship as she did for their clinical expertise. Becky respected and admired their experience brought about by many years spent at the bedside. The respect, admiration, and appreciation were mutual.

Chapter 4

The rubber soles of her well-worn running shoes whispered as Faith hurried down the freshly waxed hallway of her unit. Faith adored her patients, and her patients adored her. Her older patients, the ones who reminded her of her own Grammy and Grandpa, thrived on her gentle touch, her kind smile, and her calm, soothing words. Her younger patients were the men and women in the midst of their working, parenting, living it up years, though many of them were devastated by illness and weakened by disease.

They counted on her for compassion, understanding, and encouragement. Though Faith worked the graveyard shift when most people were home, safe and snug in their beds, with warm blankets tucked around them and engulfed by sweet dreams in the comfort of restful sleep, a few of her patients would fight the lull of fatigue just to see the kindness in her smile, or to feel the comfort of her touch.

Many caregivers whizzed in and out of patients' rooms with barely a glance at the person in the bed, let alone a sincere, "How ya doin'?"

Faith not only asked but also spent a few quiet moments listening to the responses. Bit by bit, Faith could break down barriers of fear or anxiety that kept patients from opening up to their caregivers, and she was able to pick up on subtle clues that other caregivers often overlooked.

Faith was their Guardian Angel, their adopted daughter who seemed to do her often-thankless job so effortlessly, whose love was so apparent to all of her patients and their families.

Faith never hesitated to stay at a patient's bedside when asked to do so. As the end of life approached, she would put the side rails of the bed down and cradle her patient in her arms. She whispered soft words of encouragement as she awaited the final whisper of breath from warm lips soon to be chilled by death. She had no fear of death, and as a matter of fact, she recognized the blessing it brought to so many patients ravaged by terminal disease, as well as their families.

Faith had many "favorites," but truthfully, all her patients thought they were her "favorite" because she cared for each with perfection and compassion. Her most recent "favorite" was an elderly gentleman named Mr. Savino, who had end-stage lung cancer.

Mr. Savino talked non-stop, day and night, and emphasized every detail with great big hands that emphatically waved and pointed in the air before he would drop them down on his belly with a self-satisfied nod.

Mr. Savino frequently told his doctors and nurses, "The ladies are coming soon." Rather than chalk his ramblings up to confusion or dementia, rather than drug him with medications that only kept his body quiet but did nothing to soothe the anxious thoughts that raced through his mind, Faith had listened to Mr. Savino night after night, often into the wee hours of the morning when sleep would finally claim him. Faith would distract him with questions about his family, his home, and his work.

She did anything she could to keep his mind off where he was and what was being done to him. More importantly, she helped him dodge the dreaded sense of powerlessness and loss of control over his own destiny, sadly experienced by far too many patients the moment they donned a patient gown and climbed into bed.

Mr. Savino reminisced about Sunday dinners when the menu was always the same: macaroni with the delicious tomato "gravy" that his Ma and his Sophie spent hours simmering on the stove, stirring it almost constantly so it wouldn't burn. Meatballs were pan-fried in garlic and oil and then added to the sauce. Their rich, spicy flavor infused the savory pan drippings and added a decadent bouquet to the flavorful gravy.

Mr. Savino dubbed it "Heaven, right here on earth."

"None of that store-bought nonsense in a jar that tastes like nothing from nowhere," he would say with a smile, contentment and love in his gentle old eyes. He spoke of how the family gathered every Sunday after Mass at the homestead where they had lived for over fifty years, of the same family stories that were told time and time again over coffee and pignoli nut cookies. With misty eyes, he spoke of how they would bow their heads at the end of the meal in prayer for beloved family members who had already passed, whose absence was as acutely and painfully raw that day as it had been the day they had died.

"It isn't the same anymore. Everyone is in a rush, people forget who they are, and forget their roots. Now, my own kids, my Junior, he kisses me right on the mouth every time he visits. And my Little Sophie (who, like her mother before her, could have used her round belly as a small table) can make meatballs almost as good as her sainted mother's with the hands that God gave her. And you know what? My grandchildren are at the table for dinner every night of the week. And no one wears those new-fangled jiggamabobs in their ears with that crap they call music blasting their eardrums out."

"And you wouldn't ever hear one of those carry-around phones ringing, let alone answer it at the table, 'cause if you did, Junior would probably slap the taste right out of your mouth." Mr. Savino would smile knowingly and nod his head, his hands folded across his ample belly, peace and contentment in his eyes, the pride obvious in his voice.

Then he would comment, "You know, the ladies are coming soon," and Faith would be right back where she started.

One night, shortly after Faith came on duty, she bumped into Little Sophie as she left her father's room. She had the same peace and contentment in her eyes as her father, and Faith often felt as though she had met the long deceased "Big Sophie" because Mr. Savino frequently commented on how much his daughter favored her mother.

At her heels were two young boys, the spitting image of Mr. Savino. Chatting for a few minutes about her father's condition, his comfort, and whether he was getting enough to eat, Faith could not help but remark, "You know, your father keeps telling me that 'the ladies are coming,' but only you and your brother show up to visit. Is someone coming in from out of town?"

Little Sophie chewed the inside of her lip in thought. "I can't imagine who since we're the only family here in the States. Everyone else is in the Old Country, except for a few of his nephews in New York.

"Most of his friends are gone, and even the women from church stopped coming by after Pop stopped going to Mass. Pop just couldn't understand how God could take Ma away from him and leave him here alone. For a while, he was completely lost without her. He still cries for her and for his own Mama, my Noni. He just misses them so much. I don't think he'll ever get over losing them.

"I think he's made peace with God in his own way, still says his prayers, still says the blessing before dinner every Sunday, but he hasn't stepped foot in a church since she passed." Little Sophie shrugged.

"Father Anthony told him after the funeral how we are all clay in God's hands, how He molds us according to His will, and that we must trust Him. If Pop could have thrown that clay right at Father Anthony's head… well…"

She paused for a moment and then set her jaw as if daring Faith to disagree with her. "But I do know this. He has a place in Heaven, right next to Ma."

"Well, I'll keep you posted if anyone shows up. You go on home now; I'll be with him tonight. I'm looking forward to more stories; he really loves to go on and on about all of you. He is so lucky to have such a wonderful family," Faith told Little Sophie as she gave her a quick hug.

"We're the lucky ones, believe me. They broke the mold when they made him." Little Sophie smiled wistfully as she wiped away a tear from her soft cheek and then took her sons' hands in her own. "Come on, guys, let's let Papa get some sleep."

The many hours of the night shift dragged by, and the unit was quiet for a change. Faith was able to get her work done relatively quickly, and then she spent a little bit of time with each of her patients. She tucked them in, stroked a few furrowed brows, and held the hands of those who were afraid of those lonely hours before dawn. As well she rubbed the backs of her "other" patients- the friends and family members keeping vigil at their loved ones' bedsides.

She saved Mr. Savino for last so that she could sit with him for a bit. He really did seem more peaceful when he talked about his family. Likewise, Faith enjoyed being enveloped in the warmth of his happy memories rather than swallowed up by the heartache and misery she witnessed night after night.

Her own father once asked Faith why she "settled" for being "just a nurse."

"These are the moments that make it all worthwhile," she had told her Dad and described the many tender and intimate moments she spent with her patients at some of the most vulnerable times in their lives.

"What other job allows me to do what I love most? I'm privileged to witness humanity at its finest and sometimes even at its worst. And guess what? Whatever happens, whether my patients live and go home to their families and their jobs and their lives or go home to their Maker, somehow, I'm able to make a difference. It's a gift, Dad, and I'm really lucky, blessed actually, to be able to whistle on my way to work every day. Most days, I even whistle on my way home. I can't say the same about a lot of my friends who hate their jobs, and I certainly don't want to waste my life being miserable. Life is way too short. One thing's for sure: I'll never wonder if my life mattered when I'm on my deathbed."

Faith sat thoughtfully for a moment and recalled all the patients who had passed, burdened by all the "unfinished business" weighing heavily on their hearts: regret for things left undone and words left unsaid, remorse for wrongs left unmended, guilt for choices made and opportunities missed, and overwhelming sorrow for time lost with loved ones because work had become a misguided priority.

Then Faith winked at her father and reassured him that yes, she was fine, yes, she was eating well, and no, she wasn't dating anyone. And really, she was very, very happy. Honest.

Faith walked into Mr. Savino's room and pulled a chair up to the bed. His eyes opened, and Faith apologized, "I'm sorry, Mr. Savino, I didn't mean to wake you."

"That's ok, my Angel, I'm awake. I'm just waiting for the ladies to come. They'll be here soon. I'm expecting them tonight," Mr. Savino said softly, the fatigue evident in his voice, his face somewhat paler than usual yet relaxed and peaceful. Faith opened her mouth to redirect the conversation back to stories of his family, to get his mind off "the ladies," but he closed his eyes and sighed, his soft huff followed by a gentle snore.

A coworker interrupted her, "Faith, you've got a phone call. Mr. Savino's son is on line two."

Faith tiptoed softly out of Mr. Savino's room and walked to the hall phone. She picked up the receiver, "Hey, Junior, how's it going?"

Junior laughed but then told Faith he had just spoken with his sister. "Listen, Faith, I'm worried about Dad. He's always been sharp as a tack, and this whole bit about 'the ladies' has me shaken up. It's not like him, know what I mean?"

Faith reassured him that, sometimes, the elderly get a little disoriented in the hospital, especially at night. Deep sleep interrupted frequently by well-meaning staff only trying to do their jobs, a strange environment, even certain medications could lead to the development of a phenomenon known as "sun downing." The result was disorientation and confusion which commonly occurred in the evening hours.

Fortunately, the syndrome was transient and usually resolved itself once the patient resumed a normal schedule at home and got a good night's sleep. Faith reassured Junior that his father's mind would clear as soon as Mr. Savino was back in his familiar environment.

"Maybe he thinks the ladies are from that church group, and he's just expecting them to visit."

"Don't count on it. Pa never called them "ladies," not after Ma died. He called them 'the gaggle of hens,' and that was that. The only women he ever called 'lady' were Ma and Noni. And they sure as hell aren't coming to visit!" Junior laughed a robust laugh that came straight out of his gut. So very much like his Dad, Faith thought.

"Well, like I told Little Sophie, if anyone should visit, I'll be sure to let you know. Take care now and call me if you wake up during the night. You know where to find us." Faith smiled as she hung up and walked back to Mr. Savino's room.

Faith tiptoed to Mr. Savino's bedside, and softly so as not to startle him, she pulled a chair up to the bed. As she lowered the side rail on the hospital bed, she leaned over and whispered softly to him, "Junior called to check on you, Buddy."

She gently stroked his forehead and pulled his blanket up, smoothing it around his shoulders. Faith expected him to stir at her touch, ready to tell her yet another story.

As she tucked the covers in, though, Mr. Savino did not stir. She picked up his hand and squeezed gently, but this time, Mr. Savino didn't squeeze back. Faith felt his wrist for a pulse that wasn't there, watched his chest for the gentle rise and fall of breath, and realized there was none. Despite Faith's watchful eye, despite the meticulous care and concern she devoted to all her patients, "the ladies" must have slipped by her- his beloved wife Sophie and his dear Mother- and they lovingly took Mr. Savino home.

Chapter 5

Isaac had never been so darned tired in his life. Finally, after searching for what seemed like an eternity, he found an unoccupied call room with clean sheets. As he plopped down on the cot and shut his eyes, his breath exhaled in a rush, and he prayed for a few precious minutes of what he hoped would be uninterrupted slumber.

The first day of the internship had started out badly enough, but as bad as it had been, the days only seemed to get worse. Dr. Simon had put him on call that first night, and although he had been warned time and again that he would be busy, he was blindsided by what "busy" truly meant.

An intern's life was not just "busy;" quite simply put, it was hell. In and out of the OR, in and out of patients' rooms, constantly answering pages, continually troubleshooting and doing damage control on the surgical floors, the never-ending paper trail of documentation of every single thing he had done- add it all together and Isaac's dreams of an award-winning and illustrious career as the greatest neurosurgeon who ever existed became a very distant, very dim memory.

The responsibility was relentless and overwhelming. It encompassed not only Isaac's waking hours, but also most of what should have been his sleeping hours as well. Rarely was time available for a shower or to brush his teeth, and his "freshly ironed" shirt and pants quickly became a map of wrinkles. He frequently missed dinner and quickly learned that the graham crackers, peanut butter and juice kept in the patient kitchens were exactly that: for the patients.

He was exhausted, he was starving, and all he wanted to do was cry for the first time in his adult life. He heard his pager go off yet again and groaned. If this was another emergency, he was going to die. If it wasn't, he hoped he would die anyway. At least that way, he could get some rest.

Isaac groggily dialed the extension on the pager and waited for someone to pick up the phone. His shoulders slumped and he nodded off, listening to instrumental elevator music, snoring softly as the tune played in his ear. A female voice roused him back to reality, and he had to shake his head to clear it.

"Surgery, this is Faith."

"Dr. Goldman, I was paged," he said as he fought the overwhelming urge to yawn. The yawn won out. Isaac was tempted to just agree with whatever she told him, to tell her she could write her own orders, and he would sign them in the morning before rounds. In fact, he would sign his firstborn child over to her, anything, if he could just get some sleep.

"Hey, Dr. Goldman, Mr. Savino just passed, and we need you to come pronounce."

Passed? Passed what, a kidney stone? Pronounce? Isaac mulled this over in his sleep-deprived stupor as he put his lab coat back on. He rinsed his mouth with mouthwash he found on the sink in the bathroom and said a quick prayer that whoever had used the mouthwash before him didn't have a cold or, even worse, bubonic plague.

Isaac walked over to Surgery in a mood that got worse with each step. Why can't these things wait until morning? He grumbled to himself about the audacity of a patient dying on his first night on-call, yawning yet again as the doors to the patient care unit whispered closed behind him, and walked over to the desk where a nurse sat, writing in a chart.

An unsigned death certificate lay on the desk in front of her. She looked up as Isaac stood in front of her and silently pushed the death certificate across the desk to him. Her face was a neutral mask that belied any emotion hidden underneath the surface.

Isaac immediately recognized her and thought to himself, "Oh, shit." The last thing he wanted to deal with right now was a smug nurse with an attitude.

"Where's the patient?" he asked abruptly, ignoring the death certificate that awaited his signature. He took his stethoscope out of his pocket.

Taken aback by his coldness, Faith quietly answered, "Room

205. His family will be here shortly so you can talk to them. Heads up: They're a very tight family. This isn't going to be easy for them."

"No kidding, really?" Isaac thought to himself sarcastically, and he stalked off to room 205. Angry at that nurse and totally irritated that he even gave a damn about how she made him feel, he kicked a trash can out of his way as he made his way over to the bed. He abruptly pulled down the patient's gown and placed his stethoscope on Mr. Savino's chest as he stifled yet another yawn. He listened for any heartbeat or respiration that would indicate life, then took a small penlight out of his pocket and pulled up Mr. Savino's eyelid.

He shined the light directly into his eye, looking for the tell-tale constriction that indicated life, but there was none. Isaac muttered to himself again about being tired, being bothered, and not really caring about much of anything at that point except his pillow, then turned and almost collided with Faith, who stood silently in the doorway, her one raised eyebrow silently indicating everything she thought but would not say about Isaac's bedside manner.

Faith immediately went to Mr. Savino's bedside and silently pulled his gown back up over his chest, providing him the modesty and dignity he deserved even in death. Gently, she smoothed the blankets and folded his hands over his round belly. She draped Sophie's rosary beads over his fingers, the ones that had sat on his bedside table throughout his entire hospital stay and tucked the Cross securely in the palm of his hand.

Isaac felt as though he was intruding on a very intimate moment and became flustered by the glint of tears in Faith's eyes. Uneasy with this blatant display of emotion, he began to walk out of the room but stopped when he heard Faith speak. He started to ask her to repeat herself but then realized she wasn't addressing him.

"He's new, Mr. Savino. He'll learn. Let's get you spiffed up for your family."

Isaac was confused. Mr. Savino was dead. Isaac had heard it through his very own stethoscope. Or hadn't heard it, as was the case. Why would Faith talk to him as if he could still hear her? And exactly what did she mean by "He'll learn?" Learn what?

Isaac pondered those questions briefly as he signed the death certificate but abruptly pushed them aside as he gathered the papers and looked around for the nurse. Walking up the hallway, he stopped outside Mr. Savino's room when he heard muffled sobbing, followed by Faith's soft voice as she consoled the family.

"I think he knew that they were coming for him, and he wasn't afraid. He knew he wouldn't be alone. Your Dad isn't suffering anymore. He's home safe and sound with the ladies, probably celebrating over some macaroni and your Mom's incredible Sunday gravy." He watched silently as Faith smiled at this grieving family, holding Junior's hand in one of her own and Little Sophie's in the other. Isaac could not recall any lecture in medical school that addressed the emotional aspect of surgical care, and he was out of his element, ill at ease with this blatant display of humanity in front of him.

His sense of logic prevailed. He had assessed his patient, pronounced him, and signed the death certificate. As far as he was concerned, his job was done. Again, exhaustion prevailed, and Isaac walked back to the desk to leave the papers on top of Faith's clipboard. He rubbed his eyes and stifled yet another yawn, then stumbled back to his call room.

The next morning, as Isaac flew out of his call room, he buckled his belt and tucked in his shirt simultaneously as he walked quickly to the nurses' station on Surgical Oncology. His eyes felt gritty, and his head was muddied by the fact that, cumulatively, he had slept for about fifteen minutes. Trying not to yawn, he caught up with the rest of the surgical team just as Becky stepped off the elevator.

She walked past the group to the chart rack and though she said not one word, she expected them to follow. Isaac did his best to appear awake and competent while surreptitiously scoping out the nurses' station for a fresh pot of coffee. Patients, laboratory values, tests, charts, more patients, phone calls, pre- and post-op checks- the list went on and on.

The day escaped him as Isaac struggled to keep abreast of the never-ending deluge of work handed to him, bundled together with all the accountability and responsibility that went along with saving lives. It wasn't until after he had choked down dinner that he finally had a moment to sit down with the other interns in the lounge, and then the venting began.

Becky continued her rounds after getting out of the operating room and stopped just long enough to realize that it was almost seven pm when the cafeteria closed and locked its doors. She was going to miss dinner yet again. The first few days with the new interns had been a nightmare. She had to intervene frequently and redundantly with sharp instructions for things she clearly recalled learning in medical school.

Becky sighed in relief as she remembered her half-eaten sandwich left over from dinner at Faith's house. At least this wouldn't be another night of pretzels and soda from the vending machines in the basement, about the only food anyone could find in the hospital once the cafeteria closed its doors.

In her refrigerator at home was an old box of baking soda her mother had placed on the bottom shelf the last time she visited, supposedly to absorb the stale odors of a refrigerator left empty, and a jar of eye cream in the butter compartment which she used religiously to hide any evidence of many sleepless nights spent staring at the ceiling and brooding over her patients' care.

"I thought life would be easier as chief resident," Becky thought wryly. "I could almost dredge up some sympathy for the interns." She snorted to herself, "If I had the energy…"

She shrugged as her thoughts trailed off and tried to keep in mind that patience was a better teacher than temper. As she walked into the lounge set aside for surgical rounds, Becky stepped smack dab into the midst of an all-out gripe session among the interns.

"I'm so tired; I almost fell asleep on the john. I couldn't help it. It was the first time I sat down all day."

"Lunch was a mint I found stuck in the lint in my pocket. And I haven't had anything to drink since my coffee this morning. I'm so dehydrated, I feel like a raisin."

"The next person who pages me and wakes me up had best be telling me God himself just walked on the unit."

As the door shut, all conversation abruptly ceased. Becky studied the motley crew, a far cry from the group of freshly ironed, freshly starched, energetic interns who had begun the first day of their first post-graduate year full of determination to make their mark on the world by saving lives and stamping out disease. Now, obviously, all they cared about was a hot meal, a hot shower, and a warm bed, not necessarily in that order.

Becky put one hand on her hip and cocked an eyebrow. "Bad day?"

That was all the encouragement the interns needed to spill every bit of angst about the unfairness of life in the hospital. Out came a list of complaints about the nurses whose paths they had crossed on their first day.

"I thought I was going to starve to death, and they wouldn't even give me a cracker..."

"I asked one of them to get me dressing supplies, and he walked away..."

"One of them paged me at 5 am to ask for a laxative. A laxative! At 5 am! And I had just fallen asleep…"

Becky held up her hand like a nursery school teacher and gave them the first and probably the most important lecture of their surgical career. Actually, it was more like a string of pearls of wisdom, most of which would become the key to survival in this sterile hospital world.

"Welcome to the world of hospital politics, better known as 'Sand Box, 101.' And if you can't learn to play well in that sandbox, then the next five years of your life are going to be hell, plain and simple.

"First: if you want a cracker, ask, don't take. The food in the kitchen is for the patients, period, and if every intern who missed a meal started helping her or himself, patients would be the ones going hungry, not you. If you're hungry, ask one of the nurses. Politely. They always have a snack or two tucked away and have no problem sharing.

"Any one of the unit secretaries would be happy to show you the file of take-out menus for places that deliver right up to the floors. Get to know the folks on the unit; once they realize that you aren't the arrogant jerks you've been acting like, maybe they'll include you the next time they order out.

"Second: if you want dressing supplies, get them yourselves. The nurses and the aides are running their tails off, trying to get their own work done so they can take care of our patients and still leave on time. Administration won't pay them overtime anymore, so needless to say, waiting on you is at the bottom of their list of priorities.

"Third: how bad do you think you'd feel if you hadn't moved your bowels in three days, on top of a gut full of surgical staples, to boot? If you were paged at 5 am, then it was by a nurse who was considerate enough not to page you in the middle of the night for that laxative. Personally, I'd have thanked her.

"And while you all sit back here slapping each other on your collective backs, congratulating each other on how great you might think you are, try remembering the nurses who are still out at the bedside busting their butts so that you ultimately end up looking like heroes. Those nurses will save your ass, but they sure as heck aren't going to kiss it."

Becky looked each intern in the eye for added emphasis and then left the lounge. The interns just sat where they were, stunned, not sure what to say or what to do. Eventually, it occurred to them that they still had work to do, and they all got up to find Dr. Simon again to try to get through what was left of this day, which, to Isaac, felt as though it would never end.

Chapter 6

Patients like Theresa Travio come around only once or twice during a nurse's career, and if that nurse is perceptive enough, she will realize that she has just met one of God's perfect angels. Theresa was that patient with Faith. A jolly woman of fifty-five years, as Italian as manicotti, as robust as any linebacker with probably twice the girth, Theresa had a smile that could light up the night sky and an outlook on life that could rival Pollyanna's. Nothing ever dragged her down, and she always did her best to lift everyone up to her level of joy.

Her focal point, what kept her going every day of her life, was her family. Her husband Tony, her sons Anthony and Joey, and her dreams for a future filled with grandchildren (on whom she planned to dote for the rest of her life) were the foundation of her happiness and her motivation for living. But as strong as her will had been to see her dreams come to fruition, the cancer was beginning to gain momentum, and Theresa was struggling to stay ahead of it.

Theresa was back in the Surgical Unit and had been assigned to Faith's caseload once again. As her primary nurse, Faith was well-versed in Theresa's course of illness, in her surgeries, and in her response to each of the myriad of therapies she had undergone.

As her friend, Faith was equally as well-versed in Theresa's love for her family, in her fear of what might happen to them once she was gone, and in her fervent prayers that her sons would have lives and loves of their own, just as she had had with their father.

During the family visits, with pizzas on the tray table, bottles of soda on the window sill, and munchies, snacks, and Italian cookies from the Italian bakery in Wooster Square crowding whatever space was left, Theresa would call out to Faith as she walked past her room, "Hey, Faith, you look pale, wouldja eat something, already? You're fading away right in front of me!"

Faith would walk right into the loving embrace of Theresa's family, sharing not only a snack to nourish her body in the middle of a crazy-busy shift but also the warmth and security of a family's love that enveloped and sustained her soul amidst the sadness of Surgical Oncology.

Theresa would smile, laugh at her husband's jokes, poke fun at her sons, and everyone would act as if they didn't know the truth: that this time, there was little hope, if any. For several years, the cancer had been isolated in her lung, and although its growth had been slowed by chemotherapy and radiation, this time, it had grown too quickly and had spread to her brain.

There, it had grown slowly but surely, and the news that it was inoperable was almost too much to bear for Theresa, for her family, and for Faith as well.

Like many patients with cancer, Theresa had undergone surveillance scans twice yearly just to "check on things." CAT scans in the past had shown evidence of tumor recurrence in Theresa's lung, but her Oncologist had been able to control its growth. This time, to everyone's shock and devastation, the scan revealed an ugly smudge on what should have been a routine scan of her brain. Up until now, no one had noticed anything unusual that might have indicated metastasis.

No distinct sign or symptom had jumped out to anyone; nothing had alluded to exactly how sick Theresa really was. During this admission, though, Faith had picked up on subtle cues she recognized only because of her familiarity with her patient: the fine, intermittent tremor in Theresa's fingers as she reached for a glass of water, the occasional lapses in conversation when Theresa would lose her train of thought, the increasing fatigue and frequency of her naps.

Faith would pretend nothing was wrong, keeping up the positive attitude and light banter that Theresa not only expected but demanded in her family's presence. Theresa's own tears waited for lights out after visiting hours were over when there was no one there to witness her agonizing heartache.

No one except for Faith, and it was her love, understanding, and support that gave Theresa the permission she needed to grieve for the family she would leave behind. Faith's tears often flowed as well, as she mourned not only for her friend but also for her own loss that was soon to come.

As much as Faith loved Theresa and as much as experience told her the time to "let go" was drawing near, she just could not bring up the subject of a "Do Not Resuscitate" status with Theresa and her family. When the time came, the DNR status would indicate Theresa's desire to allow nature to take its course uninterrupted.

No medical intervention would assault Theresa's body with electrical shocks to restore heart rhythm; no pounding on her chest would shatter ribs in an attempt to keep the blood coursing through her body; no tubes would help her breathe or take in nourishment. None of these interventions could possibly cure Theresa; all would merely prolong the inevitability of death.

When Dr. Goldman had approached her one evening to accompany him to Mrs. Travio's room to discuss the DNR, Faith's professional demeanor escaped her. Tears sprang up in her eyes as her composure crumpled. Unfamiliar with this display of emotion from a nurse who, by all accounts, was the Rock of Gibraltar, Isaac had absolutely no idea how to respond to it and said the first thing that came to mind.

"You really shouldn't let yourself get too attached to these patients. It probably would be easier for you to just keep your distance."

Faith's head snapped up, shocked that anyone would criticize her compassion for her patients. A momentary look of fury flashed in her eyes. "Keep a professional distance" was the one professional "rule" professors in nursing school had drilled into the student nurses' heads time and time again. Faith found it disturbing and quite unpalatable in an environment that often held so much sorrow.

Hopefully, physical pain could be managed with medication, but the emotional devastation that accompanied a tragic diagnosis such as cancer, whether terminal or not, could only be handled with compassion and sensitivity. As far as Faith was concerned, "professional distance" was just a cowardly and pathetic excuse to avoid showing the warmth and emotion so often lacking in bedside manner.

Faith kept her voice quiet and her tone even so that no one, least of all the patients or their families, could hear her. She looked right through Isaac as she struggled to contain herself. "I promised myself a long time ago if the day ever came when I stopped caring, when I could no longer find the time or energy to give a damn about my patients, I would quit nursing and go pump gas for a living. These patients, these families, are my responsibility, and if all it costs me is a little piece of my heart to allow them to live and die with dignity so that they know someone gives a shit about them, I'll gladly give it."

Faith shook her head as she left the nurses' station and cursed under her breath the "clinical detachment" so many medical schools seemed to preach to their students.

Hopefully, Faith prayed, by the time they completed residency and set up their own practices, these doctors in training would have learned some compassion and sensitivity, as well as the kind and gentle touch they would want anyone to give their own mother. They would, if she had any say in the matter.

Faith walked into "the bubble" to find some tissues and wiped the mascara from under her eyes, then plastered a smile on her face. She walked back to the nurses' station where Isaac stood and purposefully strode past him towards Theresa's room. She did not look back to see if he followed her.

Isaac was taken aback by Faith's resolve. During his second year, he had begun to let his guard down bit by tiny bit, and slowly, he realized how inaccurate the first impression he had formed of Faith on that disastrous first day of his internship year truly was. He began to appreciate her positive outlook, even in the face of profound illness and death.

He found himself watching her closely and observed the compassion in her interactions with patients and families. Isaac began to see a nurse who was more kind than not, a woman who was much more joyful than smug. He silently followed her and wondered about this nurse: who she really was, how she managed to stay so positive in the face of so much sadness, and who the lucky devil was she came home to every day.

Chapter 7

Faith led the way into her patient's room with Isaac on her heels and smiled at Theresa and her family. Tony, Anthony, and Joey sat around her bed, and familiar tins of her favorite foods littered the bedside table. As always, the centerpiece of this buffet was Theresa's favorite white clam pizza, with a liberal sprinkle of crushed garlic and wedges of fresh lemon. Everyone had a full plate in hand; laughter, jokes, and smiles of happiness-everything that was a loving and dedicated family-filled the room with an aura of normalcy and joy.

The atmosphere here was devoid of illness and all the sadness that goes along with it. With so much love in this room, no one would ever imagine the cancer monster that lurked in the corner. Certainly, no one would ever believe a darkly hooded, soulless angel of death hovered just outside the door, biding its time, waiting patiently with cruel anticipation for the opportunity to sweep in and whisk away the life that was the heart and soul of this perfect family.

As soon as Faith and Isaac walked into her room, Theresa knew something was up. Ever the protective and nurturing Mother to her family, she tried to prolong the joy and peace that enveloped them, to delay any conversation she knew was inevitable. Theresa bravely smiled and waved Faith and Isaac into the room.

"Sit down, get some dinner, and eat already! Have a little

snack or something! Tony, get some more plates. Anthony, where are your manners? Pull up another chair, we have guests! Joey, go get some more ice for their drinks! Come on, wouldja eat something already, you're fading away right in front of me!"

Faith chuckled as Theresa's family jumped to do her bidding, and her husband and sons teased her that, even from a hospital bed, she could still boss her family around and keep everyone in line.

Not sure how to begin the one conversation she had hoped never to have with this patient who defined her as a nurse and had blessed her with friendship, Faith hesitated. For the first time, she was unable to meet Theresa's eyes. Even after several years in nursing, with all the terminally ill patients whom she had cared for and loved through unimaginable sadness, Faith found this one topic with this one patient almost impossible to discuss.

She felt inept, graceless, and totally out of line in disturbing the harmony of this woman's world. As she struggled to find the words that would allow her to deliver this heartbreaking news as gently as possible, in her soul, Faith knew those words didn't exist.

Isaac hesitated, waiting for Faith to begin, and hoped that she could at least give him some direction as to how to handle this conversation. As an intern, he had spent most of his time at the hospital, running his butt off and performing the multitude of tasks that fell on the interns' shoulders. Occasionally, he spent some precious time in the OR, where he watched attentively, held retractors, and was lucky enough to staple or suture some incisions at the end of the case. As the internship passed into residency, Isaac assumed increasing responsibility for patient care and had more direct and hands-on patient contact, in addition to more OR time.

Isaac finally knew the breathtaking feeling of having an attending surgeon say to the scrub nurse, "Ten blade to Dr. Goldman," and he was granted the privilege of experiencing overwhelming power and control over a patient's destiny. He was hooked. Dr. Isaac Goldman was on his way, and he began to feel more confident that, just maybe, he could do this.

But as wonderful as those experiences had been, as proficient as he was at doctoring on a surgical unit and coordinating care for his patients, by Isaac's third year of residency, he was still a novice at handling the more emotional and intimate aspects of communication, most especially the delivery of bad news.

He had absolutely no idea how to go about discussing death. Isaac's focus was on saving lives, not allowing lives to end. To him, it was almost unimaginable that he would allow any of his patients to just "give up." Like many surgeons, he believed that a chance to cut was a chance to cure, and he wanted to deliver the best care that modern medicine and his education could provide.

Isaac had certainly been aware of patients' DNR orders, but until now he had never been in the position of broaching this topic with them. Taking part in the decision-making process was almost unpalatable. Patients often were admitted to the hospital with Advanced Directives already completed, a copy placed prominently in the front of the chart. Oftentimes, because of their long-standing relationship, the patient's Attending physician had already obtained them during an office visit.

It never occurred to Isaac that giving his patients permission to "give up" was the best and most appropriate medical care he could provide, and he was completely out of his element. He prayed the right words would come out, that miraculously, he would know what to say.

Clearing his throat, Isaac began to speak. "Mrs. Travio, as you know, your CT scan last month showed a metastatic lesion in the frontal cortex of your brain. This is an extension of the cancer that started in your lung, and while treatments in the past have been successful in controlling the spread of lung cancer, this time, it snuck in under the radar, so to speak, and made its way to your brain. At this point, unfortunately, we have no other treatment to offer you. The tumor is inoperable."

The room became deathly quiet; only the shallow breathing of all who were present was audible. Desperate for the strength she would need to keep from breaking down in front of her family, Theresa sat very still. Tony took her hand in his and held on tightly. Immediately, with their fingers intertwined, the knuckles on both their hands turned stark white, the only sign of the emotional turmoil and panic that engulfed this husband and wife.

Both boys sank down into the chairs they had pulled up for Faith and Isaac only moments before. Up until now, Anthony and Joey had remained positive and hopeful that their Mother would live to throw their future wives' bridal showers, that she would be there to hug and kiss their children, loving her grandchildren as intensely as she had loved them.

Now, their faces reflected overwhelming sadness not only for the impending loss of the one who had made them who and what they were, but also because of the devastation that went hand in hand with the loss of the perfection in their lives that only a Mother's unconditional love could bring.

Faith owed her friend the dignity and respect of complete honesty and knew that a full explanation was essential for Theresa and her family to make this last, and probably most difficult, decision of their lives. She stepped in front of Isaac and moved closer to Theresa and her family so she could look at each of them. Only then did she begin to speak.

"Theresa, because of the extent of your cancer and because

we can no longer offer you any treatment that would delay what we now know is going to be inevitable, this might be a good time for you and your family to talk about your wishes, and to take care of anything that might make it easier for all of you later. Most importantly, together with your family, you should decide exactly how much you want done so that we know what to do or what not to do when the unthinkable happens."

The phrases, "when your heart stops, when breathing ceases, when the arms that so gently embrace and protect your family go slack," though understood, remained unspoken.

With strength that could only be described as superhuman given the circumstances and with firm resolve that came straight from her heart, Theresa locked eyes with Faith. Her smile never wavered as she tightly gripped her husband's hand. With her other arm, she motioned for her sons to sit on the edge of the bed so that she was able to reach them both.

She gave to them and also drew from them the strength that only comes from sharing the same blood and the same soul. Then, she smiled. Theresa loved Faith like the daughter she never had, and ever the mother who would give her own life to spare her children any pain and suffering, she laughed out loud.

"Well, that was easy; I thought you were going to tell me we couldn't have any more parties in my room. What would I do without my clam pizza? Come now. Tony, get some plates for our guests. Eat something, wouldja? You're fading right in front of me!" Theresa winked at Faith, who saw wisdom and strength in her friend's eyes.

Faith played right along with her as she gave her family yet one more precious memory to hold on to and preserved another brief moment of peace and normalcy among them. The decisions would come, as difficult as they were to consider, but for now, no more sadness would be discussed.

As the family struggled to pick up where they left off, as the jokes became forced and the laughter hollow in their ears, Faith and Isaac kept up the charade so that hope would remain just a little bit longer. Faith tried to choke down a piece of pizza now grown cold, before she and Isaac left this family to continue celebrating their love for each other.

Isaac thought Faith was right behind him as he walked out of Mrs. Travio's room and spoke quietly over his shoulder, "I was impressed with how you handled that, and I didn't mean to offend you with, you know, with what I said before. I can see she's special to you."

He turned to look at her and was surprised to see that she hadn't followed him. He looked around in time to see her disappear into the nurses' lounge and hesitated only for a moment before following her.

Isaac cautiously entered the lounge and looked around. Chairs surrounded a small table, and a small couch was pushed against one wall. A refrigerator and a tall cupboard that, he assumed, must hold the "snack or two" Dr. Simon had told them about so long ago filled another wall, and a small cart holding a microwave and an automatic coffee pot was pushed into the tiny space behind the door. That was it.

"Not much for a home away from home," Isaac thought.

Faith stood in front of the cupboard, doors open, and muttered to herself. "Why are we always out of coffee filters when I need them?" Isaac heard her sniff and hiccup as she turned around and then jumped, startled to see him standing there.

Always so confident with his surgical expertise, always so certain about his decision-making and critical thinking in emergent situations, Isaac was clearly ill at ease. He had seemed so self-assured in Theresa's room. Faith had thought Isaac looked uncomfortable because of the role he had just played in disrupting the peace and harmony that was the norm for Mrs. Travio and her family.

It never occurred to her that Isaac might have been uncomfortable because of her. She stood there expectantly and waited for whatever it was he was going to ask her.

Faith finally asked him, "Do you need something? We seem to be out of coffee filters, but we have tea bags." She waved to the cupboard in front of her. "Help yourself."

It was only then Isaac realized Faith had been crying. He was shocked to see a crack in Faith's normally strong and, what he had assumed to be tough as gristle, exterior. Although any evidence of tears had been wiped away, her green eyes were still glassy and brilliant with unshed tears. She hastily wiped at her eyes again, brushing away any sign of emotion that betrayed her cool exterior.

When Isaac didn't respond, she told him, "Just write the orders, and I'll take care of them. I have to get back to work."

The rest of the evening was quiet and after catching up on her charting, Faith began to pass bedtime meds. As she walked towards Theresa's room, she paused in the hallway as Tony and his sons left her room, still laughing and smiling.

"Night, Ma…sleep well…see you tomorrow…" and, as always, "I love you." Their adoration for her echoed down the hallway as they made their way to the elevator, and their composure and forced gaiety lasted for as long as it took them to get out of earshot. Only then did tears and sobs give voice to their grief.

Faith quietly approached the group, hesitant to intrude on so personal a moment, but she didn't want to leave any questions unanswered or any needs unmet. Her nursing care did not begin and end with her patients who lay in bed; rather, it encompassed the patient, family, friends, and even the family pet. "The patient unit," she had learned to call it in nursing school, and Faith was determined to do whatever it took to maintain its integrity.

Theresa's family huddled together. Faith encircled the group with arms that couldn't quite reach around them all, yet her love and support for them did. She could not shoulder their burden, but she could share their pain. For the seemingly unemotional families who were unable to shed tears for fear of embarrassing themselves, Faith gave them permission to be human, to demonstrate their grief however they chose to do so.

Her compassion allowed them to give voice to immeasurable and indescribable sadness that overwhelmed the stoicism of otherwise gruff old men, and it soothed the young ones who were still too innocent to fathom the significance and magnitude of their loss. Faith's patients would never be left to die alone, and equally as certain, families would never be left to cry alone.

Chapter 8

"Many patients are far removed from their own care when they come into the hospital, and too often, they are forced to relinquish control over their own destiny and leave it at the door. It's almost as if they have to give it up when they sign the admission paperwork," Faith told the many nursing students who came to Surgical Oncology for clinical experience.

"It's up to us to help them stay in control of their care and chart their own course, to allow them to participate in the decision-making process.

"As nurses, we have become displaced from our patients' bedsides. Federal mandates, state laws, even the minutiae dictated by licensing regulations not only govern the care we give but also restrict the ways in which we are able to give it. Our priority is not the ever-growing pile of paperwork that gets pushed on us by administrators who focus more on just getting the job done rather than on how we can possibly fit it all into an eight or twelve hour shift. They certainly aren't raising our salaries to make working here so enticing that our short-staffed shifts become the exception to the rule. Our number one priority always must be patient care and advocacy," Faith emphasized this last sentence in frequent lectures she gave to the students.

"Your patient care does not begin and end at your patient's

bedside. Help them find available resources to facilitate proper care in the community. Educate patients and their families so they can maintain their health at home. If we prepare them well enough, we can keep them out of the hospital and ultimately save tax dollars, which may be better directed toward preventive health care. Remember that you and I will be retiring someday. I'd like to think all that money I've fed into the government coiffeurs all these years will stay in the Medicare pot and in my Social Security fund as well. Someday, you'll be counting on that money, too.

"Our second priority is to figure out how to tend to all the demands dictated by administration while still delivering the quality care we are taught to give in school. It's not easy. In fact, if you throw the nursing shortage and all the short-staffed shifts into the mix, sometimes I wonder if healthcare is on a slow and steady spiral down the drain. I don't know how healthcare will survive the crisis we are in, but I do know this: nursing care will be its saving grace."

"I've come to one grand conclusion: the expert nurse is NOT the one who knows pathophysiology and pharmacology like the back of his or her hand. The true expert is the nurse who, even if he or she doesn't know the answer to the question, he or she knows where to find it to create a safe and effective plan of care. Then, that care is delivered with compassion and sometimes even with a sense of humor. It's an amazing feeling to know that we, as nurses, can do this. It's also unbelievably empowering to know that, on so many levels, we are able to impact healthcare as a whole."

Some of her students would look completely shocked, trying to figure out what on earth they had gotten themselves into. Others rose to the challenge, empowered and determined to be part of the solution. Faith could see it in their eyes. These were the ones who shared her passion, who would be an asset to the profession, and to the many patients they would treat during their career. The other group would slowly but surely leave nursing if they even completed nursing school.

Burnout was common. The frustration of too much paperwork, the long hours, lost weekends, missing Christmas dinner or Seder supper with family, and the weekly paychecks that paled in comparison to the substantially higher salaries of friends in other professions which required less education and preparation…well, burn out was no surprise.

Faith took a few deep breaths and closed her eyes for a moment. She frequently joked with her patients, both men and women, that Lamaze breathing was not only for childbirth. The deep breaths and focus of the process could be used by anyone, whether to relax a patient before a painful procedure, to calm a patient who was unable to sleep, or to give herself a moment to collect her thoughts.

Faith assumed a confident and cheerful demeanor she didn't

feel and went back into Theresa Travio's room. Theresa lay quietly on her side, and the smell of garlic hung thick in the air. Everything had been cleaned up, pizza boxes were in the trash, and the extra paper plates and plastic utensils that always seemed to be readily available for the family parties were tucked away out of sight.

Faith marveled that in the midst of such profound heartache, the Travios would use their time and energy to clean up despite reassuring them time and again that she would take care of it. The room was always left spotless. Once again, Faith was struck by the irony that such heartbreak would strike their family.

"It is so unfair," Faith thought.

"Hey Theresa, how're you doing?" Faith whispered as she smoothed the sparse, gray fuzz that had replaced the luxurious brown waves that were, at one time, Theresa's crowning glory.

Silence hung in the room like a dark, suffocating blanket, broken only by the sound of ragged breathing and the occasional sniffle. Then Theresa spoke.

"I hate that question; I have no idea how to answer it. What difference does it make, anyway? Shitty, I guess." Her face appeared pinched, and her ever-present smile was now gone. Eyes that sparkled when her family was present were now dull and hooded with despair. Faith knew Theresa had a right to be depressed and angry; in fact, she anticipated it.

Not wanting to press her friend or force her to talk about things she wasn't yet ready to discuss, Faith simply asked, "What can I do?"

Theresa looked at Faith incredulously and then snapped, "What the hell do you think you can do? Fix me. Make me better. Or kill me right now because trying time and again to beat this fucking disease is driving me crazy. I can't take it anymore. I pray over and over for something or someone to make it all go away. Even God doesn't listen. I've puked my guts out from the miserable poison that asshole oncologist told me would get rid of it. I've had pain like you can't imagine after surgery that was supposed to 'get it all,' to use that moron's own words. A direct quote, mind you," Theresa scoffed at the memory.

Then Theresa's brave front crumpled. "Cure me," Theresa whispered to Faith, desperation and agony so evident in her voice. Then she started to cry, and not the loud, effusive kind of crying with sobbing hysterics, full of anguish and heartache. Theresa shed big, silent tears filled with pain and disbelief that her life was going to end far too soon. She would never see her sons marry or welcome her new grandbabies into the family, and she would never make love with her husband again. Her biggest fear remained unspoken.

As she grew sicker and weaker, she would be a burden to those whom she loved so much. Ever the consummate "Mommy,"

Theresa Travio was used to taking care of everyone else. She could not bear the thought of having to rely on someone else to take care of her home and her family, and she was utterly humiliated to think that someone else would have to take care of her.

Theresa drew in another deep, ragged breath as the hopelessness in her voice flooded Faith with sadness. Then, abruptly, anger returned once more.

"I never thought cancer could be so demoralizing. At first, the oncologist told me that after surgery and chemo, I could live a normal life. I'd love to know what the hell 'normal' is. It's all so relative, that's what it is. My 'normal' is spending my days trying to forget about the chemo that I just took for six weeks, which made me feel like absolute shit and left my head as smooth as a baby's bottom. Then, once I thought the worst was over and I assumed I was "safe" again, I spent my days trying to forget what I had just gone through to fight this fucking disease, even though I saw the reminder of it in the mirror every day."

Faith handed Theresa another tissue which she immediately crumpled into a ball in her tightly clenched fist. "Then 'normal' was saying every damned Novena I came across, and please, Dear God, once the chemo was over, that the cancer would become a really horrible, distant memory, that it wouldn't come back."

Incredulously, Theresa huffed and then shook her head

vigorously as if to cast away the memory of her most fervent prayers denied, of her dream for a future with her precious family shattered for a final time. She paused for a moment, her eyes unfocused, staring off to a time in her life too agonizing to revisit, utterly disheartened that, yet again, she was living it. Her voice became a pained whisper.

"The first time it came back, I had surgery again and, oh sweet Jesus, that fucking chemo. Once it was gone, once all that torture was over, it became impossible to live the normal life that son of a bitch told me I could live because if it had already come back once, and my prayers obviously weren't answered the first time, why would I bother hoping and praying anymore?" Theresa shook her head, bitterness plainly written all over her face.

"So then I just hoped. What else could I do? 'Normal' just meant that I spent my days waiting for the other shoe to drop, for the cancer to come back again…and again…and then yet again. I can't even work up the energy to hope anymore. But I can't give up. I'm not ready to sign a DNR. I still have a life to live. I have too many dreams left, dreams that I can't just take to my grave. So you and that Doctor can take those DNR papers and shove them straight up your collective asses." Theresa set her jaw and glared at Faith. Her expression challenged Faith to tell her she was wrong.

Faith's gaze never faltered from Theresa's as she sat down

on the bed and then wrapped her arms around her patient as far as she could reach. She loved this patient as if she was her own mother and truly "got it" when it came to understanding the myriad of emotions and gut-wrenching devastation brought about by this horrid disease. Faith rocked Theresa gently and allowed her all the time she needed to grieve for what the future would bring, as well as for what would never be.

Chapter 9

Isaac lingered in the Surgical Unit the next morning after rounds with Dr. Simon and methodically wrote his notes in the patient records. He spent more time reviewing lab results on the computer than was necessary and sipped coffee that had long since grown cold as he stared at the same chest x-ray hanging on the bank of lights that was there just for that purpose.

"Must be something really good, what's up?" Becky glanced briefly at the x-ray and then frowned in confusion at the healthy set of lungs on a routine post-operative film. She turned to Isaac for an explanation. Isaac looked over at her and Becky got a clear view of his face.

"You, Doctor, look horrible, and you weren't even on call last night. What's up?"

Isaac looked like hell, like he hadn't had a decent night's sleep in days. Most nights, after he had spent the day scrubbed in the OR and then spent the evening reviewing surgical cases scheduled for the next day, Isaac would sleep like a baby. Last night, however, was different.

Isaac had gone home the previous evening following rounds with the intern who would monitor his patients overnight on Surgical Oncology. He sat in his living room, beer in hand, a hamburger and fries long grown cold on the coffee table in front of him. He stared at the wall, lost in thought, and struggled to make sense of the whirlwind of unfamiliar emotions that flooded his mind. He had started his intern year off confident, positive about his decisions, comfortable with his capabilities, and sure that his expertise would continue to blossom and that his learning curve would be short.

Those feelings had quickly evaporated into thin air with one screw-up after another. By January of that first year, Isaac had been convinced of one thing only: he was completely out of his league in the hospital world. He was not cut out to be a surgeon, let alone to have the title of "MD" following his name.

Every waking moment outside the hospital was spent immersed in medical literature and textbooks to learn, absorb, and retain the droves of minutia every doctor was expected to know. He not only had to know it, but he also had to be able to retrieve it in an instant and regurgitate it with accuracy, especially in a critical, life-threatening emergency.

While other interns looked forward to nights and weekends off to relax and unwind with family and friends in that part of their life not enmeshed in medicine, Isaac remained oblivious to a world in which preparation for his future as a neurosurgeon did not predominate. It became a daunting and overwhelming task. Isaac began to think he was better suited to make French fries at some fast-food restaurant than to bear responsibility for a patient's health and well-being.

Flash forward to residency, however, and Isaac's feelings of inadequacy were soon replaced by renewed confidence in his abilities. As well, he quickly began to appreciate what a certain nurse was bringing to his professional practice. He pondered the nurse in Surgical Oncology with admiration for the clinician she was and for the determination and persistence she showed in caring for these sick patients day after day.

Honest appreciation for her skills and her confidence had replaced the resentment he felt for her because she witnessed his first major gaffe at the very start of his career. He also had to admit his day seemed so much brighter when she was in it.

Isaac looked forward to her contributions at rounds every morning. Faith just seemed to have it so "together" and managed to overcome the seemingly insurmountable tasks of mountains of paperwork, fewer staff, and acutely ill patients who were much sicker than the ones he had worked with in medical school, with little effort. Whatever happened to simple, uncomplicated surgical patients who were in and out of the hospital in two or three days?

Isaac was awed by what Faith knew, and he found himself following Faith's lead during early morning rounds. Frequently,

Faith would comment under her breath before going into a patient's room, "His breathing was off, and he looked a little punky, so I ordered an arterial blood gas. Look at the results; he's hypoxic. Maybe Bi-pap?" Faith's insight and advice would often point Isaac in the proper direction, with necessary test results already in hand to guide his treatment plans.

Other times, Faith would say, "Something just isn't right, but I can't put my finger on it. I went ahead and ordered a chest x-ray for you and did some labs. The films are up on the wall." Sure enough, the patchy whiteness on the x-ray and the elevated white blood cell count proved Faith's instincts to be dead on, and Isaac would start the intravenous antibiotics, which would lead to recovery from pneumonia.

Isaac begrudgingly admitted to himself that, as a matter of fact, many of his "success stories" had more to do with Faith's and the other nurses' assessment skills and keen insight gained by spending so much more time with patients at the bedside, rather than his medical expertise brought about by years spent in a lecture hall. He had learned quite a bit from Faith about patient care, about professionalism, and probably most importantly, about treating patients like human beings rather than an assembly line of diagnoses.

Far from being totally comfortable with the human side of

patient care, he knew for a fact that he was becoming a better surgeon because of her.

"No, I'm fine, I was just studying late. You know how it is," Isaac tried to chuckle, but it came out as a coarse bark. He thought about asking Becky what she knew about Faith, but he also knew of their friendship and was hesitant to have his question get back to her. He had achieved quiet peace with the nursing staff on Surgical Oncology and didn't want to rock the boat by becoming fodder for gossip over the coffee maker.

His days of being the fledgling on the unit were over, thank God, and the last thing he needed was for Faith to think he was as naïve and inexperienced with relationships as he once had been with patient care. He left the bank of lights and began rounding on his patients in the unit.

Although he appeared to be deep in thought, Isaac looked around for her. He was anxious to find out if Faith had made any progress with Theresa Travio, if she had had any luck with helping this patient decide her fate. The truth was, he was anxious just to see her. Isaac found Faith in her usual morning spot at the nurses' station, black pen in hand, the ubiquitous charts laid out in front of her.

"So what happened after I left last night? How did Mrs. Travio do?"

Faith looked up at him, the familiar black smudges ever-present under her eyes, and he thought he saw them ever so slightly soften. Wisps of her hair escaped the confines of her barrette, and Isaac was immediately struck by the thought that no one had ever looked lovelier.

His mind quickly went blank, and he forgot what he had asked her. Instead, he wondered about Faith again: her life, her world, what made her happy, and what made her sad. He knew that his life would never be the same if he didn't learn everything he possibly could about her. Equally as certain, he knew his life would never be the same once he did.

Faith's voice startled him away from his thoughts, and she replied, "She's not ready to sign the DNR. She knows her time is coming, she knows we can't cure her, but she's not yet ready to give up on whatever future she has left. And seriously, I can't blame her, even knowing what will happen to her if and when…"

Faith's voice trailed off as she closed her eyes for a moment. She took a deep breath, haunted by many memories that ran through her mind: of patients who had coded over and over, who had ribs broken and second-degree burns branded on their chests from electric paddles applied time and again to restore a heartbeat, whose bodies were assaulted with the application of modern medicine, all in an effort to save a life that, one hundred years before, would have passed on with no questions asked.

While some code efforts were successful, while some patients defied death and ultimately returned home to their families and their lives, Faith fought the heartbreaking image of the "failures:" patients whose hearts started to beat again but whose minds never came back, leaving empty shells seemingly in suspended animation, with no chance of returning to their present lives.

She saw the families who would cluster around the patient's bed, initially relieved to know their loved one had survived, anxiously awaiting the first movement or eye-opening, and pleading with the patient to just wake up and squeeze their hands. The hope would continue for a week, maybe two, and then it would begin to fade into desperation for just one sign, any sign. Initial joy melted into misery as hopelessness haunted their eyes.

As time dragged on, the families' fear of death and loss turned into horror at the shell of their loved one, once a strong, capable, beloved human being with a family, friends, pets, and a life.

Now, that shell was suspended in a dimension that was beyond life, yet not quite reaching death despite showing no purposeful movement or action and no evidence of conscious thought. The guilt would come, slowly but surely, that they had not signed the DNR. Enmeshed in guilt was the knowledge that, by not doing so, they had condemned their loved one to a useless, meaningless, purposeless existence.

Grief would follow, but this time, the grieving process would be long and drawn out, prolonged by breathing machines, feeding tubes, bed sores, and pneumonia that would sometimes drag on for months or even years. Death always brought sadness, but this second scenario indefinitely extended the grieving process with indeterminate closure.

The wounds inflicted on loved ones were seemingly much more devastating. Families were left to wonder, understandably, what they or the patient had ever done to deserve such cruelty and pain. Although a beating heart remained in the bed, and although a familiar face rested on the pillow, for all intents and purposes, their loved one was dead and would never awaken again. For these families, closure, mercilessly, was elusive.

Faith looked to Isaac and expected some response from him, or at least something to indicate that he comprehended this patient's dilemma, but Isaac just stood there and stared at his feet. He wanted to invite her to coffee, to continue their conversation, only this time, he wanted to talk about her. Maybe later, he thought, after rounds ended.

A call bell went off and Faith hastily excused herself to answer it, leaving Isaac in the nurses' station. She realized it was

Theresa and hurried to her room, only to find her patient fully dressed, make up shakily applied, a bright and colorful scarf tied around her fuzzy head and a hopeful smile on her face.

"How's it going today, Lovey? How are you feeling?" questioned Faith, noting that Theresa was steady on her feet as she gathered and packed her belongings, calm but determined.

Her voice was strong and insistent as she told Faith, "It's time to go home. I have a family to take care of, and by now, I'll bet my laundry room is overflowing." Her smile broadened, and her eyes bore a look of courage and strength that only a woman who was as dedicated to her family as Theresa was, could display.

Before Faith could get a word in edgewise, Theresa reverted to her ever-present role of Mommy. "Faith, you're wasting away. Wouldja eat something already? Here, have my toast and some juice. The hours you stay on your feet are amazing, or torture, or maybe just stupid. I can't quite decide which it is yet." Theresa winked playfully as she teased her, like she often teased her sons.

Faith groaned. "I had one of your cannoli at 3 o'clock this morning with my coffee. If I eat anything else, I'm going to explode right out of these scrubs!" Faith laughed and playfully patted her trim, flat stomach.

"What would I do without you, Tree? You're always looking out for me." Faith looked wistfully at her beloved patient for a moment and struggled to hold back unshed tears.

Theresa held her hand and rubbed it in the same soothing and relaxing way Faith's own mother did before she would go to bed as a child. "Even when you expect it, it's never easy. You miss your own Mother, don't you?"

Faith rarely discussed her personal life at work, although she had shared with Theresa a few details of her mother's illness and that she had passed when Faith was young. Her patients had enough going on in their own lives, and their plates were overwhelmed with their own trials and anguish. Faith did not want to burden them or their families with any sad stories of her own. She brushed off her friend's astute observation with a lighthearted shrug.

"Well, sometimes, but I get to take care of people who become my own family, and it helps me remember what a gift you all are to me. Not all people get to love their jobs as much as I do, and honestly, I feel bad for them. This," Faith waved her hands around her, "is what's important."

Faith took a deep breath, stalling to think of anything she could possibly say to this patient/friend who wanted to go home but who still required nursing and medical care to at least stabilize and strengthen her enough to get there. Although Theresa was not as weak as some cancer patients, Faith doubted she would be able to attempt even a fraction of the housework she was accustomed to doing daily or to care for her family the way she wanted to, the way she expected to, the way she always had. Faith had witnessed her friend's exhaustion after so much as walking to the commode.

She worried about how she would handle physical limitations that quite possibly would prevent her from taking care of housework, let alone allow her to remain safely at home. Faith knew in her heart, however, that Theresa was bound and determined to get home to her family and her life, and as her nurse and strongest advocate, she was obligated to help her get there.

"Theresa, are you sure you are doing the right thing?"

Theresa looked at her friend, head held high, eyes glistening, and nodded her head. Then she sat down on the bed, drew in a shaky breath, and blew it out slowly. She pursed her lips and furrowed her brow.

"I don't know, Faith, I honestly don't know. But it's time to find out now before it gets too late to even try."

Faith exhaled equally as slowly and nodded. "I'll go get Dr. Goldman, and we'll see what we can do to get you out of here."

Faith knew in her heart that advocating for her patient and supporting her wishes were her priorities; however, her sense of practicality forced her to consider the reality of helping her friend with what just might be her final wish. She struggled with the constant tug of war between life and death and realized, in Theresa's case, it was inevitable that death would win.

Out of respect for this God-sent angel/patient who had done more for her than she had ever done in return, not only as her nurse but also as her friend, Faith's heart prevailed. Theresa still had a life to live, and she was not about to waste it in the hospital.

Chapter 10

Isaac sat at the desk with an open chart in front of him when Faith returned to the nurses' station and told him of Theresa's plans. "Mrs. Travio is dressed and ready to be discharged. She's just waiting for her family to come pick her up. I can do the discharge instructions with her while you finish up your paperwork. Oh, and can you write out her prescriptions, too?"

Isaac's pen halted mid-sentence, and he sat back in his chair, dumbfounded that Faith could possibly believe this patient was able to leave the hospital. His professional demeanor snapped.

"She's in absolutely no position to go home, and I can't approve this discharge. It certainly is not in her best interest to leave the hospital; at least here, we can control her pain. What if she needs IV fluids? What if she can't even swallow her pain pills? What about when that tumor gets too big, and she seizes, or worse, strokes out? I will not be held responsible for that. Stop letting your emotions get in the way of common sense; do you want that to happen to her at home? I cannot in all good conscience allow her to just go home and hide in her bedroom to die."

Faith was equally dumbfounded by Isaac's vehemence, and just as quickly, she became angry. Pulling her petite frame up, hands on her hips, eyes flashing, Faith walked right up to Isaac until she was directly in front of him, eye to eye, practically nose to nose. She lit into Isaac in a way she had never spoken to a physician before.

"Stop making this about you, Dr. Goldman, and as far as emotion overruling common sense, exactly whose best interests are you worried about, yours? She's the priority here, not you. Do you honestly think anything you do is going to make a difference now? That dear woman is going to die, and you are not going to save her. And quite honestly, none of the Travios gives a crap about your approval of this discharge, or even your 'good conscience' for that matter. Get over it. She is going home."

Faith took a deep breath and dropped her head, and then she shrugged. "There is no harm in honoring a patient's life by respecting her wishes, whether you think it is in her best interests or not."

Throwing his pen down and picking up Theresa's chart, Isaac stood. Before he walked away from the desk, he said angrily, "That woman is not ready to die yet. She just needs to beef herself up and become stronger, and then she'll be able to go home safely. I can't discharge her knowing I haven't done everything possible for her."

Despite all her efforts at demonstrating the human side of patient care, despite trying to impart to interns and residents time and again that sometimes medicine had to take a backseat to a patient's final wishes regardless of what was written in the medical textbooks or what their professors in medical school had taught them, Faith resigned herself to the fact that she was never going to get through to this doctor. She shook her head and lowered her voice to a very modulated level, and rebuffed Isaac's attempt to have the final word.

"Well, I'm sorry you feel that way, but Theresa Travio wants to go home, and you, Doctor, have no right to stop her."

Faith turned on her heel and stormed to the phone. As she picked up the receiver, she looked Isaac right in the eye and then dialed the phone. Loud enough for him to hear, she paged Dr. Simon to Surgical Oncology and made sure to add that the page was "ASAP," as soon as possible, so that returning to the surgical unit would become Becky's priority.

Isaac stared back in total shock and disbelief, then stomped over to the desk and threw down Theresa's chart with an angry thud. He muttered under his breath and tried to justify his reasoning.

"Who does she think she is, questioning my judgment? I'll be damned if that patient leaves this hospital. No doctor in his right mind would deem her stable. She's not ready. I'm the doctor, and she's my patient, dammit. I'll make that decision when I'm darned well ready to make it, period."

He began to write furiously in Theresa's chart and outlined all the barriers to discharge-reasons this patient should not leave the hospital just yet-and almost drove the tip of his pen through the pages with the force of his angry pen strokes.

A few minutes later, Becky hurried into the unit. Isaac stood to talk to her, to explain what was going on with their patient, to describe how weak and sick and debilitated she remained. He was none too pleased when Becky turned to Faith first and asked, "What's going on?"

Faith ignored Isaac as she outlined the morning's conversation with Theresa Travio and told Becky of her desire to return home. "She's dressed and ready to leave, and she already called Tony to come get her."

Becky looked irritated that her day had been interrupted by this. "So, what's the problem?"

Faith just looked at Isaac expectantly with one eyebrow raised, arms folded across her chest, waiting for him to tell his side of the story. Becky looked at Faith quizzically and then over at Isaac. The realization dawned on her that there was more than just a slight difference of opinion here. Dr. Goldman obviously did not agree with the plan that Faith had outlined, and equally as obviously, he was angry that she not only disagreed with his professional judgment but had gone over his head.

"Ok, guys, let's get subjectivity out of the picture. Physically, what is going on with her? And how did she respond to the discussion about DNR status yesterday? If she agreed to the DNR and signed the paper, then this discussion is moot."

Faith talked over Isaac as he attempted to get a word in edgewise and directed her words to Becky with no acknowledgement of his attempts to speak.

"She's not ready to sign, and if you listen to what she has to say, you can't blame her. Given that each one of us knows she is going to die, why can't she just die at home, in her own bed, if that's what she chooses to do?"

Faith paused for an answer, and not receiving one, she continued.

"Personally, I think Theresa just wants to spend one more day in her house and one more night in her own bed, next to her husband. We can certainly set up palliative care for her with home nursing. Once she and her family are ready to let go, or once she gets to the point when she knows she is close, maybe then we can talk about hospice. It must be their choice. If her family is unable to care for Theresa at home, then she can be re-admitted here for hospice care.

Faith became desperate. She put her hand on Becky's arm and pleaded with her, her composure weakening more and more by the minute.

"Come on, Beck, what's the harm in this? Why can't we just give this family a few more happy memories? Who knows if another opportunity to go home will happen again? If we can't honor the wishes of a dying woman, then we are giving into that damned disease and letting it get the best of all of us. We can't do that to her."

Faith willed herself not to cry and waited for Becky to respond. Having no written DNR in the chart significantly muddied the picture. She could understand Isaac's concern that, if he agreed to discharge Theresa, he could be considered negligent in his care of his patient. Ultimately, however, it was the memory of her mother's illness which strengthened Faith's determination to prevent anything similar from happening to one of her patients. Though she had tried time and again to block certain memories from conscious thought, she was unable to suppress them when patients were reliving the experience right in front of her.

Visions of her mother wasting away in her bed at home, the look of helplessness and desperation that seeped into her father's face when he realized he couldn't manage her pain anymore, and memories of the final hours of her mother's life spent in a cold, sterile hospital environment came flooding back, and Faith had to shake her head to chase them away. She dropped her hand from Becky's arm and backhanded the tears she could no longer contain. Faith waited for her decision, which, as Isaac's senior resident, would be the final word.

Becky's eyes softened as she listened to Faith, and she thoughtfully considered Theresa's case. To buy herself a moment to weigh both arguments, she reviewed the day's lab results and the pages of nursing notes that outlined Theresa's progress over the past few days. Then she put the chart back in its rack. She returned to the desk where Isaac and Faith remained standing, their posture stiff and defiant with arms crossed across their chests. They purposely avoided looking at each other.

"Dr. Goldman, your assessment of Mrs. Travio is accurate, and your plans to strengthen her by improving her nutritional status, in addition to managing her pain, are certainly appropriate. As with many cancer patients, it would be ideal to proceed with these measures to support a safe discharge plan."

Faith gaped at her friend and could not believe what she had just heard. Faith and Becky had sat up many a night, commiserating over a Bass Ale, on the state of healthcare in the United States and the inability of so many physicians to let go when there was obviously no positive outcome to be had by any of the "extraordinary measures" offered by modern medicine. They agreed on one thing: at a certain point, heroism had no place in healthcare.

As professional care givers, they could only do their best to provide the safest care they could give, as meticulously and compassionately as possible. They both worked hard to effect positive outcomes, but when the time came, if their best efforts weren't good enough, they would allow their patients to pass on to their next life with dignity, respect, and complete certainty that someone who truly cared was on their side. Was Becky turning her back on the beliefs she had shared with Faith so many times? Faith could not believe it and opened her mouth to argue with Becky.

"However," Becky said pointedly and silenced Faith with a look that spoke volumes of her respect for her friend. "In Mrs. Travio's case, it is inappropriate for us to assume that what we have to offer her in terms of treatment aligns with her definition of "best interest," or that it fits in with her plans for whatever time she has left, however long or short that time may be. And we know that what we do have to offer her is only going to prolong the inevitable. 'Cure' is unrealistic at this point. Even though Mrs. Travio isn't ready to sign a DNR, that doesn't mean we disregard her wishes or ignore her desire to go home to her family.

"We don't know her agenda, and quite honestly, it isn't our business. She is in the driver's seat here, and it's up to us to support her in whatever way we can. Faith can set up home nursing services which will provide palliative care and keep her comfortable, as well as safe. And honestly, she'll be better off in the comfort of her own home, in familiar surroundings, with Tony and her sons around her. I'll sign the orders. Faith, you take care of coordinating the discharge planning. Now, is there anything else?" Becky stood expectantly and directed her gaze to Isaac, sensitive to the fact that he was upset and probably embarrassed that his plan had been overturned. She gave him her full attention and waited patiently for his response. When none came, she quickly changed the subject.

"Good. Now, I've got a Whipple procedure this afternoon. This patient has a big tumor on the head of the pancreas, wrapped around everything. Nasty as hell, and I've never seen anything like it. I don't usually let anyone but another fifth-year General Surgery resident help with anything this extensive. It's not neuro, but you'll never even see a Whipple, let alone assist in one, in your specialty. Why don't you scrub in? Come on, let's get coffee and review the best approach to getting this tumor out. Parts of this operation are tricky. Then, we'll discuss the postoperative course. These patients go directly to intensive care, and the complications…"

Becky and Isaac walked down the hall with their heads together, their pace quick and purposeful. Faith did not notice the quick and confused look on Isaac's face as he briefly glanced back over his shoulder at her; neither noticed Becky glance back at Faith as well.

Faith turned back to Theresa's chart. She knew Becky was trying to help him save face, and she respected her for that. Even though she didn't agree with Dr. Goldman's approach to Theresa's care, she knew he meant well. Actually, she admired his drive to do well for his patients. Letting go was hard. Any nurse with a heart and a few years in the trenches knew that, but the learning process to reach that level of acceptance was brutally difficult, mentally as well as emotionally. It not only took its toll on the spirit, but it also left an indelible imprint on the heart.

For many physicians, it took a strong dose of humility to accept the fact that someone much wiser and more powerful than he or she was writing the orders and creating the care plans, humility that many surgeons achieved only after losing the battle against a stronger opponent many, many times. It took an unbelievable degree of arrogance to assume the audacity to invade the human body with a scalpel, to change what God Himself had created. Allowing nature to take its course was not the same as giving up, and it did not mean admitting defeat. Curing was not always the goal. Caring was.

Chapter 11

"I thought for sure Goldman was going to burst a blood vessel over Theresa Travio, but the Whipple was a pretty good diversion. What did the attending say when he saw him scrubbed in?"

"I'm not sure he even noticed. I started the case and isolated the tumor; he showed up for the glory of resecting it, and then he left. We reconnected everything, finished up and closed. Goldman did a pretty good job. I was impressed with how well he handled it, given that he really hadn't had time to read up on the procedure. Cripes, I remember those days, being so busy you couldn't possibly hope to study everything you needed to, and then going into the OR on a wing and a prayer, and maybe one cup of coffee if you were lucky. I give him credit, though; he never brought up the Travio issue. I think he may have even learned a thing or two from you." Becky tipped her bottle in Faith's direction and then downed several gulps of her beer. She rested her head back on the couch and closed her eyes for a moment.

"Well, at least she's home, and probably happier than she's been in a long time. You must feel pretty good about that," Becky opened her eyes and glanced at Faith.

"Honestly, no. This is just the calm before the storm, Beck. I'm glad she's home with her family, and I'm sure they are thrilled as well, but it won't be for long."

Becky looked at Faith in surprise. "We know she's terminal, but she's probably got some time left. From the looks of the past few days, it may even be a bit longer than we thought. At least she won't spend that time on the surgical floor. And her pizza will certainly be a lot hotter straight from her own oven." Becky tried to lighten the moment with humor, but her attempt didn't have much impact on her pensive friend.

"You're probably right," Faith replied, but experience and a strong gut feeling told her otherwise. Changing the subject, Faith asked, "So tell me about Isaac Goldman. What's his story? He doesn't say much when he comes around; he just does what he needs to do and then moves on. I've tried to chat with him a few times, but he really keeps to himself, although I can't say I blame him for that."

Faith sounded a little bitter after the last statement, and the message behind it wasn't lost on Becky. She remembered a few painful dating disasters Faith had experienced, compounded by the subsequent humiliation of knowing her personal business became food for gossip during slow periods at the nurses' station.

Fraternizing amongst colleagues was never a good idea, working as closely as they did on a daily and nightly basis, and it could only lead to disaster when the relationship ended. It was an occupational hazard to work so closely with other people in so intimate an environment, and both Becky and Faith had learned to keep their personal lives out of the professional arena. Becky could personally attest to that point. Faith was more mature than most and always the consummate professional, but that kind of stress in the workplace had the potential to make a difficult situation almost unbearable.

"I don't know much. He's been about as 'chatty' with me as he has been with you. I know he's brilliant, and he's obviously going to be a gifted surgeon. Neurosurgery, now that's a calling if there ever was one," Becky mused, watching Faith's face closely and trying to gauge her response to that last bit of information.

Becky knew all about Faith's mother and had observed her time and again as she took care of patients with devastating neurological cancers and other diseases. Strokes, aneurysms, tumors- they reminded Faith every day of what her own mother had gone through. As well, they reminded Becky of what Faith, the youngest daughter who was forced to grow up in a hurry at the tender age of fifteen, relived every time one of them died.

It couldn't be easy for her, and Becky was well aware that every time one of Faith's patients passed on, a little piece of her heart went with him or her. She worried about Faith and constantly wondered how much more of her heart was left to give. She marveled that there was anything left of it at all.

Becky paused for a minute, watching Faith with her peripheral vision as she sipped her beer, and then off-handedly asked, "So what's the deal between you two? I couldn't believe how angry you both were."

Faith's hand froze as she brought her beer up to her lips and then abruptly put it down. She cleared her throat and tried to keep her voice even as she ignored the question and wondered aloud, "I wonder what made him decide on neurosurgery? Better surgeons than Isaac Goldman have yet to perfect any kind of surgical technique that is curative, especially for cases like Theresa's."

"Haven't a clue. I give him credit, though. His goals are certainly admirable. I wish I could say my goals are as grand. Honestly, after five years of residency and a fellowship, I think I'll finally be ready to just go hang out my shingle, remove gallbladders, and resect colons for the rest of my career. Maybe freeze off a wart or two. I never really thought surgery would take over my life, but it has. You're so lucky, Faith; you can leave it all behind when you go home, especially when you've used up every last shred of emotional energy with your patients. I feel like I never get away. I hope Isaac Goldman understands what he's up against. I hope he's not shocked to realize how much he's going to give up in the process. There is just no way to practice surgery half-assed. You either give it your all, or you remove gall bladders, resect colons, and freeze off a wart or two for the rest of your life," Becky tried to laugh, but it belied the hope she had had for something different, something better.

Faith couldn't have agreed less with Becky but kept silent. She brought her work home with her every day of her life; she certainly didn't leave it sitting on a desk in an office. She couldn't imagine anything more gratifying than being responsible for a neurosurgical breakthrough of that magnitude, something that carried the potential to affect as many lives as a surgical "cure" would. She couldn't help but wonder: had her mother been diagnosed a decade or so later, could someone, maybe even Isaac Goldman, have found a way to save her?

To lighten the mood, Faith nudged her friend and got up to get them both another drink. "Don't sell yourself short. I'd let you operate on my hemorrhoids any day."

As she popped the top off another bottle of beer, Becky managed to spray them both with foam. She laughed and teased Faith, "No problem there, you are definitely my favorite pain in the ass!"

A comfortable silence settled over Faith and Becky as they sat side by side on Faith's couch. So many conversations between good friends took place with no words at all, and although both felt quite comfortable offering advice warranted by the situation, most of the time, each knew what the other one was thinking. It just wasn't necessary to fill the airspace with extraneous noise. Becky reached over, squeezed Faith's hand, and then intertwined her fingers with hers. Faith smiled tenderly at her friend.

The beauty of their friendship and sisterhood was simple: each recognized the fact that, although they didn't always agree on everything, although certain topics carried different meanings for each, they respected each other's views enough just to agree to disagree. Despite their differences, despite conflicting views, each felt admiration, respect, and affection for the other. No disagreement, no matter how huge, could affect their friendship.

Chapter 12

Faith had a few days off and desperately tried not to think of work. She struggled against memories of her mother's illness and death years before, yet somehow, they frequently managed to blindside her when her guard was down, especially when patients to whom she had grown close were slipping closer to death.

Thoughts of her mother would creep into her mind for no reason at all, and Faith would find herself distracted from her everyday tasks: staring at the dust rag in her hand and wondering how it got there, holding the receiver up to her ear and listening to the dial tone only to forget who she was trying to call; stopping at a stoplight and snapping out of her reverie only when horns blared behind her.

Memories of her mother's final days haunted many dreams in which she struggled to escape nightmares of her past; other nights, she would toss and turn during the many troubled hours when sleep evaded her. Often, she climbed out of bed feeling unrested and unsettled, blankets and sheets in total disarray, her pillowcase damp with her tears.

Her father heard it in her voice during their weekly phone call. "What's wrong, Baby, tough time at work?"

Faith's father could read what was printed on her heart as

clearly and as easily as he read the Boston Globe over his morning coffee, and as only a father could, he was the one person on earth who knew Faith better than she knew herself. It was pointless to try and hide anything from him. Faith's breath escaped her in a rush, and she broke down sobbing.

"Ok, ok, I'm coming to get you. I'll be there in a couple of hours. You just throw some things in a bag and wait for me…." her Dad hurried to say, and Faith could hear him rustle around as he gathered up his keys and his coat.

"No, Daddy, really, I'm fine. It's just a tough time, that's all, and I have a little bit of a headache. Besides, I have to work." She paused, and in the silence, she heard her father take a deep breath.

Faith was well-versed in her father's forth-coming litany of reasons she had to take care of herself, but before he could begin, she quickly added, "I'm off next weekend though, and I could really use a break. And, well, I miss you. I miss…"

Faith tried to rush her words to keep from breaking down again. A gigantic sob threatened to escape, and she bit her lip to control it. "It's just been a tough time."

Her father waited in silence for her to continue, but when she didn't, he changed the subject. "I'd love a ride down to New Haven, and maybe some pizza in Wooster Square. Then we can jump back in the car and come home for the weekend. You can always take the train back to New Haven on Sunday night. It's always nice to have some quiet time in the car to chat, and you know your brothers will smother you as soon as you get home."

At the mention of pizza, Faith started to tear up again but forced her voice to be light as she responded, "How 'bout I save you the drive and just take the train up in the morning after work? I can nap on the way up and have the rest of the day with you. Who needs sleep, anyway? We'll find time together, Daddy, I promise. We always do."

Despite the hollow ache in her chest, Faith smiled. A trip home would do her well. Time with her family, especially with her Dad, would do wonders to brighten her world. Maybe some time with him would help her learn how he had managed to survive that time in his life, how he had lived through the turmoil of his wife's illness and the tragic loss of his life partner. As well, perhaps Faith could figure out a better way to cope with the sadness she witnessed every day at work.

Slowly, through the course of Theresa Travio's illness, as well as with other patients, Faith had begun to feel like a fraud. She guided her patients and their families through tragedy with compassion and skill all the time. She nursed their sorrows and their ills, and her shoulders supported them when they needed support; her compassion carried them when they needed to be carried. On the inside, however, she felt completely inept at processing all the conflicting emotions she felt, working amidst so much heartache. As heavy as this burden could be, Faith knew in her heart it was only a matter of time before the weight of sadness began to impact her ability to practice according to her own high expectations or before it affected her ability to adhere to the standards she had set for herself so long ago.

She did not want to be a hypocrite who comforted her patients and dried their tears but who was unable to do the same for herself. In her lifetime, she knew of only one expert who would be able to give her the answers she needed, who would even begin to comprehend the meaning behind her questions. Doctors and colleagues at the hospital could answer any and every clinical question she had in her head, but only her father held the answers to the myriad of questions she had in her heart.

Becky found Faith in her usual spot at the desk in the nurses' station at the end of her shift, rushing to complete all the charting she did not have time to finish during the night. Becky rested a comforting hand on Faith's shoulder.

"Maybe a long weekend away will give you some peace of mind, and you can come back with a fresh outlook." Last evening as she rounded on her patients, she had watched as Faith and Isaac duly avoided each other's paths on the unit. She also observed as each one cast quick, furtive glances at the other, knowing in her heart what those glances meant. Becky contemplated the evidence before her and tried to suppress feelings within her own heart, ones that hovered just beneath the surface, feelings that were hidden by the stiff and toughened exterior she had been forced to mold around her heart during her surgical internship.

"It will do you some good," she added and then squeezed Faith's shoulder. She looked up in time to see Isaac Goldman walk off the elevator, and not wanting to witness what she hoped was not happening, she hurried to get to the OR. Isaac approached the desk and stood before Faith.

She tried to keep her head down until finally, she was unable to ignore his presence any longer. Her eyes met Isaac's, and something flashed between them. Faith felt it in her heart, and as her face reddened with heat, she felt the warmth radiate to her soul. Isaac sensed something as well but was unable to define it, and it remained nameless.

Afraid to speak to Faith, Isaac reluctantly turned around and silently left the unit. Faith watched as the elevator doors closed behind his back, then shut the chart in front of her and placed it carefully back in the chart rack. She looked around briefly to make sure she had left nothing undone and hurried to grab her coat and suitcase out of her locker. As exhausted as she felt, an amazing sense of anticipation and hope enveloped her as she left the hospital for the train that would carry her home to her family.

Faith climbed aboard the train at Union Station and found an empty seat. She stowed her suitcase in the overhead bin and then stuck her ticket in the headrest in front of her so the conductor would not have to wake her. She had no sooner rested her head back in complete exhaustion than she fell into a deep slumber.

The train left New Haven, then New London, then Providence, and soon enough, pulled into South Station in the heart of Boston. Through the hazy fog of deep sleep, Faith heard the conductor's voice boom loudly, "South Station! Final stop, South Station!"

Chapter 13

Faith hurried to gather her suitcase and rushed down the aisle, then out onto the platform where she looked both ways for a familiar face. Already, she felt enveloped in a sense of warmth, a sense of peace that only family could give. Faith was overwhelmed to see five beloved faces rushing towards her, family with whom she shared not only resemblance, but also the common bond of heritage, history, and many, many memories.

All five swarmed her and surrounded her in a tightly knit, circular hug, and all talked at once. Her youngest brother took her suitcase, her two middle brothers each took a hand, her father walked behind her with his hands on her shoulders, and her oldest brother ran ahead of the group to get the car. She realized that no matter how much she loved her job and her life in New Haven, this was still home.

While surrounded by her family's love, her heart and soul secure in the familiarity of their warm embraces, she could await the answers she sought and forget the sadness she had left behind at St. Mike's for just a while longer.

Scott, the youngest of the four brothers in her family, the one to whom Faith secretly felt closest, carried her suitcase up the stairs and put it on her bed. "I'm so glad you're home. Dad said you sounded like shit."

Faith's smile did not reach her eyes. "His words?"

Scott shrugged. "I knew what he meant, and I know he's worried. So, what's up?"

Faith sat down on her bed and hugged an old pillow covered with crooked embroidery, one of her first Daisy Scout projects. She remembered how she had struggled with the embroidery, how she had pricked her finger time and again with the sharp needle, after which she fell on her mother's lap and sobbed her heart out. Her mother had soothed her and rocked her and then dried Faith's tears and sat with her on her lap.

She picked up the sewing needle and patiently, time and again, guided Faith's hands to make the tiny, crooked stitches on the pillow. In the corner was an ever-so-tiny speck, rusty in color, the remnant of a drop of blood her mother had been unable to wash out.

She sighed deeply as she buried her face in its softness, and Scott waited silently for her to speak. Finally, she looked up, and Scott could see the mist as it clouded the same green eyes shared by all the O'Brien siblings. The concern in Scott's voice was all the permission Faith needed, and one solitary tear began to flow silently down her cheek. When Scott sat down beside her and put his arms around her, she finally allowed them to break free.

"Sometimes it just gets to be too much. I know it's nothing I'm doing wrong, but I struggle with knowing that, regardless of what I do, so many of my patients will get sicker, and so many will die, sure as I'm going to die, and sure as you're going to die. I know that; I'm not so naïve as to believe I will be the one to make everything all better." Faith's words halted, and she gazed off into the distance.

"Sometimes I feel so guilty because I'm always lying, telling them it's going to be ok, but I know it's not, not for my patients, not for their families. I know what it's like, Scott; we both know what it's like. I hate like hell that I keep telling those poor families everything will be just fine and dandy when I know damned well it won't be. They'll relive every second of it, every day, for the rest of their lives."

Scott knew exactly what his sister meant, as he had relived the same hell repeatedly since the day it happened. He remembered how helpless he felt, how disappointed he was in himself that he had not been able to do more, to help more, but he had been immobilized by his own grief.

Rather than try to work through it, he buried it. It killed him to see his sister like this. He knew what she did every day at work, and he comprehended better than she did that it was in honor of her mother's memory, to try and erase the guilt she felt at not being able to do more for their mother when she was so sick.

Faith palmed away the tears that left shiny streaks down her cheeks. "I must look like the cat just dragged me in. Maybe I'll take a quick shower."

"Well, hurry up because Dad has dinner all planned, and he wants us to eat at 6 pm sharp."

They both laughed. Ever the perfectionist, when Dad called his family to the table for dinner, they hurried to the dining room, although their haste was grounded more in not wanting to disappoint their father than in fear of any punishment.

"Front and center" was his standard call to order. Despite the drill, dinner itself was always festive and loud, with light-hearted banter and teasing. Since so many of Faith's siblings no longer lived at home with their father, this kind of celebration only happened on the rare occasion when they all managed to rearrange their own crazy schedules to gather under one roof.

Scott hoped that time with family would give Faith the permission she needed to unload whatever it was that had brought her home.

Faith looked around the table and listened in on several conversations at the same time.

"Did you see Big Papi belt it out of the park last night?"

"I'm up for promotion soon to manager, and the boss said if I play my cards right, I could make shift supervisor by next year."

"Jennie's this new girl I met at school last semester. I'm thinking of bringing her home sometime."

"I've been thinking about applying to med school. The M-CATs are coming up, and I've been reviewing math and science, especially "O" chem. Man, organics just about killed me the first time around…."

Faith sat quietly and soaked it all in. The hospital world was crazy, but because her unit was so short-staffed, she could not justify leaving the other nurses in a bind to come home on a regular basis. Now she realized how badly she needed her family, and how empty her life had been without them. Her father glanced over at her, and he smiled a familiar, gentle smile.

"You're not saying much, Baby. Is everything OK?"

Faith looked at her family sitting around the dinner table. "Right now, it's just perfect. I couldn't be happier, and I'm so glad I could come home for a few days. I've missed you all so much. I've missed you, Daddy." Faith reached over and squeezed his hand. She smiled fondly at the man who had become both Mother and Father to her at a time when he should have been coming to terms with his own loss, and his own grief. Instead, he had managed to keep Faith together, made sure she attended school and kept her grades up, in addition to doing all the normal "things" any other teenage girl would do, any girl who still had her mother.

"Well, we've certainly missed you," then hurriedly added, "But we understand how busy you are." He squeezed her hand back, lifted it to his mouth and kissed it, then smiled at his youngest child, who still had his heartstrings wrapped tightly around her little finger.

"Why don't you turn in early and get a good night's sleep? Just sleep in, and after you wake up and we have some breakfast, we can take a ride together. Would you like that?"

Faith smiled back and raised her father's hand to her cheek. She knew where he wanted to take her, and while she always accompanied him to her mother's grave when she came home, this time was going to be especially hard. Although she had accepted long ago that her mother could never have come home again after her last trip to the hospital, that she had gone there to die, it was a reality she didn't want to face right now.

In her heart, she knew Theresa Travio probably would not be home long either, and that fact just reanimated the grief she had lived through years ago, carrying it forward to join the impending heartache that would accompany the loss of her friend. They say it gets easier, Faith thought. Well, here's a news flash: it doesn't. If you are lucky, you become numb to the pain or accustomed to it, but easier? Never.

After getting the best night's sleep she had had in months, Faith woke to the smell of the fried eggs and bacon she loved so much but never made for herself because it was too much trouble. She pulled on jeans and a Red Sox sweatshirt and then hurried down the stairs and into the kitchen to find her father pouring coffee into two mugs, the newspaper folded by her plate, save the business and sports sections which lay next to his own. They ate their breakfast in comfortable silence with only occasional comments on the news or anecdotes about day-to-day life in the neighborhood in between bites.

As Faith cleared the breakfast dishes, her father excused himself to warm up the car. Faith smiled at the familiarity of his routine. He never went for a drive without giving his old Chevy time to warm up and "shake the willies off," as he liked to say. "Willies" or not, the car was her mother's, and after all these years, it still ran like a charm, thanks to her father's diligence.

They drove to the cemetery in a small town just outside of Boston, in a setting that could only be described as idyllic. Although it lay just beyond the hustle and bustle of the "Hub" of craziness that was the city, her mother's final resting place was like stepping back into a quieter, simpler time. Faith often felt as though time had just stopped inside its gates. As they drove, each pondered his or her own memories of the woman who had been the center of their family's world for what seemed to be such a brief time. Faith tried not to cry at memories that remained fresh and felt scars on her heart tear open yet again. Subtly, she tried to wipe a tear away before her father could see, and he pretended not to notice.

"So, how're things at the hospital? You ready to run the place yet?"

Faith had to laugh; her father always knew what to say to make her smile. "The hospital is great, Dad. And no, I'm not ready to take it over just yet." Faith sobered as she continued, "Really, I don't think I'll ever be able to leave the bedside. I don't know. I just really feel like I have something to contribute to my patients and their families. I know I can maybe offer them something that other nurses can't, at least the ones who don't have a clue what it is really like. Wearing a suit to work every day would make me nuts, and I'd feel so useless."

"Oh, I imagine they'd find a use for you! Seriously, Baby, whatever you put your mind to, I know you'll do well. You've always excelled at taking care of people, and you work so hard." Her father shook his head, pride in his voice.

"Such determination you had! I remember watching you with your mother, how strong you were, how you took care of everything without being asked, and you never seemed to tire. And so, so gentle, my goodness. I remember Mother saying you had a gift, that as soon as you came into someone's life, they would know they had been graced by an angel."

They rode in silence for a few minutes and then turned left

through the gates of the cemetery. They parked the car and walked down a long row to a headstone of rose-colored marble, lovely in its simplicity. It was carved with a humble inscription: "Grace Casey O'Brien-Beloved wife and mother."

Father and daughter held hands tightly and bowed their heads in prayer. After a softly whispered "Amen," Faith's father stepped forward and rested his hand on his wife's headstone. Comforted by the familiarity of the cool marble under his hand, he turned to Faith and beckoned her with the other.

"Look who's here, Grace, it's our Faith, home for the weekend. It's been a while, hasn't it?"

He smiled at Faith and continued to speak. "That's ok, she's doing what she does best, Mother, isn't that right?"

Faith noticed a small bundle on the grass in front of the stone and picked up a small bunch of lavender, now dried and withered, obviously well past its prime. Faith was still able to detect the subtle perfume of the now-grayed blossoms, the pure and gentle scent that had filled her mother's bedroom, a gift from the husband who had wanted to blanket his wife in the comforting smells of the garden she loved so much. She rested her head on her father's shoulder, no longer able to hold back the sadness that had been threatening to bubble over since their phone conversation several days ago.

Scott had just nipped the surface, so to speak, last night

before dinner, but Faith had not been ready to speak of it then. Now, though, she couldn't hide it. Faith began to cry and tilted her head up so that her face was buried in her father's neck. His arms pulled her close and held on tightly, and he rocked her as he had so many times when she was just a child.

Several moments later, Faith pulled away but stayed within the circle of her Father's arms. She looked down at the ground and then over to her mother's headstone. She drew in a deep breath and let it out in a long, slow breath. Faith then gazed up at the sky, as if looking at the many "perfect angels" she had cared for but had lost despite her loving care and guidance.

"How on earth did you make it through it all, Daddy, through the worst experience of your life, and still stay on your feet for me and the boys, or on your own feet, period? I mean, how do you get through something like that and still go on?"

Her father sucked in a deep breath and pursed his lips. As he scratched the back of his neck, he tried to think of a way to answer Faith, to explain how he had managed to get out of bed every morning to face another day without the love of his life, the other half of his heart and soul, by his side. The day he and Grace were married, they envisioned their world, to have and to hold, for the rest of their lives. Now, the rest of their life was passing before him, but Grace was no longer by his side.

There was no easy answer, he thought to himself. No handbook to follow, no instruction manual, no magic key to help any of his family survive what, so cruelly, the fates had delivered to them. Out of habit, he unconsciously brushed back hair that no longer existed on the top of his head.

He exhaled and answered Faith, "You just do it. You stay busy. You get on with your life and try not to be consumed by what fate handed you. I can't really explain it, Baby, I wish I could. Your mother died because of a God-forsaken, merciless disease. She would have killed me if I had given in to it, if I had just given up and let it destroy me, too. So much sadness in our lives, and you, even at fifteen, you were still a child. I didn't just have to get myself through the day. I had to get you through it, too."

"I never knew how you managed to stay so strong, Daddy. You never seem to let it get you down. How do you do it? I think, at this point, I'm just so numb to it. I understand loss and all, but I'm afraid that if I think about it too much, I'll fall apart."

Her father smiled a sad, little smile and held his daughter's face in his hands. "Faith, honey, you can't avoid pain. The more you try to shield yourself from it and the more you ignore it, the more you wall up your heart. Eventually, you'll be shielding yourself from the things that really matter, and you might miss something really good and really special. You are wonderful with your patients, Faith, and I know you've touched many lives with your compassion and understanding. You are able to empathize with them in a way no one else who hasn't experienced such a profound loss of someone so dear possibly could. But when are you going to start nursing yourself? You don't have to shoulder everything for everybody all the time."

"Remember that last office visit? Your mother and I just couldn't believe how strong you were, standing up to the doctor like that." He shook his head, a look of amazement mixed with pride on his face.

"What a pompous fool he was; your mother hated him. I think she just became a lab experiment to him after a while, you know, 'Let's try this,' or 'Maybe this will work.' 'Maybe.' I hate that word. It gives you hope, but then 'maybe' becomes 'oh well,' or 'better luck next time,' and hope goes right down the toilet. I wish I had been as strong as you. That night, we laughed about it, how speechless he was with his mouth hanging open. I'll bet he's still talking about it."

Both smiled at that memory, though it certainly was not a happy one. "I still marvel at you, though, how you…"

His voice drifted off as they both remembered the weakness that progressed to the point of incapacitation; how day after day Faith would tend to her mother's increasing needs as well as the physical demands of helping her father with household chores and tasks, how she tried to shoulder as much as possible so her father could remain at her mother's bedside.

Then, when her mother could no longer be managed at home, when the pain became too much for her, when the bedsores began, and the smell…

"I just wish she could have stayed at home. I feel like I failed her," Faith's voice trailed off, and her father cut right in and firmly took her by the shoulders.

"Now stop it and listen to me! What else could you have done? You do this for a living now. You know what's involved in caring for patients, day in and day out. What could you have done to make it any better or any easier?

"Think about it and answer me honestly. If one of your patients was dying, and her fifteen-year-old daughter was standing in front of you right now asking what else she could do, what else she could take on in addition to what she already had on her plate, what would you say to her? What would you tell her to help her realize that nature doesn't give a damn what we want, that there is absolutely nothing anyone can do to stop it? You are so great at being a nurse, Honey, but first and foremost, you were her daughter. Give yourself permission to let this go and just be sad because your mother is gone. That's it. You didn't have to 'fix' anything. You did everything you possibly could have done. There was no way she could have stayed home. As sad as it was for all of us, your mother knew that. And you know that as well. I know you do. Now you just have to allow yourself to believe it."

Chapter 14

"Vacations never last long enough, do they?" Faith said in greeting to Becky as she made her morning rounds on the unit.

"Back already? You just left. How was it?" Becky juggled a cup of coffee, a donut, and two charts under her arm until Isaac Goldman came up behind her and relieved her of the charts.

"Hey, Dr. Simon, let me get those for you," Isaac added her charts to the stack in the crook of his arm, plus morning lab results and the OR schedule. He smiled shyly at Faith and hurried over to the desk to begin his morning work.

Her eyes followed Isaac as he walked away, then Faith smiled and sighed, "It was so great to see everyone, and my Dad is wonderful, as always. I can't believe I'm back already, even though it was just for a few days. My visits home always end too quickly. Hey, are you up for a quick dinner tonight? I switched a night with one of the other nurses, so I'm free, and my Dad did my laundry for me before I left, so I don't even have that to do."

"Think your Dad would want to adopt me? I swear, I have so much laundry to do. Thank God the hospital washes my scrubs. Oh, crap, which reminds me, I don't have any clean underwear. Shit. I think I'm going to be camped in at the Laundromat, sorry. Rain check?" Becky laughed at the disappointed expression on Faith's face. "To tell you the truth, forget the underwear. I'll just borrow a pair of yours. Please tell me you have some normal granny panties that won't embarrass me when I change my clothes in the locker room!"

Faith howled, "Granny panties? Are you kidding me? Even my own mother didn't wear Granny panties. How about a nice pair of white cotton undies that I promise won't floss your behind? Your mother would be proud; heck, your Granny would be proud. Just come over after you get out. Maybe we'll order Indian?"

Becky shook her head. "Nope, real food just isn't going to do it tonight. Ice cream, it must be ice cream, and lots of it. We'll throw on some fruit and nuts, so we don't feel so guilty. Oooh and there's calcium in ice cream. This is getting better and better. I'll pick it up on my way over; don't you worry about it. I'll see you tonight."

They parted ways, Faith went back to her patients, and Becky walked over to the desk where Isaac sat. They reviewed the lab work and diagnostic workups together, and discussed the clinical implications of each, as well as the list of differential diagnoses. At this point in his residency, Isaac had become clinically proficient, and their morning rounds consisted of more collaboration and less instruction.

Becky nodded in agreement with Isaac's outlined plans of

care and ducked into the bubble for a few moments of peace so she could eat her donut and gulp down her coffee. Two lengthy surgical cases stood between her and an evening with her friend, but if she skipped lunch, she could get to Faith's apartment that much sooner. She really wanted to hear what her friend had to say about her visit home.

Something was missing from Faith's life, and Becky thought she knew what it might be. She suspected it was probably what was missing from her own life as well. As she was about to push the unit doors open, she briefly looked back at the desk where Isaac sat scribbling notes in his patients' charts.

At the same time, Isaac nonchalantly lifted his own head and looked around the unit. When his eyes rested on Faith's head bent over a mountainous pile of charts, his face softened, and his pen stopped midway through a sentence. What was it that made him feel this way around her like he wanted to follow her, carry all her charts, bring her a fresh cup of coffee as a quick pick me up at two in the morning?

He shook his head self-consciously at a mental image of himself, Dr. Isaac Goldman, a love-sick puppy, who had no clue how to address a young woman or how to talk to her, especially one as brilliant and as beautiful as Faith. Faith, what was her last name? He gave himself a mental slap on the forehead that he had never thought to ask her. Even if he could get up the nerve to try and call her, he'd never be able to look her up in the phone book without her last name.

Becky pulled at her lower lip as she stared at Isaac, who stared at Faith. She noticed a questioning look in his eyes, along with a hint of disappointment. As brilliant as Becky was with her wealth of medical knowledge and surgical expertise, this time, it was woman's intuition that took over, and she resigned herself to a truth she did not want to admit. She sighed as she walked over to him and leaned down.

Very quietly, she asked, "What do you want to know?"

Without waiting for his questions, which she already knew without even asking, she answered him, "Faith O'Brien. Big, Irish Catholic family. Mom passed, Dad still lives in the family homestead outside Boston. Four older brothers, Faith's the baby."

Isaac put his head right back down into his charts as he attempted to feign indifference. Then he sighed, threw down his pen, and sat back in his chair. He looked up at Becky and simply said, "It's that obvious?"

"I've seen you staring at her when you think she isn't looking. And except for the pissing contest between you two over the change in plans for Theresa Travio, you've been hanging on every word she says in rounds. I think you've even learned a few things from her, although you'd never admit it." Becky again turned to leave, and Isaac cleared his throat.

"Thanks. Um, Dr. Simon, I was wondering. I really shouldn't be asking you this, but…."

Becky held up her hand and beat him to the punch. Her voice became even softer so that all the inquiring minds who lived to know other people's business, let alone embellish it and spread it around on the hospital grapevine, wouldn't hear her. "No, she isn't seeing anyone. No, she hasn't mentioned you. And in case it's your next question, no, I won't fix you up with her." Becky couldn't bring herself to make that gesture; that would be like stabbing herself in the heart. She inwardly sighed and then left to spend the rest of the day in the OR. Isaac picked up his pen and then stared down at the chart, lost in thought.

Chapter 15

Faith groaned and dropped her spoon into the empty soup bowl that had held the most decadent ice cream sundae she had ever eaten: three scoops of ice cream, fudge, strawberries, bananas, nuts, and enough whipped cream to smother the bowl. At the bottom of the bowl there remained a small puddle of melted ice cream. She used her finger to wipe up a small trickle of fudge sauce that had dribbled over the side of the bowl and licked it off, then leaned back on the couch and shut her eyes. Her hands rested briefly on her belly, and then she unsnapped her jeans and groaned again.

Becky leaned back on the couch and stretched her arms over her head, then dropped them limply to her sides. She sighed in complete bliss and smiled in agreement. "That was perfection. I've been looking forward to that all day. Do you think the fiber in the nuts and strawberries was enough to cancel out all the calories?"

"Absolutely, calories are illegal in anything that tastes that good. Besides, that's why they make scrubs so loose. Truthfully, though, if I had them on right now, I'd have to use a shoehorn to get them off."

Faith sniffed and then rationalized, "Oh, who cares, anyways? No one is going to see this body any time soon. Besides, you don't eat all day long when you're in the OR. Maybe you should have seconds."

Faith winked at Becky and laughed as she gathered up their bowls and spoons. "The heck with doing the dishes tonight; I'm just going to leave these to soak. I can barely move; I think I'm about to go into a sugar coma."

"Well, move over, I'm right behind you. What a way to welcome you back from your mini reprieve. How's the family doing, by the way? Is your dad staying busy?"

"He's great, Beck, I just marvel at how positive he is and how focused he is on making every day perfect like he's living each one for both himself and my mother. I guess if he enjoys each day twice as much, it will be as if he's sharing it with her."

"He sounds like such an amazing man." Becky smiled as she recalled the photos Faith had shared with her of her big, happy, Irish family. "And how're the bros?"

"They're unbelievably well and so incredibly busy. Sean is taking his M-CATs, can you believe that? He's always been so driven to succeed, he'll do well in medicine," Faith smiled at Becky.

"Or surgery. I'm not sure in which direction he's really leaning. Scott is still living the life of Riley, always busy, still follows every Red Sox game like his life depends on it. Ricky has a new girlfriend, and she sounds like she might be the one. He wants to bring her home to meet us. Can you believe it?"

Faith looked off wistfully, almost sadly. "They are all so busy, and their lives are so rich and full. Even Patrick is taking on a management position at the construction company."

Becky looked intently at her friend and wisely kept silent as she waited for Faith to go on.

"I don't know, Beck, I don't know what's wrong with me. I love my job. I love my friends. My family is such a blessing, but…"

Lost in thought, Faith paused as she considered the 'shield' her father had mentioned surrounding her heart. "I guess sometimes the loneliness just gets to me, you know? I really wish I could reach out in bed at night and feel someone lying next to me, with another toothbrush hanging in the bathroom and two placemats on the breakfast table.

My parents had the perfect marriage, the perfect family. I grew up with a wonderful example of what life is all about. I want that, I'm ready to have my own perfect life. I want to wake up to the same thing my parents woke up to every day. I'm ready for something different, to share my life with someone special, too." She looked wistful as she remembered her father's advice and misted over at the wisdom and insight he had into matters of her heart.

 Becky reached over to squeeze her hand, and Faith squeezed back as she dabbed her eyes with a tissue.

"I know you'll find it, sometimes it's just a matter of looking around. You never know who might be right in front of you..." Becky was cut off by the shrill ring of the telephone. The hospital phone number popped up on the caller ID.

"What are they calling you so late for? It's your night off, for Pete's sake. Let the answering machine get it."

"No, it's ok. If they have an issue, they know they can call me with questions anytime. It's not a big deal." Faith answered her phone, and with a look of complete confusion, she asked, "Who is this? Oh my God, no, I'll be right there."

Faith ran to the closet to grab her coat and slipped shoes on her bare feet. Her voice cracked as she struggled to cover the panic in her voice.

"I've got to run, Beck. That was Isaac Goldman. Theresa Travio was just readmitted, and it doesn't look good. Lock up, would you mind?"

She didn't wait for an answer and ran out the door. It never even occurred to her to wonder exactly how Isaac Goldman got her phone number or why he had thought to call her at home in the first place.

A dozen different scenarios raced through her mind as Faith flew from the parking garage across the hospital campus and then up the stairs two at a time to Surgical Oncology. She prayed all the while that she would find Theresa in her room and that this was just a false alarm. The cancer couldn't have grown that quickly. This was surreal. Theresa had just left the hospital and had been home for less than two weeks with her family.

She barely had time to gain enough energy and strength to create just a few more happy memories to sustain her husband and sons through what she had hoped would not occur for at least a few more months. Throwing her coat on the couch in the bubble, Faith frantically scanned the patient ID board to find Theresa's name and room number. She struggled to hold her tears back and fought a wave of panic when she realized Theresa's name was not listed on the assignment board or even in the unit census. She spun around in desperation and almost knocked Isaac Goldman over in her haste to find her friend.

"What happened? Where is she? Am I too late?" Faith's voice cracked as sheer panic threatened to overflow. She grabbed both sleeves of his lab coat in her fists and looked at him desperately.

"I tried to get here as fast as I could, but I hit every damned red light, and the construction on the fucking "Q" Bridge is, of course, blocking everything." She didn't think to censor her choice of words, but Isaac didn't bat an eye.

"Mrs. Travio is in ICU. She's stable now, but she came in

obtunded, and her respirations were really depressed. We reversed her pain meds with Narcan, and she's breathing more normally now. I'm going to leave her in the unit overnight to keep a closer eye on her."

Faith's eyes shut as her head dropped forward. "Oh, thank you, dear Jesus and His Blessed Mother," she whispered in sweet relief and then looked up at Isaac. "So, this was drug-induced, not tumor growth? I mean, if Narcan reversed the problem, she'll be ok, right?"

"She's ok, but honestly, just barely. She evidently had a grand mal seizure, that's why Mr. Travio called the ambulance. We loaded her with anticonvulsants, reversed the narcotics, and primed her with steroids to decrease the pressure in her head. For now, she's stabilized, but the onset of seizures can only mean her tumor has grown and her disease is progressing. We'll schedule an MRI for tomorrow morning to evaluate the extent of it. I'll take you to the unit now. Once Mrs. Travio was stabilized and settled, her husband asked for you."

Faith's head dropped again, but this time in relief and she took a few deep breaths to get her wits back about her. She swiped at her cheeks to dry them. An intuition that came from years in nursing, as well as the hard-won instincts of a motherless daughter, told her the unthinkable was about to happen, yet again. She whispered a quick prayer to her mother to give her the strength she would need to support Theresa and her family through what she knew would be an incredibly difficult time.

Chapter 16

The Intensive Care Unit in any hospital is a world of its own, with a life of its own. Although integrated into the hospital system and intertwined with other patient care units, the ICU is an island in many ways. Once the electric doors swoosh closed, it is isolated from the rest of the hospital by virtue of high patient acuity, advanced technology, and the heightened stressors of a minute-by-minute battle between life and death.

ICU nurses, with their extensive education and background, make life-or-death decisions on a constant basis, often with no physician present. With finely tuned assessment skills and the ability to troubleshoot a crisis quickly and efficiently, they are experts in appropriate management and treatment of any situation that might arise at any hour of the day.

Isaac Goldman had given her a brief rundown of the course of events that had brought Theresa back to the hospital, but when the sliding doors of the ICU softly swooshed open, it was only natural for Faith to seek out the expert who would know the "real story," the nurse who could give her the answers she so desperately needed, in the language that only a fellow nurse would understand.

Faith found Susan standing at Theresa's bedside. Her skilled eyes watched the rise and fall of Theresa's chest and simultaneously noted her vital signs on the monitor located above the head of

Theresa's bed. She observed the relaxed expression on her sleeping patient's face and carefully watched for any subtle indication of pain or distress. Even in an unconscious patient like Theresa, pain required meticulous titration of medication to prevent the recurrence of the slowed and inefficient respiratory pattern that had existed only hours before.

Although Sue kept a gentle smile on her face as her warm and motherly hands smoothed back the sparse fuzz on Theresa's now almost-bald head, Faith knew that her analytical mind correlated everything she saw on the monitor with what she observed during her continual scrutiny of her patient. Faith whispered a prayer of gratitude that Theresa was in the ICU because here, she would be under the astute surveillance of sharp-eyed, expert nurses who lived this scenario every day.

"Mama Sue," as she was known to the multitude of new nurses she had mentored over the years, as well as countless staff she lovingly nurtured through the course of their lives, trials, and tribulations, motioned to Faith to follow her out of the room. They stood just outside the room, watching Theresa through the plate glass window but out of earshot so as not to disturb her restful slumber. Susan talked to her friend as she jotted notes and vital signs onto the flow sheet.

"Ok, take a deep breath and relax, Faith, she's ok. Vital signs all look good. She's breathing well and doesn't even need the face mask for oxygen. We're using nasal prongs as a precaution. She's dry because she hasn't been taking much fluid by mouth, so we're hydrating her with some IV saline. And I haven't seen any more seizure activity. She's stable for now and will probably go to the floor tomorrow."

Although Faith was used to doing the same on a less intense basis as her patients tended to be more stable, she still marveled that Mama Sue could watch her patients, chart the details, and talk to Faith at the same time.

"Thanks so much, Sue. I was scared to death when they called me. Where's Tony?"

"I sent him home. He was just a mess, crying and begging Theresa not to die. It was heartbreaking. Her sons are no better. Once we knew Theresa had stabilized and we got her settled, and once they saw that she was comfortable, I convinced them that the best thing for everyone was to be well-rested and able to think clearly when she woke up. They are going to need their strength in the days to come, and it isn't going to help Theresa at all if one of them collapses at her bedside," Susan explained, and she looked at her friend with unspoken meaning in her eyes.

The explanation was moot at this point. Faith knew that Theresa's time was limited.

From years of experience, Mama Sue knew Faith needed permission to leave her friend's bedside. Her professional advice, coupled with her motherly sensitivity, made Faith's decision to do so easier.

"Look, I know this is your first night off after your vacation. I promise I'll call you if anything changes, but you need to go back home and sleep. Call me if you need to check on her for your own peace of mind. When the Travios get back, I'll let Tony know that you were here. Go on, Theresa is in good hands."

Sue reached out to Faith and pulled her into her warm embrace to give her a much-needed hug. She rubbed her friend's back with gentle, loving hands, which had soothed so many patients, family, and friends over the years. Mama Sue whispered to her as only a mother would so that only Faith could hear.

"She has a gift in you, Faith. Tony told me how they love you like a daughter, how good you've been to all of them. Go home. I'll call you if anything changes, I promise."

Faith looked back over her shoulder as she slowly and reluctantly walked away from Theresa's room and walked right into Isaac Goldman, who had come up to check on his patient. Startled, Faith latched onto his arms to keep her balance, and Isaac grabbed her by the shoulders to keep her from falling.

"Whoa, steady there. How's she doing?" Isaac looked at

Faith with concern, which Faith interpreted as professional concern for his patient.

"She's stable, thank God, and she's in great hands with Sue. Her family went home. I can't believe Sue convinced them to go. Theresa is so lucky she's on tonight." Faith looked back again at Theresa's room.

Isaac noticed for the first time the flecks of gold in Faith's eyes. He saw a flash of raw pain, which was quickly replaced by the profound strength he was so used to seeing. He wondered again about this nurse who had captured his eye not too long ago, and suddenly, he wanted to know much, much more, but this was obviously neither the time nor the place.

Before he could even speak, Faith continued. "I'm sorry I was so short before, and I didn't even thank you for calling me. I really appreciate it," Faith paused for a moment and then quizzically looked up at him.

"How did you get my number, anyway?"

Faith suddenly was aware Isaac was still holding her by the shoulders, and she, his arms. They stepped away from each other almost self-consciously but continued to study each other. Faith waited patiently for his response, and Isaac opened his mouth to answer her.

He wanted to tell her that, as soon as Becky had told him her last name, he had looked her number up in the phone book and committed it to memory. He wanted to tell her that, for months now, he had been watching her on the surgical unit, wondering where she learned to be so kind and gentle. He admired her seemingly effortless way of making every patient feel special, speaking freely to patients and families while juggling a full caseload with no complaints.

Despite what must have been hundreds of patient and family interactions during his residency, he still felt uncomfortable with the degree of intimacy with patient care that Faith embraced so freely and fiercely. His own efforts felt clumsy and hollow in comparison. He wanted to tell her he noticed every morning how exhausted she looked yet made an effort to smile at every patient and say "goodbye" before she left for home.

He wanted to tell her how beautiful she was, with the black smudges under her eyes, her unruly hair always escaping her barrette, and her scrubs crinkled after a chaotic twelve-hour shift. More than anything, he wanted to tell her that his life would never be the same if she didn't at least have a cup of coffee with him and tell him everything there was to know about herself and about her world.

"I was able to get your number," was Isaac's vague response.

"I knew you were close to the family. It was only natural that you should be here."

Isaac looked over Faith's shoulder and off into the distance, and silently cursed himself. As high as his IQ was, as much as he was able to memorize surgical techniques and then perform them with precision after one or two supervised procedures, as easily as he could speak in front of a conference room full of Attending physicians and fellow residents, he was unable to invite her for a simple cup of coffee, let alone tell her what was building within him.

Faith felt a brief flash of disappointment. "Well, thanks. I guess I'll go home then. I'm back tomorrow night; I should get some rest." Faith slowly walked toward the elevator with her hands in her pockets and her head down. She didn't look back.

Isaac stuffed his hands in his lab coat pockets and followed her with his eyes until the elevator doors closed behind her. Then he walked to his on-call room and unsuccessfully tried to get some sleep.

Chapter 17

It was all Faith could do the next day to keep herself from driving back to the hospital, to check on Theresa Travio and see with her own eyes how she was doing. She had called Susan as soon as she got home to check on her to see if anything had changed, then called again an hour later because she couldn't sleep. Finally, after two cups of herb tea and a mile of mindless pacing, she crawled into bed and fell into a restless, dream-filled sleep.

Flashes of her mother's death passed behind her eyelids, and interspersed among these scenes were flashes of Isaac Goldman: his cool demeanor in the face of so much chaos in the hospital world, the strength she felt in his surgeon's hands as they grasped her shoulders, his clumsiness in trying to talk to her on a level beyond that of mere colleague. During wakeful moments, Faith would stare at the ceiling, and her thoughts went from Theresa to Isaac and back again. She prayed yet again for the strength she would need to watch another one of her beloved patients die.

Calling the intensive care unit for the third time before Susan reported off to the day shift, Susan reassured her yet again that yes, Theresa was still stable; no, there had been no more seizure activity; and of course, someone would call if her condition changed. Realizing that she was going to accomplish nothing by staring at the ceiling, Faith got out of bed to begin her day. She filled it with mindless activity, anything to keep her mind off the hospital, but time and again, her thoughts returned to Theresa and the Travio family.

She lay down for a quick nap before work but was unable to fall asleep, so she got out of bed and put on her robe. She microwaved a piece of leftover pizza for a quick dinner and mindlessly nibbled at it. Finally, she threw it away, wiping her hands and mouth on a dish towel. She put her scrubs on and left for work two hours early.

Faith was relieved to find that Theresa had, in fact, been transferred back to Surgical Oncology and her name was now written up on the ID board. She hurried down the hall but then hesitated in the doorway before walking into Theresa's room. Gathered familiarly around Theresa's bed were Tony, Anthony and Joey, but the room was eerily quiet without the usual chatter, laughter, or jokes. Absent was the ever-present pizza.

No tantalizing smell of garlic permeated the air. No cups or plates littered the windowsill or nightstand. The subtle rise and fall of Theresa's chest were the only movements discernible under the sterile white top sheet, and the stillness was broken only by the raspy sound of her slow, agonal breaths. Theresa's shape seemed more shrunken, even more wasted away, than the previous night when

Faith had seen her in the ICU. Tony held Theresa's left hand and Faith was startled to see that Theresa's wedding ring was missing.

Tony noticed her expression, and when she looked up at him, he held up his left hand. On his ring finger, where Theresa had placed it over thirty years ago, was Tony's wide gold band. Next to it, above the second joint of his pinky finger, was the thinner gold band that he had placed on Theresa's. He closed his fist around the ring to keep it safe within his grasp.

"Neither of us has ever taken our ring off. Theresa even refused to take it off when she had all her surgeries; she made the nurses tape it in place in the OR. Yesterday, when the paramedics put Theresa on the stretcher, her hand flopped over the side and the ring came off. It came right off and just rolled across the floor." Tony's head dropped into his hands, and he sobbed.

Faith rushed to his side and put an arm around his shoulders. She placed her other hand on Theresa's arm and gently rubbed it.

"Hey, Tree, I'm here. Where's my piece of pizza?" Faith softly cajoled Theresa as she whispered a prayer that her friend would open her eyes and laugh at everyone for looking so grim and then sit up and begin ordering her family into action.

Theresa's eyes remained closed, her chest rising and falling slowly and shallowly, her face pale and almost mask-like. Faith looked over to Theresa's sons, and Anthony just shrugged as a single tear ran down his cheek. Joey kept his head down, and occasionally, he would backhand his cheeks in a feeble attempt to hide his tears.

Their eyes were reddened and swollen, and the two looked small and innocent in stark contrast to the blanket of somber emotions that now enveloped them. Faith hugged Tony and excused herself with reassurance that she would be right back. She walked out to the desk in search of Theresa's chart, and with it tucked under her arm, she went into the bubble and shut the door behind her. She opened the chart to the Progress Notes section and began to scan notes written since Theresa's admission yesterday evening.

"ICU Admitting Resident Note: 54-year-old female with a history of lung cancer, multiple recurrences with brain metastasis, now presents to the hospital with sudden onset grand mal seizure and severe respiratory depression. Full Code Status…"

"ICU Nurse's Note: vital signs stable, no evidence of seizure activity. Responds intermittently to family. Unresponsive to staff. Exhibits purposeful movement to noxious stimuli only…"

"General Surgery Resident Note: transferred to Surgical Oncology. MRI of the brain reveals extensive metastatic disease, profound edema noted with midline shift, and limited response to high-dose steroids overnight. Brain stem herniation imminent. No purposeful movement was noted in the family's presence. In light of rapid and profound deterioration in physical condition and mental

status, Do Not Resuscitate status discussed with family who agrees to comfort measures only..."

Faith shut the chart and closed her eyes for a minute, then went into the nurses' lounge to splash some water on her face. After drying her face in the mirror, she fluffed her hair a little and pinched her cheeks to bring some color and some life back into her own pale face. Then, she practiced smiling until she could do so without breaking down.

Faith smiled brightly as she walked into the room. "Ok, when was the last time any of you ate something?"

Tony and his sons just stared at her blankly. Food? Seriously? They looked at each other for an answer, but no one responded.

"I thought so. Ok, you guys, out. Go get something to eat, please, before you all fall over. Go on, I'm here now, and my shift technically doesn't start for another hour. I'll stay here with Theresa in case she wakes up. Go. We'll be fine until you get back. Won't we, Tree?"

Faith looked down at Theresa and smoothed her brow with one hand, shooing Tony and the boys out of the room with the other.

Each son tenderly kissed his mother and told her he loved her. Tony hesitated until the boys left the room and then kissed his wife so gently, so tenderly. He rested his cheek against her forehead and allowed his tears to flow silently and freely. As the wetness fell on his wife's face, Faith saw Theresa's hand move ever so slightly on the blanket as if trying to reach up and stroke the back of her husband's head, as she had seen her do to comfort him so many times before.

As Tony left the room, he stole a glance over his shoulder as if he were trying to find some small sliver of guilt-relieving permission to leave his wife's bedside. He wondered if something as simple as a sandwich was allowed at a time like this. Not sure he was doing the right thing, he found some solace that Faith would be with Theresa to watch her and comfort her until they returned. He promised himself it would only be for a little while as he turned away and followed his sons down the hall.

Faith pushed a chair back from the bed and out of the way and then put the side rail down. She sat down gently on the sterile white sheets and clasped her patient's hand in her own, then kissed it with the love of one who had grown to adore this patient as much as she adored her own family.

Faith spoke softly to Theresa of happier times, of memories that would remain to comfort her family. She reassured her of the family and friends who awaited her arrival in the next life. Time, though seemingly interminable for those left behind to mourn the loss of someone so precious, would pass in an instant. Her family would soon be with her, once again secure in the loving comfort of her arms. Faith's words were tender, words she had whispered to her own mother as she lay dying so many years ago when her own family stood gathered around a similar hospital bed, conceding to the imminent truth but desperately wanting to believe otherwise.

As she stroked her patient's face, the nurse in Faith saw the change of rhythm in the rise and fall of Theresa's chest and felt the coolness seep into her hands. She witnessed the pale color of Theresa's face fade slowly to the creamy ivory color of death. It happened so quickly, too quickly, and she didn't have time to summon Theresa's family back from the cafeteria.

The daughter in Faith remained seated on Theresa's bed so she wouldn't be alone. She held her hand and stroked her brow, even as she allowed her own tears to flow. When Tony and his sons returned, they found their wife and mother lifeless, breathless, and seemingly cold now that the warmth of her soul had slipped away. Her hand, however, remained warm and snug, clasped tenderly in the hands of her cherished nurse.

Chapter 18

Faith's childhood could best be described as a fairy tale. The youngest of five children, she arrived after four sons whose ages ranged over a twenty-year span. Faith was the miracle baby who had arrived unexpectedly after her mother had turned forty years old.

"Our gift from God," Faith's mother called her after she awoke from the anesthesia given in those days for childbirth, and Faith was placed in her arms for the first time.

"My baby girl, look how perfect her hand is," her father said in total wonder. His daughter wrapped her tiny fingers around his pinkie, which seemed gigantic in comparison.

In later years, Faith's father would laugh as he told her, "It was actually me who was wrapped around your little finger, not the other way around."

Even as a newborn babe, Faith had the eyes of an old soul, as if she had already lived one hundred years and carried the weight of many life lessons and hard-earned wisdom on her shoulders. Intently studying the world around her, she demonstrated empathy for and understanding of others with a maturity that belied her young age.

A testament to the love and care her family showered on her with such tenderness and joy, Faith began to show a nurturing and caring side at a very young age. As she grew older, she demonstrated uncanny insight into the feelings and emotions of people in the world around her, as well as an unconscious awareness of what others needed. Mature beyond her years, her mother's friends often commented that Faith was never truly a child but rather an adult in kids' clothing.

Faith was dubbed "nurse" at a very young age. At first, caring for her precious dollies and stuffed animals that littered her room, Faith soon became the caregiver on the school playground to whom many of the younger children ran for comfort and a kiss after skinning a knee or falling off the monkey bars. While other children would point and stare at others who were "different"- people who walked with braces, who rode in wheelchairs, or who had other physical challenges- Faith would smile, invite conversation, or simply sit quietly, providing company on an otherwise lonely day.

To the kids who sat in the "special" classes, who tried but never quite caught up with the "normal" kids in school, Faith would coax and encourage them, celebrating every milestone and hard-won achievement, praising their efforts and hugging them like any buddy would do. Faith was a friend, ally and protector of all, and she would defend those who could not or would not defend themselves. When asked why she cared so much, why she spent so much of her time taking care of others, Faith would respond quite simply, "How could I not?"

When Faith turned fifteen, during her sophomore year of high school, her mother developed headaches. Horrible and blinding, made worse by light or loud noise, the headaches pounded mercilessly inside her mother's skull with every heartbeat. Faith would return home after school to find her on the couch with lights off and blinds drawn, a pinched and pained expression on her face.

Faith would place a cold facecloth on her forehead, shushing and clucking like a mother hen, doing everything that her fifteen-year-old self could think of to make the agony end. Faith would try to massage the pain away, rubbing her mother's head and neck to relieve the tension and stiffness brought about by struggling against its grip, both desperately willing it to subside.

Occasionally, the pain would diminish, and Faith's mother could once again get herself up off the couch or out of bed. She would try to shrug those dark periods of agony off, blaming them on "the change," owing them to the stress of managing a household, trying desperately, but hardly succeeding, to laugh the misery off as a result of worrying about world peace and global warming.

After a month of trying to ignore the pain that had so brutally interrupted her life, as the brief periods of relief became even less frequent, Faith's mother gave in and agreed to see the doctor. Her father took a rare day off from work to accompany his wife, and when Faith came home from school that day, she found her mother and father sitting together on the couch. Her brothers sat on kitchen chairs pulled into a tight, close circle with their parents, and they all leaned forward, their shoulders touching, as if in a protective huddle around their mother. Faith felt a hollowness spread in her chest as her heart plummeted to her feet. Seeing the reddened and puffy eyes on everyone's faces, she knew immediately that something was terribly, horribly wrong.

Faith sat down in the one empty chair between Scott and Patrick and looked around at those who loved her the most. Her knuckles blanched completely white as she clenched the edges of the chair, and she braced herself for whatever her family was about to tell her. In the time it took for her father to explain to her that her mother had a tumor, it was malignant, but the doctor was optimistic that chemotherapy and radiation might help her, Faith's adolescence came to a screeching halt, her innocence shattered by the cruel devastation of a beloved parent's life-threatening illness.

Over the next nine months of her life, Faith's fairy tale world drastically changed. Her once carefree existence, filled with the celebration of life and love for the family who surrounded her, became a redundant schedule of school, home, caring for Mom, making dinner for her brothers, housework, and finally, homework. Bedtime came later and later, and her alarm clock often jolted her awake after only five or six hours of sleep that was fitful at best. Faith's cheerful façade began to fade, and in its place evolved a woman with the visage of a teenager but the heart and soul of a sage. She became the living portrait of a young woman whose life was interrupted abruptly by the worst tragedy imaginable.

Faith became the caregiver her mother used to be. Once upon a time her mother would make hot cocoa and fresh brownies for an after-school snack, when loving and attentive conversation would be squeezed in between all of Faith's extracurricular activities. Now it was Faith's turn to bring her mother a fresh glass of ginger ale to sit with her and keep her company on many lonely days and pain-ridden afternoons.

When the lines of tension on her mother's face became pinched and drawn, Faith would measure out the correct dose of pain medication and ensure that the pills were given at the correct time. Through meticulous observation of her mother's response to medication, Faith would notify the doctor herself when the prescribed dose no longer eased the throbbing pain in her mother's head and would call for refills when the bottle was almost empty.

Despite being just a high school student, overnight Faith felt as though she had become a full-fledged caregiver. As her mother's illness progressed, she became an active participant in her mother's care, not only tending to her mother's physical needs but also coordinating the many appointments that filled her mother's days. She became accustomed to rushing home after school to help her father get her mother into the car, and once at the oncologist's office, she would run in to get a wheelchair for her mother to spare her the debilitating exhaustion that merely walking into the office would cause.

After a full course of radiation left her mother too weak to attend to her own personal needs, with reddened and painful radiation burns on her head already bald from several rounds of toxic chemotherapy, Faith found herself sitting in the oncologist's office along with her father. Grace, with an exhausted and pained expression on her face, sat hunched in her wheelchair between them, too weak and frail to hold her emaciated body upright.

She clasped her eyes shut and kept her head down as if to shield herself from the unbearable weight of what she knew to be bad news. Faith clasped one of her mother's hands, her father clasped the other. Calmly, Faith asked the doctor what, exactly, the torture of "medical science" was supposed to be doing for her mother?

The doctor sat back in his chair and looked at Faith in surprise, then looked at her mother and father. He scratched his head and rolled his pen between his hands, sighing as if to communicate exactly how busy he was. Then, he assumed a condescending smile and shrugged.

"The CAT scan did not show any regression in tumor size after the radiation treatment. Quite frankly, I had hoped for a better response. I am scheduling you for a new chemotherapy protocol in two weeks. It's experimental, but I am confident that this regimen will offer you some positive results." With that, the doctor turned his attention to the chart on his desk and began to scribble his notes and thus ended the discussion.

Faith watched in horror as her bald and shrunken mother seemed to wither even more. Grace crumpled in on herself, and silent tears flowed through closed eyelids, her mouth clamped tightly against overwhelming despair that hope had betrayed her for the last time.

With her head bowed, her mother whispered, "Oh, please, not again. Make it stop. Please, please, please, make it stop."

The doctor did not acknowledge the agony so apparent on his patient's face, the distress so obvious in her voice. He did not look up from the chart in front of him.

"I'll set up the appointment, and the nurse will speak to you about your prescriptions before you leave. We'll do some labs today to get a baseline." He stood up and walked to the office door and stood expectantly with his hand resting on the doorknob in silent but apparent invitation to leave.

"No, Doctor, that won't be necessary." Faith was as surprised as her parents by the quiet, unexpected strength in her voice.

"You didn't hear my mother. She's done. We're done. It's time to go home now. Come on, Mom, let's go." She began to back her mother's wheelchair up and turned her around. The doctor stood with his hand on the doorknob, his mouth agape, as Faith wheeled her mother out of his office.

The doctor curtly admonished them as they proceeded up the hallway, "I strongly advise against ending treatment now, or we won't have a chance. Do you understand what I'm telling you?"

With overwhelming conviction she was doing what was best for this amazing woman who was the center of her family's world, Faith stopped and turned to face the doctor.

Equally as sternly, she replied, "You are missing the point. 'We' aren't in question here, Doctor, my mother is. She just said she's done." Turning back to her mother, her father beside Grace holding tightly and resolutely to her hand, Faith gently pushed her out of the doctor's office for the last time. Without another glance or consideration for anything but family and their commitment to each other, they took Grace home to die.

She and her father struggled for several months to care for Grace at home, to allow her the blessing of passing in her own bed, with family and unconditional love surrounding her. They almost succeeded. All the while, however, Grace became weaker, frailer, and more emaciated. They had worked around the clock, and each took a turn nursing her while the other slept. They exhausted themselves in an attempt to keep her clean and to prevent the bedsores that seemed almost inevitable despite superhuman efforts to turn her and massage her and support her withered body with the softest pillows they could find.

Eventually they both had to admit that their efforts were futile. They just could not keep abreast of the backbreaking amount of work involved in caring for their beloved wife and mother. Too tired and shell-shocked to work up even the slightest energy to cry, Faith, with her brothers gathered around her, clasped both of her father's hands in her own. The agony and heartbreak in her eyes said all that needed to be said, and with silent tears that flowed freely, her father gave in to the disease that his wife had struggled so relentlessly and so courageously to overcome.

Almost imperceptibly, he nodded and admitted defeat. Faith's oldest brother called the ambulance that would carry their mother away from her home for the last time in her life and then joined the family in the embrace of a tight-knit circle around her bed. With strength that could only come from a lifetime of loving memories and shared heritage, they embraced each other with the loving support they would need to get through this nightmare.

Faith's mother was taken back to the hospital she hated, under the care of the doctor whom she resented for the pain and misery his relentless "treatments" and his "hope" that it might work "this time" had inflicted during the last few months of her life. Faith, her brothers, and their father spent her mother's final hours being ushered in and out of her hospital room every time the nurses turned her, or changed her, or performed the tasks that, by this time, were meaningless.

When death finally approached, Faith's father and brothers were standing at the foot of her mother's bed, heads down and shoulders touching, speaking softly. They did not see her breaths grow shallow, did not watch her withered body fade bit by bit into the stark, sterile whiteness of hospital sheets. Faith was the only one who bore witness to her mother's transition from this world to the next.

As she clasped her mother's hand in her own, she caught a very quick glimpse into her mother's soul, where her own future and purpose flashed before her. Faith sensed the moment her mother's soul escaped her body as her last shallow breath escaped her mouth. It caressed Faith's cheek with soft and gentle warmth and lingered just for one fleeting, precious moment. It paused briefly among this family and bestowed a mother's final blessing on her children and husband. Before it dissipated for good, it blessed Faith with what proved to be the most profound and most meaningful gift Grace had ever given to her daughter. Tragically, a mother had died, but out of that profound anguish, through a mother's loving legacy, was born a nurse.

Chapter 19

Faith sat at the desk and stared at the phone as if delaying notification of the covering physician would put off the inevitable. The death certificate sat on the desk in front of her and Faith glared at it, cursed it, damned it for signifying the end of any life, let alone her friend's. She reached for the phone, dropped the receiver back on its cradle, and then picked it up again. Before she could change her mind, Faith dialed the page operator and asked for the surgical resident on-call.

She was shocked to hear Isaac Goldman's voice, "Dr. Goldman. I was paged?"

Faith swallowed. "Hey, Isaac, it's Faith." She cleared her throat and sniffed, then continued unnecessarily, "I'm the nurse taking care of Theresa Travio."

As if I wouldn't recognize your voice…

Her voice shook as she struggled for composure, determined not to cry. "Theresa just passed, and you need to come pronounce her." She paused momentarily, waiting for his answer, but then blurted, "Wait, weren't you here late last night? You should be off now."

Isaac tried to sound offhand and matter of fact as he responded, "Someone else needed the night off, so I switched."

What he didn't say was, "It cost me a favor to get someone to take tonight off and work Saturday night for me instead so I could be close to you."

What he couldn't say was, "I've never met a woman whom I needed to speak to so badly, whom I needed to be close to just so I could breathe. What do you dream about at night? What makes you happy? Will you let me spend the rest of my life trying to make you smile?"

The thought almost shocked him as he realized the truth behind it. He also knew that, except for one brief moment last night in the ICU, Faith had shown absolutely no interest in him unless it was related to patient care, and even that was pretty mundane and straightforward.

Distracted by the task at hand, Faith didn't acknowledge Isaac's explanation and continued, "Theresa's family is still here, they are just saying goodbye. They are all pretty torn up and…" Faith could no longer hold back her emotion and felt a sob ready to escape.

Her voice cracked as she quickly added, "If you could just come pronounce her and sign the death certificate, her family can go home." She abruptly hung up the phone before her tears began in earnest.

Faith walked softly to Theresa's room and tiptoed just inside the doorway, hesitant to intrude on so intimate a moment. Theresa's sons knelt on the floor as they gripped her hands, their heads bowed onto her chest, weeping softly. Tony clasped one son by the neck and reached across the bed to the other to stroke the back of his head as Theresa had done so many times before, a touch that was so familiar to all of them. Nothing was said. What could anyone say in response to every son's worst nightmare, to every husband's deepest fear, that would make this scenario even remotely bearable?

Faith paused in the doorway, giving this family time to grieve and to prepare to say a final goodbye to the woman who was the world in its entirety for each of them. Finally, the boys stood up and one last time, they kissed Theresa's forehead, and then each of them hugged their father. Tony stood motionless as Faith motioned to Joey and Anthony to follow her into the hall to give Tony some precious time alone with his wife.

They stood just outside the doorway and heard the sobbing and pain of the father left to pick up the pieces for his family. When Tony finally came out of his wife's room, he silently walked to Faith and put his hands on her shoulders, kissing her forehead as tenderly and with as much love and affection as any father might kiss his daughter, then pulled her to his chest and held her tightly for a moment, gently rocking her, as if to comfort this daughter/nurse who had become such a cherished part of their family. Then, silently, he took each of his sons' hands in his own and led them to the elevators without looking back.

Faith went back into Theresa's room and there Isaac found her, looking down on Theresa, her face still wet with tears. Wordlessly, he put his stethoscope in his ears and listened for Theresa's heartbeat. Hearing none, he reached into his pocket for his penlight and lifted each eyelid to shine it into her eyes.

Noting no response in her pupils, Isaac pronounced softly, "Time of death, 7 pm." He thoughtfully pulled her gown back up over her chest and replaced the sheet over her body, as he so often had seen Faith do. Then he stepped back from the bed. Faith walked around the bed to where Isaac stood and with no explanation, she stood up on tiptoe and kissed his cheek, then walked out of her patient's room. Isaac watched her leave, lost in thought, and then he left the room as well.

Becky came onto the General Surgical Unit the next morning, two cups of coffee in hand, her clipboard tucked under her arm. She found Faith at the desk in her usual 6 am position, charts in front of her, keeping an eye on the call lights, ready to multi-task and answer the many questions that were fired at her while she tried to finish up her own work.

"How was your night?" Becky handed Faith the cup of fresh coffee from the donut shop across the street to save her from drinking the black sludge that had been sitting at the bottom of the unit coffee pot for hours.

"Same shit, different shift." Faith answered flatly, her face expressionless as she looked at Becky. The brightness of unshed tears in Faith's eyes was the only visible sign of the pain and turmoil going on inside of Faith's mind, apparent to only those who knew her well.

Becky lowered her voice to a very soft pitch so that only Faith could hear her. "You've got to know she's in a better place, Faith. She was blessed with a great, loving family, and she was blessed with the care of the best nurse in this hospital. You gave her the greatest gift anyone could have given to her at the time she needed it most. You gave her back her dignity and helped her get her wish: to go home, even for as brief a time as it was. Her family will never forget that."

Not waiting for an answer, Becky raised her voice. She looked around and asked, "Where are the residents? I can't believe the OR schedule today is totally packed. Some Attendings must have their kids' tuition payments coming up because they seem to be cramming more and more cases onto the schedule," Becky shook her head and headed towards the elevator.

"Drinks tonight, at your place? I've got books all over my living room and a week's worth of dirty clothes still sitting on my bathroom floor. OK?"

Becky smiled at her and then rushed out, coat tails flapping behind her in their usual flurry. Faith hurried to finish up and go home so she could climb into bed and forget the sadness of the hospital, though she knew that even in the deepest of sleep, she could not escape it.

Chapter 20

Before leaving for the day, Becky returned to the unit for final rounds. She read through the patient charts and co-signed some verbal orders she had given over the phone while she was in the OR. She reviewed labs and x-rays, did a few quick patient visits to evaluate all the tubes, drains, and dressings that go hand in hand with general surgery, and slipped out of her lab coat as she headed for the elevators. She stopped to rub her neck and then arched her back to relieve the kinks caused by hunching over the surgical table for hours on end.

The elevator doors opened, and Isaac Goldman rushed out. The two almost collided in their haste to reach their destinations.

"Hey, I already did the post-op checks and wrote the notes. I gave report to the on-call resident, so I'm out of here." Isaac looked to Becky for approval and then glanced around the unit.

He looked back to Becky and off-handedly asked, "Is Faith on tonight, by any chance? I just wanted to see how the Travio family had done. I didn't get a chance to speak with them before they left."

"I'm not sure. I saw her this morning, but just for a quick minute before I went into surgery. She seemed ok but sad, though. I have to run, I have plans. See you tomorrow."

Isaac jammed his hands into his lab coat, his real questions unanswered. What do you do in a case like this? Send flowers to the nurse who worked so hard caring for her patient, knowing she would never see him or her again? Offer a trite, "So sorry for your loss" the next time he saw her on the unit? Pretend the whole thing hadn't happened and move on? More importantly, what do you say to the woman whose mere presence in the unit made it a better place? Whose smile made him forget everything but her and made him look forward to getting up at 4:30 AM just to get to work? Whose gentle touch on her patients' hand was the same gentle touch he hoped to feel someday, himself?

"They sure as heck didn't teach us this in med school," Isaac grumbled to himself as he slowly walked back to the elevator and pushed the button, head down, frowning at his shoes.

Walking out to the garage, Isaac wondered how on earth people did this, day after day. How on earth do you take care of terminally ill patients, knowing they most likely aren't going to be here next month, or quite possibly even next shift?

Although he couldn't exactly say he had grown close to any of his patients, Isaac had found himself attempting to follow Faith's lead and tried to get to know at least something about each one to make the experience somewhat more personal. It was so easy for Faith, Isaac thought. His own efforts to ask gentle questions and then to seem genuinely interested in his patients' answers seemed so clumsy and forced, so unnatural to him. So many of his surgeries were completed uneventfully, and the patients recovered in a few days, returning home to their lives and their loved ones, and he never saw them again. Isaac wondered why anyone would bother to get to know these patients, as transient as the patient population in a hospital seemed to be.

The hospital, the daily routine, and the patients - at times, Isaac felt as though he was just traveling a route so predictable he needn't pay much attention to redundant scenery along the way. His efforts required focus only on the mechanics and technical details of a specific surgical procedure that would help a patient recover and get well.

Faith obviously thought otherwise. He marveled at all the information Faith retained, not only about her patients' diseases and treatments but also all the other details he might otherwise have considered insignificant. Something as simple as a flavored popsicle might seem trivial, but one day, after overhearing Faith on the phone trying to track down a root beer popsicle, he quickly learned that, to a patient who hadn't been allowed to eat for days or even weeks, the very first taste of a favorite, icy cold treat may very well offer a tiny glimmer of Heaven.

Isaac thought of another time he walked into a patient's room, only to find Faith standing on the lid of a trash can, balanced precariously as she sang along with her teenaged patient to a song on the radio while taping a poster of a young actress on the ceiling. Once Faith explained her patient's activity was going to be restricted for several days to lying flat on his back following his lumbar and thoracic surgery and that counting ceiling tiles would be his only activity until his family was able to visit in the evening, Isaac began to realize the pure genius behind Faith's seemingly "silly" intervention on her patient's behalf. Isaac began to appreciate the many small gestures Faith made for her patients, simple gestures that made such a genuine difference in their days.

Isaac marveled at the serenity and peace that emanated from Faith despite the stress and sadness of Surgical Oncology. "I wonder how she does it." Isaac said to himself. Equally as loudly, a voice in his head said, "you idiot, drive over there and find out!"

Isaac ran back to the elevators and repeatedly punched the button to get to Surgical Oncology. Growing impatient as he watched the numbers flash far too slowly, Isaac bolted for the stairs and took them two at a time to the surgical unit, where he plopped himself down in front of the computer in the bubble. He reverse-Googled her phone number, the one he had committed to memory, the one inscribed on his heart.

"25A Kenneth Street, North Haven, CT" popped up on the screen, and Isaac thanked God for the photographic memory that saved him the precious seconds it would take to hunt down a pen and paper. Then he flew back down the stairs and out to the garage, in search of the answer to so many of his unspoken questions, in search of his life.

Chapter 21

"I don't think I ever would have forgiven myself if I wasn't with Theresa when she died. I feel like I was as close to her as I was to my own Mom. I wonder how Tony and those boys will manage without her? She kept everyone, everything, in line. She kept perfection in their lives. What do you do when that kind of love leaves you?"

"Well, how did you guys do it? I'm sure your brothers couldn't have been much help. I mean, they're guys. What did your father do? How old were you anyway?"

Faith's eyes grew misty at memories that were as fresh now as they were that awful day her mother died. "Well, I was there at home. I was fifteen, but it was just sort of assumed that I would take over the household stuff. My Dad kept himself busy, to distract himself from how lonely he was. He tried so hard to be both Mom and Dad for me, although at my age, I don't think he really knew how to do that. The boys were either already out of the house, or well on their way. He just didn't know what to do with a fifteen-year-old daughter.

"He tried, though." Faith looked wistful for a quick moment. She pulled out glasses, vodka and juice. "Beer isn't going to do it tonight, Beck, sorry. I need this drink more than oxygen right about now."

"I hear you, Faith. That sounds good to me. I think we both could use a little 'sedation.'" They both chuckled at the trite euphemism, even though it wasn't funny.

The drinks went down smoothly, and both women sat in silence as the alcohol worked its magic. Faith went into the kitchen to make another drink for them both without asking Becky whether or not she wanted one. She hoped that if she got sufficiently schnockered, she might sleep free of the nightmares that frequently tormented her after a beloved patient passed. They were always the same, similar to the ones that haunted her after her own mother had died: the ones about what she might have done differently, or what she might do better the next time, the ones that made her question, "If only…"

"Do you have any munchies? I won't be able to drive home if I drink too much on an empty stomach."

"I'm sorry Beck; I didn't even ask if you had eaten dinner. Want to order a pizza? I have some cheese and crackers if you'd rather." Faith popped up off the couch and headed into her kitchen. While she was out of sight, Becky hedged around the question she had started to ask the other night when the ringing of the telephone had interrupted her.

"That Goldman seemed to do well with that whole situation. I wondered in the beginning if anything would crack that shell he keeps around himself, but he's been lightening up a bit. Wonder what the deal is?" mused Becky.

"Mr. Travio appreciated his attention, I know that. I've got to tell you; I was shocked he called me at home. I figured one of the other nurses on the floor would let me know when she was readmitted, but Mama Sue didn't know how close I was to Theresa, and the other nurses in ICU had no way of knowing the extent of my relationship with the Travios. They never would have thought to call me. I really owe him for that one." Faith walked back into the living room with a small plate of cheese and some crackers and placed it down on the coffee table. She picked up a cracker and mindlessly began to nibble one corner.

The partially eaten cracker forgotten in her hand, Faith continued. "You know, when I first met him, I thought he was just another one of those yahoos who knew everything and had no problem making sure everyone else knew it as well. He's brilliant, that was evident right away, but as smart as he is, he's so damned awkward at the bedside. Everything comes out so clinical, like he's speaking to one of his professors. Sometimes I see the patients' eyes glaze over, like they just can't understand his language. And then I finally figured it out. He just doesn't know how." Faith's expression softened. "Maybe he's one of the lucky ones who has never lost someone close to him. Maybe he has no clue what it's like to have his world ripped out from underneath him. I don't know. Maybe he was never taught, or maybe he was and just can't translate it into practice.

Faith nibbled another corner of her cracker again, lost in thought. "But lately..." She paused to take another sip of her drink.

"I don't know how to explain it, and I almost want to laugh at times because you can tell he's trying but isn't quite sure how to go about it. He finally realized that just standing in the patient's doorway while giving bad news isn't such a great way to deliver it, so slowly but surely, he started easing himself inside the room. Sometimes he almost looks comical, but inside, I know his heart is good and I think he really does care. He just doesn't know how to show it."

"I wonder what makes him tick. I guess we all have a reason we went into this profession." She mulled over her last statement.

Becky just sat quietly, watching Faith with wise eyes that missed nothing. As Faith rambled on about Isaac, Becky's mind was hard at work trying to process what was playing out before her. Shadows of sorrow that were so readily apparent in Faith's face when Becky brought her coffee this morning began to dissipate, replaced by a subtle softening of the furrow in her brow. Becky felt a flash of disappointment, but she recovered quickly and reached for a piece of cheese, no longer able to look at her friend. It almost broke her heart to say, "Maybe he just needs someone to show him."

Faith didn't seem to hear her. "Do you know anything about him? I always want to ask, like, where he came from, where he went to school, you know, the usual. I don't want to invade his privacy, though. Some of the docs keep themselves pretty removed and I can't blame them. The hospital is just too damned small sometimes."

Faith shook her head ruefully. Experience was a harsh teacher. She had watched the new and naïve nurses, time and again, who came to a teaching hospital with dreams of marrying a doctor and living a privileged life. What most of them found out, and usually the hard way, was that at the end of a five-year surgical residency, the vast majority of those doctors would move on, alone, and make their lives elsewhere with people who didn't eat, sleep, and breathe the hospital.

Not waiting for Becky to answer her question, she answered it herself. "Well, he's probably going back home to his high school sweetheart when his residency is over. What about you, Beck? After you are done, when is it going to be your turn? When are you going to settle down? Do you ever think about sharing your life with a special someone?" She stared absently at the ice cubes in her drink and swirled them around, unaware of the sadness that fleetingly clouded Becky's face, the subtle wilting of her posture.

"Well, actually, I've wanted to talk to…"

Her words were cut off abruptly by loud, insistent knocking

at the front door. "What the heck?" They both looked at the front door, and then at each other.

"Who the hell is that at this hour?" Becky looked at Faith worriedly. "Let me get it."

Becky walked to the front door and looked through the peep hole. She turned around and looked at Faith, then turned back to the door and slowly opened it. There, on the top step with his hands jammed into his pockets, stood Isaac Goldman.

Before he realized it was Dr. Simon and not Faith who was standing in front of him, he began to say, "Sorry for dropping in so late…" but then stopped short. Isaac hesitated momentarily and focused on Becky. Then, as if this were any typical social call on any typical evening after work, he looked her straight in the eye and calmly asked, "Is Faith here?"

Startled to hear a man's voice, Faith put her empty glass down and walked toward the front hallway. She stood at the end of the hall, shocked to see who was standing at her front door. She looked at Becky with a puzzled expression on her face, her head tilted to the side, not quite comprehending what was happening.

"OK, well, I was just leaving. Faith, I'll see you in a few days. Take it easy and get some rest." Becky hugged her friend and kissed her on the cheek, then walked back into the living room to grab her coat. Isaac stood glued in the same spot and looked only at

Faith.

"See you around, Goldman." She nudged his arm as she walked by and thought to herself, Isaac Goldman wasn't as dense as she had once thought.

Faith stood silently, not moving. She stared at Isaac, and he at her.

Finally, he asked her, "Do you mind if I come in?"

As if pushed from behind, Faith started forward, "I'm so sorry, let me take your coat. Come in. Do you want a drink?" She led him into the living room and without waiting for a response, went into the kitchen. She returned to the living room a few moments later with two fresh drinks and then abruptly stopped. She looked at him in total confusion.

"Wait, what are you doing here?"

"I know it's late, and I'm sorry about barging in on you. I was afraid you'd be in bed, but, well, honestly, I couldn't wait."

"Wait for what?"

Isaac didn't respond. Instead, he took the drinks out of her hand and placed them on the table. Standing less than an arm's length away, the confused look in her eyes grew soft as a rush of hope filled her with warmth. She hesitantly reached out to him and put her hand on his arm.

"Isaac?"

Isaac reached into his mind, into recesses uncluttered by medical minutiae, where only pure emotion and the sensitivity he had been taught to repress in the hospital setting were hidden. He searched for the courage to do what he wanted to do, to say what he wanted to say. He swallowed once and opened his mouth to speak, then just as quickly closed it again. Finally, he realized there was just one thing he could do, and giving in to hopeful possibility, he pulled her into his arms.

Isaac held Faith close and rested his cheek against the beautiful curls he had never seen free of the barrette she wore at work. As he closed his eyes, he knew he held in his arms the most perfect woman God had ever created. Part of him was afraid she would push him away yet as he took a deep breath, he felt her body begin to mold his own and she settled into his embrace. He didn't speak; he just held her and swayed gently back and forth. One of his hands cradled her head against his chest and as he took a deep breath, he breathed in the purest scent of lavender on an Irish hillside.

A gentle sense of peace enveloped his soul. Isaac sensed the flutter of angel wings in her heart which beat so close to his own, and then he heard a soft, hesitant intake of breath. The only allusion to the pain of her loss was a whisper as soft as a tiny kitten's first purr, filled with the innocence of a child. He tightened his embrace and clasped Faith more closely, as if only he could protect her from the misery of a world which often defied explanation and offered no apology for the cruelties it inflicted upon so many. Isaac finally realized his purpose in coming to St. Mike's and felt contentment and the peace of belonging for the first time in his adult life.

Isaac leaned back to look into Faith's eyes, still bright with unshed tears, and his thumbs gently traced the silver tracks of those that had already dried on her cheeks. He stepped back but was stopped as she circled his neck with arms now intent and purposeful on their own mission.

Faith pulled him back against her heart where reason told her he belonged, knowing all the while that, finally, love was speaking to her. She looked up at him, her eyes meaningful and searching, and whispered softly, "What took you so long?"

Lowering his head to hers, Isaac gently kissed her, and Faith leaned fully into his embrace. Overwhelmed by a sense of completion, they realized that the answers to life's questions rested right there, in each other's arms.

Outside, on the top step with her hand still on the doorknob, stood a woman who had spent much of her life in search of her own perfect love. Decimated by sadness for unspoken questions that had been answered abruptly by an unexpected knock on the door, Becky mourned as her own dream for her future slipped out of her grasp and into the arms of another, and sorrow filled her heart for the love that had gone unnoticed by the one she had cherished above all else. Dr. Isaac Goldman would spend the rest of his life adoring the soul mate she had spent her life searching for; she would spend the rest of hers mourning the loss of a love that was never meant to be.

Chapter 22

Isaac woke the next morning as usual at 4:30 and opened his eyes only to realize he lay next to an angel. Afraid to move for fear of waking her, or of waking himself for that matter from the most magical dream he had ever had, Isaac watched her sleep. Even in slumber, with her curls now mussed over her face and her hands curled together and tucked under her chin, as she gently snored and then exhaled in a soft hush, Faith was still the most beautiful woman he had ever seen. He looked back over the previous night, coming to Faith's apartment in search of his future, firm in his conviction that he could not live another moment without her.

He sought what had eluded him all his adult life, and somehow quite miraculously had found himself enveloped by the heart and soul of an angel. What was once just a fantasy now filled him with determination and hope for his future. Isaac reached out and touched her cheek with one finger, ever so softly, as if it were the fragile wings of a butterfly. His lips grazed the tip of her nose tenderly and he leaned back to watch her awaken. As Faith began to stir, her eyes fluttered open and her gaze settled on his own. She smiled through the thick fog of sleep and reached to cradle his face in her hands.

"I thought I was dreaming," she whispered as she smiled, then kissed his chin and rubbed his nose with her own. "Where did you come from, Isaac Goldman? And where have you been all my life?"

Isaac gathered her into his arms and pulled her close, then tucked her head underneath his chin. "Two puzzle pieces," she thought, and snuggled even closer. It was then she realized the only thing separating them was a pair of white, cotton, bikini panties.

Faith looked under the covers, fell back with one arm across her eyes, and groaned. "I thought I had dreamt it. Oh my God, please tell me we didn't…"

Mortified, Faith pulled the covers up over her face and groaned again. She heard a soft chuckle and lowered one corner of the sheet just enough to peak out at Isaac.

Isaac smiled at her teasingly and waggled one eyebrow at her, then laughed out loud as he pulled her back into his embrace.

"I knew you had been drinking last night, but I didn't realize how much until we walked back to the living room, and you weaved a bit. We sat there and talked for a while, and you made another drink. When I got back from a quick trip to the bathroom, you were sound asleep."

Faith lay on her back and clutched the sheet between her fists, then allowed it to drop just a bit to her chin. "I can't believe it. I never drink that much, not since college. I'm so embarrassed." She reached up and grabbed the pillow from under her head and hugged it over her face, then replaced it. "If I fell asleep, how did I get here? Who took my clothes off?"

Matter of factly, he responded, "Well, it was a mutual effort. I carried you, and you half-helped me get your clothes off before you fell back to sleep. I just put them on your bureau." Isaac rolled over onto his belly and folded his hands under his chin. Resting them there, he looked at her, a serious expression on his face.

"After the day you had yesterday, I'm not surprised you got a bit toasted. I know it wasn't easy for you. I know how much you loved her." Isaac paused for a moment and then looked at Faith intently. "I'd like to talk to you, about last night… about us."

Faith lay in silence, almost afraid of what he might say to her. "Thanks, but no thanks," or "I'll call you," came to mind. He wouldn't call, though. They never did. Weeks would go by as hopes faded and disappointment set in, and then ultimately, humiliation. Maybe he had a girlfriend at home, with a big, shiny diamond on her finger. Maybe he was just biding his time until he set up his surgical practice and settled down on the other side of the country. This would be yet another example of what happens when you let your guard down and open yourself up too much, Faith thought flatly. She grabbed her ratty bathrobe off the foot of her bed and swung her legs over the side as she simultaneously slipped it on, modestly exposing as little of herself as possible.

Faith kept her back towards Isaac so she wouldn't have to meet his eyes and focused on tying her bathrobe snuggly closed. "So, what do you have planned for the rest of the day?"

Surprised by the abrupt change in direction the conversation had taken, Isaac grabbed Faith's wrist and pulled her back down to sit on the bed. She wouldn't turn to face him, so Isaac put both arms around her and gently pulled her back into his embrace. He held her tightly in his arms and rubbed her back, trying to comfort her and provide her with the reassurance he knew she so desperately needed to hear. "What would you like to do?" He used one finger to stroke her arm up and down; its soothing and repetitive motion almost hypnotic as it eased her mind and relaxed her body.

"What would I like to do? Um, I don't know." Faith knew what she wanted him to say yet was afraid that he wouldn't. She held her breath.

"How about we start with dinner?"

Faith's breath escaped in a rush of relief. "Dinner? Ok, dinner sounds good." Faith shut her eyes and snuggled against him. Then her eyes opened again. "What do you mean 'start?'"

Isaac laughed. "Last night wasn't really what I had expected for our first 'date,' Faith. I'd love for it to be something less predictable than dinner, but I have to work today. I probably won't leave the hospital until around 6:30 this evening and I'm on call tomorrow. I'd really like to see you tonight."

"You're on call this weekend?"

"Well, I had to do a little finagling to switch my schedule at the last minute. I only have to take call on Saturday, so I'll be off tonight. I really wanted to be at the hospital in case, well, you know..." He didn't add that Faith was the reason he wanted to work, just to be near her, to find a way to ease her pain and support her.

"Dinner's fine, I mean, great." Faith grew pensive. "I really want to thank you for being so thoughtful, calling me about Theresa and all. It meant so much to me to be able to be with her, I guess you could tell she was someone pretty special to me."

"I know. I knew you cared about her very much, but I didn't realize exactly how much until the issue with her discharge plans. I always meant to apologize to you for that. Had I really stopped to consider it from all angles, I would have realized how important it was to get her home. You were doing what you do best, and I shouldn't have been so angry at you for trying to help her. It just doesn't come naturally to me not to want to exhaust every intervention in the book. I didn't stop to think about what Mrs. Travio wanted, and for that I apologize. I'm sorry I doubted you. I'm sorry I didn't listen to both of you."

Faith lifted her head in surprise, and for a moment, could say nothing. "I don't think a doctor has ever apologized to me before, Isaac. Thank you," she added, simply.

"Faith, in your life, I don't want to be a just a doctor you work with." He smiled at her and laughed at the pink flush that rose in her cheeks. "But we should probably wait until tonight to talk about it some more. If I don't hit the shower, I'll be late for rounds."

Faith laughed, a bit disappointed, still wanting to know what he meant by "start" with dinner. He got out of bed and headed towards the bathroom, and she laughed out loud as he walked away from her. Isaac turned around, his hands on his hips, a smirk on his face, "And you are laughing because...."

"I was convinced I was the only one who had undies on. I thought you were, you know. I was afraid to look." Faith blushed, and then Isaac laughed along with her. "Towels are in the cupboard under the sink. Do you want me to make coffee?"

"You go back to sleep; I can grab something in the cafeteria when I get to the hospital." Isaac walked back to the bed and sat down next to Faith. His gaze softened, and tenderly he brushed a wisp of hair back off her forehead, and then traced her cheek, and her lips. Faith leaned towards him slowly and closed her eyes in anticipation of his kiss and let her breath out in a rush as she felt his lips gently brush her forehead, the tip of her nose, and then slowly, almost hesitantly, her lips. The kiss, though brief, spoke of promise and of hope, and then reluctantly, Isaac went to take his shower.

Rolling onto her back, Faith pulled the sheet back up under her chin and absent-mindedly stroked her lower lip with one finger, closing her eyes as she imagined how soft his lips were, how gentle his touch was. A smile of contentment on her face, Faith stretched her arms above her head in a relaxing, blissful stretch, and listened to the water running in the shower. She wondered about this man who had walked onto the unit several years ago, who had caught her eye as he cared for their patients yet caught her interest but a few months ago. Just before sleep engulfed her once more, Faith allowed herself the slightest glimmer of hope and the promise of possibility.

Chapter 23

Isaac rushed onto the surgical unit. He simultaneously struggled to drape his stethoscope around his neck as he wrestled his arms into the sleeves of his lab coat and precariously passed a cup of coffee from hand to hand. He cursed his luck as a few precious drops spilled on his sleeve. Without his coffee, he knew he wouldn't make it until lunch. Already he felt the need to shower again and scour the fog from his mind. He had to make a conscious effort to keep his last image of Faith in the back of his mind, to prevent any distraction from his patients' well-being and care.

As he joined the group of interns and residents on rounds with Dr. Simon, Isaac dropped his clip board. Becky interrupted her grilling of the intern who had been on-call overnight just long enough to raise one eyebrow at Isaac and glare at him and then turned back to the intern to critique his assessments and care of her patients. Once satisfied with answers that assured her the patients had been well taken care of in her absence, she turned down the hall to begin rounds. Her surgical team scurried after her like a group of ducklings waddling after their mother.

When rounds had ended, Isaac approached Becky, looking sheepish. "I'm sorry I was late, I overslept and just couldn't get out the door," he fibbed, not quite ready to share the subject of Faith with anyone. It would not have mattered if he did. Becky was in too much of a rush to get away from him.

Becky muttered something unintelligible under her breath and then admonished Isaac to get to work. "By the way, I pulled you out of the OR this morning. There are two patients coming in who will need complete workups before we take them to surgery. Both are complicated gut cases. Get the MRIs sent up to the OR, then get central lines into both of them and prep them. We'll plan on taking them to surgery later this afternoon. Oh, and don't forget the labs."

Isaac cursed under his breath. Any intern could perform a pre-operative work-up on a surgical patient; to a resident this far along, this was as monotonous as the scut he had been condemned to as a medical student. At this point in the year, any intern would be proficient at central line insertion, even in a patient with the most tortuous of veins. Isaac was confused. Big abdominal cases were scheduled first thing in the morning for good reason. When they took place later in the afternoon, all the parties involved knew they would be writing post-operative orders and rounding close to midnight. Obviously, he would never be able to make it to Faith's apartment in time for dinner.

Becky noticed the disappointment in his face but dismissed it. "Get moving, Goldman, you've got a lot of work to do." Isaac stared after her as she hurriedly walked off the unit. He cursed the day ahead of him, and then cursed his senior resident who, for some unknown reason, seemed intent on punishing him. He had no clue why.

Before he headed to pre-op, Isaac dialed Faith's phone number and as he heard her breathy hello, it took Isaac a moment to remember exactly why he had called her. He forgot about Dr. Simon as a warm sensation traveled through his body and enveloped him with peace.

"Hello?" Faith repeated a second time, this time her voice puzzled. "Who is this?"

"Hi."

Faith smiled as she replied, "Well, hi there, yourself. How's your day going?"

Isaac could see Faith as she lay in bed this morning, her beautiful curls all tousled, and her hands once again drawn up under her chin in the simplistic, childlike pose of deep slumber. He could almost smell the lavender, and he allowed himself a moment to imagine an Irish hillside, he and Faith lying together, blanketed by its Heavenly fragrance.

Isaac shook his head to clear it and, not wanting to say anything to disturb the peace he heard in her voice once she realized it was him, he replied, "Great, so far. Even better now…" He didn't complete the thought as his voice trailed off, and he listened to Faith breathe softly into the receiver.

Faith smiled and replied, "I think mine just got better as well. How many surgeries do you have today?"

Isaac took a deep breath and let it out in a rush. "Well, the schedule is a little more complicated than I expected. Dr. Simon has two big belly cases scheduled for this afternoon, of all things. She wants me to do the work ups this morning, but I'm afraid we won't be done in time for dinner tonight. I'll be surprised if I'm out before midnight. I'm so sorry."

"Isaac, please, don't be sorry. We'll just plan for another time, that's all." Faith hid the disappointment she felt and tried to keep her tone light.

"Look, let me get this day under control and I'll have a much clearer picture of my schedule once I evaluate the patients. I can…" The blaring of Isaac's beeper stopped him cold, then without waiting for Faith's response he said, "I've got to fly, one of the pre-ops just coded. Call you later!"

Isaac focused intently on his patient, an obese and middle-aged man, as a respiratory therapist rhythmically inflated his lungs with oxygen. An orderly, in concert with the respiratory therapist's rhythmic squeezing of the ambu bag, rapidly compressed the man's chest to pump oxygenated blood to his body. Isaac quickly assessed the situation and then began to ask general questions of the team players who also responded to the "Code."

"What have we got?"

A nurse, one who had been with Mr. Iacovino since his admission to Pre-op, stepped forward to provide the patient's background in brief bullet points. "Seventy-year-old male, three-day history of progressively worsening abdominal pain, admitted for Exploratory Laparotomy for questionable bowel obstruction. Past medical history of diabetes, hypertension, and high cholesterol. His labs haven't come back yet. We were giving him IV fluids because his blood pressure was a bit low."

"Add a lactic acid to his labs, get an arterial blood gas, and I want them all Stat. More IV fluids wide open."

Isaac initiated the Advanced Cardiac Life Support algorithm and impatiently awaited the lab results which would confirm what he already knew. The patient's body habitus, his past medical history, his advanced age-Isaac suspected that even prompt surgical intervention would not have prevented this outcome. The laboratory results which seemed to take an eternity to return confirmed his suspicions. They were completely disarrayed and indicated that Mr. Iacovino did not have a simple bowel obstruction. His gut had shut down, a surgical emergency caused by loss of blood flow to the entire bowel. Better known as "dead gut" in hospital slang, the poisons given off by rotting tissues had seeped into his bloodstream and ultimately had stopped his heart. Too many cannoli, a lifetime of cholesterol-laden dinners, lack of exercise, high blood pressure and poorly managed diabetes had all worked against him to create the perfect storm which had overwhelmed his body several days ago. Had he come in immediately when his belly pain first started, he might have had a chance at beating this demon but now, it would take nothing short of a miracle.

Ever the consummate surgeon, refusing to give up if anything he could do might offer his patient a chance at life, Isaac pressed on.

The heart monitor traced an erratic, jagged line across the screen which indicated this patient's heart was not beating but merely squirming like a bag of worms. "Charge the paddles, we have to defibrillate!" He grabbed the electric paddles and held them out expectantly for conduction gel to prevent the electrical shock from burning and blistering the patient's skin. He rubbed the paddles together and once the machine beeped to signal it was fully charged, he applied them to the man's chest.

"Clear!" Isaac pressed the buttons and instantaneously, the patient's back arched and his arms flexed, and then flopped back on the bed. Isaac stared at the EKG monitor and silently willed it to convert to a regular pattern of normal sinus rhythm, but still the erratic and jagged tracing persisted.

"Again!" The entire sequence was repeated, and after what seemed like an eternity to those staring at the monitor, Isaac saw one beat, then two, and then a slow but steady rhythm of uniform complexes marched across the screen.

"Check for a pulse," Isaac said, then waited expectantly for a response.

An intern called out, "I've got a…dammit!"

"Get another amp of Epi! Charge the paddles! Clear!" The sequence was repeated three more times, interspersed with chest compressions. On a few occasions, an isolated heart complex would appear on the screen but just as quickly, it would decompensate to the chaotic rhythm of a heart trapped in the struggle between life and death. Finally, the fine squiggles of V Fib flat-lined to nothing, an absence of any rhythm at all. Known as Asystole, Mr. Iacovino's heart was dead, lifeless, and his body was being kept alive only by the efforts of the respiratory therapist who manually inflated his lungs with oxygen, and the orderly who performed CPR.

Isaac looked at the clock. Twenty precious minutes had gone by, minutes during which this man's brain cells were starved of vital blood flow and oxygen. It became obvious to everyone that their attempts were futile, that nothing more could be done.

"Alright folks, we're done here. Time of death, 9:10 AM. Thanks, everybody."

Isaac donned shoe covers and a surgical mask, then entered the OR where Becky focused intently on a television screen. The image of a gall bladder was transmitted to the screen via a laparoscope. In her hands she held two long wands with which she performed surgery that once upon a time had involved a wide, gaping abdominal incision, days in the hospital, and weeks of recovery time. Much less invasive, this technology afforded her patients shorter recovery time and possible discharge home that very same day. Isaac waited until she was at a point during which she could be interrupted safely and then cleared his throat.

Becky looked up and, noting the tension in Isaac's eyes above his surgical mask, curtly asked, "What happened?"

"Mr. Iacovino, the bowel obstruction scheduled for this afternoon, just coded. From the sound of his history, he was pretty far gone when he got here. We'll know more once the autopsy is complete, but it's clear-cut necrotic bowel and septic shock. He just crashed, and we couldn't get him back."

Becky thought for a minute. Desperate to blame Isaac and lash out at him again, she finally admitted to herself there was no way they could have anticipated this. Without making eye contact, she replied, "Alright. Do you think you can handle the next case with an intern? I want to finish up here and round at a decent time."

Isaac was not sure if Becky was still in a bad mood or was

being sarcastic. At this point in his residency, Isaac had performed many solo surgeries, and often the attending surgeon showed up long enough to simply stick his or her head in the door and say "Hello" before leaving. Rather than risk more scut, he repressed a smart retort and simply nodded. "No problem. I'll see you after."

As he started to leave, Becky surprised him by adding, "Just leave when you are done. The intern can handle post-ops. You aren't on call tonight anyway."

The afternoon procedure went smoothly and ended much sooner than originally anticipated. Isaac quickly changed out of his scrubs and hurried to the phone.

Faith was dumbfounded. "Are you kidding me? Since when do residents get out early, especially on a Friday?"

"I don't have a clue. She just told me to finish the surgery and leave. Which leads me to my next question: if you haven't made plans yet, how about we spend the rest of the afternoon together? We can still have dinner, but I thought it might be nice if we do something fun, maybe go downtown and check out one of the museums at Yale. I loved to go to them when I was in medical school."

"That sounds fantastic."

"Great. I'll pick you up in a little while."

Chapter 24

Faith opened the door before he could knock a second time and was caught up short by an Isaac Goldman she had never seen before, one who wasn't in scrubs or professional attire demanded by the hospital environment. He was freshly showered, and Faith wanted to run her fingers through hair that looked soft and wavy. She imagined burying her face in it, feeling its softness, thinking it must smell like sunshine after the rain. He was dressed in jeans and a pink button-down shirt, with a tan windbreaker and boat shoes. Knowing her face was probably as pink as his shirt, Faith said hello softly and opened the door wide enough to invite him in.

Isaac kept his hands in his jacket pockets and followed Faith into her apartment. Noticing her laundry basket of freshly folded clothes, Isaac jokingly asked, "Did I interrupt something?"

Faith laughed and responded with sarcastic humor. "You did, indeed, something terribly important. Laundry takes precedence over everything when you have to rely on the Laundromat. One of the hazards of apartment life, I guess," and she waved her hand around her.

She added, "It's done, though, and I'll put it away later. Would you like to sit down?"

Isaac stared at Faith's form as she walked over to her couch. She was wearing jeans and a green sweater that, Isaac thought, matched her eyes. He marveled at how beautiful she was and how she seemed oblivious to that fact. He imagined his hands running over her body, learning and committing to memory every curve, every line. Her curly hair was restrained once more by the ever-present barrette, and he found himself wishing he could run his fingers through her hair, hugging her close and feeling its softness once more under his cheek, smelling lavender, immersing himself in her essence.

As Faith turned to Isaac, she caught him staring at her. "What?" she smiled self-consciously.

Her hand went up to her hair as if to smooth it back. "I wasn't sure where we were going; I figured a sweater would dress my jeans up a bit..."

"Well, actually, you could change just one thing..." Isaac encircled Faith with his arms and pulled her close. As he hugged her to his chest, he looked over her shoulder and surreptitiously reached up to unlatch her barrette. Putting it in his pocket, he reached up again and stroked her hair tenderly over her shoulders, mesmerized by its softness. Faith's eyes closed and her head fell back, lost in the hypnotic sensation of his gentle touch.

"There, that's perfect." Isaac stepped back from Faith and took her hand. "Honestly, why don't we just go to the museum now? Then we can grab a quick drink downtown and go to dinner in Branford. There are some great seafood restaurants out there on the shoreline."

Startled out of the blissful reverie of his touch, Faith grinned and grabbed her coat, slightly disappointed that the moment had ended so soon. On their way to the car, Isaac linked his hand with Faith's and squeezed it gently.

"I think I forgot to say 'hello' and to tell you how beautiful you look today." He looked at her and smiled, then released her hand to unlock the car door. He held his hand out to help her into the car and closed the door firmly, and then he walked around the car and climbed in on the driver's side.

"Wow, I'm not used to that."

"My mother always says common courtesy is a lost art. My Dad always did it for her, so I grew up with a great role model."

Smiling at another small thing she had learned about this man, Faith folded her hands in her lap and sat back happily.

"Thank you," she said, then reached over and took Isaac's hand. "So, let's get this day rolling. Where to?"

The British Museum of Art in downtown New Haven is a sight to behold. Filled with glorious paintings and stunning masterpieces of artists who had lived hundreds of years before, depicting their magnificent interpretations of the world around them, Faith was awestruck by the grandeur of the works of art. As she stood wide-eyed, staring at painting after painting, Isaac watched her. Emotion for this beautiful woman brimmed over in his heart and engulfed him in a rush of warmth.

Periodically, he would reach out to her, touching her shoulder and leaning in with the excuse of telling her about the painting she was admiring or whispering an anecdote about an amusing peccadillo of the artist. Faith would nod as she soaked in the information, not realizing that the real reason Isaac whispered so quietly in her ear was to get close enough to breathe her in more deeply… to get close enough, period.

Faith noticed that Isaac was awfully quiet, lost in thought, as they walked back to his car. She smiled at him and said, "Quarter for your thoughts."

Isaac laughed out loud, and he disengaged his hand, pulled Faith into his arms, and swung her around. Faith laughed even louder and shrieked at him.

"You're going to break your back!" she breathlessly laughed.

Isaac reluctantly put Faith back on her feet. He put his arm around her shoulders and pulled her close, then smiled as he thought, "My book bag weighs more than you."

Kissing the top of her head, he said, "Interested in a cocktail before dinner?"

"Sure. There's a place down on the water, the Skipper. We can sit out on the docks, relax, take it easy, and maybe go to dinner later."

The Skipper was a landmark down by the harbor in New Haven. A big restaurant, it had a comfortable, friendly bar and attracted a nice crowd of more mature adults and business people. Its atmosphere was one of relaxation, not the chaos and noise that were commonplace in downtown college bars near campus. They would have a chance to talk here without struggling to hear each other over the din.

"We'd like to sit out on the dock for cocktails," Isaac told the hostess, and they were taken out to a quiet table at the end of the dock where just a few other patrons sat several tables away, giving Isaac and Faith plenty of privacy to get to know each other better and to get to know what life was like for the other outside of the hospital.

As they waited for their drinks, Faith sat back in her chair and breathed deeply. "Someday, I'd love to live on the water. Can you imagine waking up to that smell every day?"

Making a mental note of something to do together on another date, Isaac asked her, "How did you like the museum?"

"It was awe-inspiring. It's amazing to me how you can look at the world through the eyes of artists who have been dead for two hundred years and know exactly what they were thinking. I think that's what they meant by 'seeing the world through someone else's eyes.'"

The waitress brought their drinks and placed them on the table. "Anything else?"

Faith smiled and shook her head, and Isaac thanked her. Lifting his glass, Isaac looked at Faith and smiled, "To second dates and new beginnings."

"Dinner, the museum, everything was wonderful. Isaac, thank you so much." Faith looked up into Isaac's face as they stood on her top step.

"I really enjoyed our evening."

Isaac looked down at Faith, knowing what he wanted yet afraid to shatter what he hoped was growing between them. He was afraid of offending this woman who represented everything good, everything pure, in his world. He reached his arms around her and clasped his hands behind her back, then closed his eyes and pulled her close.

"I'm glad you did. So did I." When he felt her sigh and relax into his embrace, Isaac squeezed her tightly, then abruptly let go of her and stood back.

"Well, I should probably go."

"Would you like to come in for a drink or maybe some coffee?" Faith looked at him hopefully, then laughed, embarrassed.

"Coffee, that was silly, you probably should get to bed. I know how brutal weekend call can be. You'll need a good night's sleep."

Isaac stood there somberly and pulled her back into his arms. Quietly, he said, "If I come in, it won't be for a drink. And if I come in, I'm not leaving any time soon." He leaned back and held her face in his hands, then kissed the tip of her nose.

"I'll give you a call tomorrow when I get a chance. Thanks for a great evening, I really enjoyed myself." Without waiting for a response, Isaac hurried down the stairs before his resolve to do the right thing waivered. Faith stood on her top step and watched his car pull away, its taillights growing dimmer until finally, they disappeared into the night.

As she undressed for bed, folding her sweater and jeans out of habit, she pulled her hair back and clipped it up off her neck. She donned her bathrobe and absent-mindedly hugged the familiar comfort of it close to her body, then closed her eyes as she thought about Isaac. She sat on the edge of her bed and contemplated the evening, then allowed her mind to wander as she envisioned another evening with Isaac Goldman and dreamed of possibilities.

She looked over her shoulder at her pillows and grabbed the one that Isaac had laid on, the one that still held the faintest smell of sunshine after the rain and buried her face in it. Then she promptly plopped it back on the bed, patted it into place, and walked back into the living room to pick up her laundry basket.

After she put away the last of her clean clothes, Faith took the barrette out of her hair and shook her curls free. She smiled at the sweet memory of Isaac's gentle hands as he stroked her hair, how heavenly his touch felt. She imagined those hands gliding over her body, and she closed her eyes as goose bumps covered her arms. She jumped as the telephone rang and jangled her back to her senses.

"Hi," she said and hoped in her heart it was he who was at the other end of the telephone line, though she knew it was before he even spoke.

"I forgot to say goodnight," he said, "and I wanted to thank you again for this evening."

Faith smiled as she quietly answered him, "You are welcome. It was a lovely evening. The restaurant was wonderful."

"Was it? I hadn't noticed."

The meaning behind Isaac's words warmed her soul. Faith felt her face flush and she held her hand there as if to contain the warmth and to prevent its escape.

They sat quietly and listened to each other breathe. Neither said a word, comfortable with the silence which encompassed them both. The meaning of unspoken words was not lost on either of them.

At the same time, they began to speak.

"I'll be off call Sunday around noon, how 'bout I pick you up?"

"Would you like to come for dinner Sunday night?"

They laughed, and Faith said, "Ok, you first."

"I'll just have to give report to the intern Sunday morning and should be out by noon at the latest. Why don't I come pick you up, and we can do something?"

"Won't you be exhausted after being up all night? What about sleep?"

"Trust me, I'm used to it. Besides, it will be worth it." Pausing for a quick moment, he added, "I'd love to see you again."

"I'll be here, just come over when you are done at the hospital."

"Great. Well, goodnight, then."

"Goodnight, Isaac."

Neither hung up and after a minute, they both laughed again.

"I feel like I did back in junior high."

"Oh my gosh, so do I! Ok, you go first."

"Ok." Isaac swallowed, not wanting to hang up, not wanting this night to end.

"Ok," Faith repeated.

"Goodnight."

"Goodnight, Isaac." Waiting for the dial tone that didn't come, Faith smiled and gently placed the receiver back on its cradle.

Isaac listened to the dial tone as the phone hung in his hand, lost in thought. He placed his phone back in its cradle and rested on top of his bed, still fully clothed. He stared at the ceiling. Thoughts of Faith swirled through his mind, intertwined among his memories of the softness of her curls tucked under his chin and the image of her body, all warm and wonderful, curled up next to his own. As sleep crept up and carried him away with his dreams, his last thought was of the two of them and of what the future might hold.

Chapter 25

Isaac stood by his patient's bedside, sweat staining the armpits of his scrubs and glazing his forehead. His back and arms ached from his efforts to compress the chest of a 275-pound patient. The family hovered around the bed as well, silent and tearful, anguish readily apparent on their faces. The team of doctors and nurses who had participated in the code efforts to save their father and husband's life, the professionals who had pounded his chest and administered medications and inserted tubes and lines, all filed out of the room.

Isaac remained to explain the goings on, what would happen after the patient was transferred to intensive care, and what was to come over the next twenty-four hours. He explained this patient's condition: that because of the cancer, his lungs had filled up with fluid and caused his heart to fail. Exhausted and weakened, it stopped beating. Isaac described what had been done to get his heart beating again and what he hoped would transpire as his condition began to stabilize.

"Hope," Isaac thought, and he pondered how that one simple element could make any dim situation that much easier to bear, how it could even make the world seem that much brighter. Hope was what he had been doing ever since he realized how important Faith was to him. I hope that she feels the same way. Hope.

"He's not out of the woods yet, but the next twenty-four hours will tell us a lot," Isaac explained to the family because even though this patient was critically ill, even though he had a breathing tube down his throat and a tube in his bladder and an intravenous tube inserted into his neck during the code, their husband and father was alive.

Isaac sat at the desk and finished his charting. He outlined in detail his assessment of this patient, all the interventions he had performed during the code, and his follow-up discussion with the family. It seemed to take forever, and by the time he finished and signed off his note, it was 8 o'clock. He closed the chart and placed it back in the chart rack. If he hurried to finish rounding on all the patients, he could grab a sandwich out of the vending machine and call Faith.

"Faith," he whispered as he smiled to himself and hurried to finish his work.

"Code Blue, ICU. Code Blue, ICU." Simultaneously, his beeper began to shrill. Isaac bolted up and out of the nurses' station and ran up the flight of stairs to the intensive care unit, where his patient, who had coded not an hour before, had coded once again.

"What happened?" He looked around the room and saw one of the nurses performing compressions on the man's chest and another injecting medication meant to restore his heart rhythm into an IV line. The tracing on the EKG monitor was erratic and chaotic, not the steady, rhythmic beating of a normal, healthy heart.

For the second time in as many days, Isaac initiated code protocol. As he awaited lab results, he called for an echocardiogram and as the image of the patient's heart came into view, the source of the problem became glaringly obvious. The sac around the patient's heart had filled with blood and was bulging, stretched to capacity, essentially compressing the heart inside an inelastic bag and holding it immobile. Aptly named Cardiac Tamponade, it prevented the heart from not only filling with blood but also from contracting to deliver that life-sustaining blood to the body.

The chemotherapy meant to kill the cancer and save this man's life had inadvertently killed him instead by thinning his heart muscle, and it had ruptured. With the few inefficient contractions his heart was able to generate, blood pumped directly into the pericardial sac until it was stretched to the point of stretching no more. Isaac could try to aspirate the sac and remove enough blood to allow it to expand and contract again, but until this patient was on an OR table and his chest had been opened, there was no way to repair the tear in his heart muscle and correct the problem. As impossible as it was for him to give in to defeat, Isaac had to admit that further efforts were futile.

"Time of death, 11:55 PM. Thank you, everyone."

Isaac left the patient's room and went to the lounge to speak with the patient's family. Pausing outside the door, he ran the code through his mind and contemplated what he would say to this family. Logically, he could think of nothing to explain why this particular patient had suffered such a complication from his chemotherapy and why another patient receiving the exact same treatment had not.

Isaac remembered his first patient death during intern year, Mr. Savino. After Isaac had pronounced him, as he was leaving the room, he recalled Faith's words to her now-deceased patient, "He'll learn."

In truth, Isaac mused, he hadn't learned a thing. Hope was one thing; he had learned to be comfortable with hope and had grown to understand that on occasion, it was hope that kept his patients alive and not him, his brilliance, or his surgical expertise. Death was another; there was no softening this blow, no matter how hard he tried, and there was not a darned thing he could do about it. Even though medical school had tried to teach him otherwise, no patient could escape its grasp.

This was the second patient death in as many days. Faith seemingly had mastered the enigma of death, had made sense of its inevitability, and on countless occasions had helped her patients' families and friends not only survive its startling permanence but also, eventually, to move beyond it.

Isaac finished up the necessary paperwork to release this patient's body to the funeral home. He yawned and stretched and then looked at his watch.

"Shit," he swore under his breath. It was after one o'clock in the morning, and there was absolutely no way he could call Faith at this time of night.

"Shit," he said again and headed for his call room to try and get some sleep.

Chapter 26

Faith opened her eyes slowly and squinted at the bright sunlight that glowed around the blinds in her bedroom. She stretched lazily, and then her hands flopped down behind her head. She smiled to herself, glad it was her Sunday off so she could relax, read the paper, toast a bagel, maybe even… then she sat up in bed abruptly.

"Oh, crap, what time is it?" she thought to herself and looked at the digital alarm clock on her nightstand. The numbers glared at her: 8:27AM. Faith looked around her bedroom and saw her telephone on the bed right next to where she had lain all night, in case he called. Her clothes were on the floor where she had climbed out of them at about 2 AM.

"He didn't call," Faith thought to herself, slipping her arms into her ratty old bathrobe. She stooped to pick up yesterday's clothes and threw them in her laundry basket, then sat down on her bed once again and stared at the phone.

"Ring, dammit," she glared at the phone as if by sheer mental telepathy, she could send a message to Isaac Goldman and force him to dial her phone number. Common sense took over, and she began to rattle off a list in her mind of all the reasons he hadn't called.

"He was scrubbed in the OR all night and didn't have time…"

"He got tied up with a new admission and didn't have time…"

"A trauma came in and he was up all night and didn't have time…"

Faith's head snapped up as she was startled by the shrill ring of the telephone. She snatched it up with both hands.

"Hello?"

"Faith, Baby, how are you?" Faith smiled at her father's familiar endearment, her heart growing soft as she leaned back on her bed to talk to her father.

"I'm fine, Daddy, how are you doing? What are you up to this weekend?"

"Oh, you know me. I can't complain one bit, just trying to stay out of mischief!"

In her mind, Faith could see her father wink as he joked with her. The comforting familiarity of his banter warmed her and, in an instant, Faith felt as though she was sitting across from him at the breakfast table. She listened to him as he told her all about his latest golf game, what her brothers were up to, and the goings on in the neighborhood.

"The Johnson's youngest, Timmy, is going overseas soon, and his family wanted to have a party for him before he leaves. It seems like just yesterday the two of you were collecting frogs and then losing them in your bedroom. Poor Grace, she was always the one who found them, usually about two or three weeks later!"

"He's such a great guy, Daddy. Remember how he and I used to play up in the boys' tree house when we were little? They'd get so mad at us, but we'd just close the trapdoor and sit on it so they couldn't get in."

They both laughed at the picture in their minds of Faith and Timmy teasing her brothers mercilessly, finally relenting and letting them all come up amidst good-hearted threats of torture and torment. This, in turn, would bring about hysterical fits of giggles, interspersed among promises to never do it again until the next time Faith and Timmy had the good fortune to run up the ladder before her brothers could get there first.

"It was all in good fun, but your mother and I used to laugh at poor Timmy. I felt so bad for him. I don't think he ever realized your brothers would never do a thing to hurt either one of you, but boy, they sure did like to tease you two."

"Poor Tim. I'll bet if all the O'Brien's showed up at his party, it'd scare the pants off him. Retribution, twenty years later! Can you imagine?"

"I'll let everyone know you'll be home, then. I don't think it will be too difficult to round your brothers up again, they all love a home cooked meal, even when I'm the one who cooks it! Gosh, twice inside of two months. This will be a real treat." Faith could hear the love in her father's voice and felt her eyes misting over with emotion. As many miles as were between them, sometimes Faith could feel his arms around her, and she wished he was closer so she could hug him back.

· "I'll call you to let you know what time my train comes in. I'm so glad you called, Daddy, I love you."

"I love you too, Baby. I'll talk to you soon."

Faith hung up the phone and lay back on her bed with her eyes closed, smiling to herself, thinking about the many blessings in her life and now Isaac Goldman. Sighing, Faith snuggled down into her pillow and pulled her robe more tightly around her. "Just a few more minutes…"

Knock, knock, knock!

Faith's brothers banged on the trapdoor to the old tree house, but Faith and Timmy sat on it firmly, their combined weight too great for her brothers to budge. A couple of times, they succeeded in raising the door a few inches, but Faith and Timmy were too heavy and the door would thump back down again.

Knock, knock, knock!

"Don't let them up, Timmy, hold on tight!" Faith and Timmy laughed hysterically, then screamed as her brother Scott managed to push the trap door up a few inches before it slammed down yet again.

Knock, knock, KNOCK!

Faith's eyes flew open for the second time that morning. She picked her clock up and squinted at it, then put it back down on her nightstand. 10:00 AM. Faith groaned to herself. Becky was the only one who ever came over in the morning, bringing coffee and donuts, full of energy and ready for anything. She thought of what she was going to tell Becky about her plans for later that day and wondered if she was ready to admit to anyone what was happening in her life and in her heart. It was still too new, too precious and special, and she wanted to revel in her own magical secret before she shared her news.

Faith rubbed the sleep out of her eyes and ran her fingers through her mussed-up hair as she walked up the hall to the front door. She yawned as she opened the door and said, "Becky, you have got to get a life," and then she stopped short.

In front of her stood a very bedraggled Isaac Goldman in wrinkled scrubs, his shirttails overflowing his waistband and a full day's worth of scruffy growth on his face. In his arms were a gym bag, a newspaper, and a white wax sack from the bakery across the street from the hospital. His face radiated a smile filled with joy at the sight of her.

Chapter 27

"You aren't Becky," Faith said flatly, utter shock apparent on her face. She clasped the lapels of her bathrobe tightly in her fist and just prayed that yesterday's mascara wasn't smeared down to her chin.

"I'm sorry, I should have called first. Were you expecting Becky this morning?" Isaac smiled at Faith, who looked as beautiful as if she had spent hours getting ready just for him.

"No, but she's the only one who ever comes by on her mornings off. I just thought it was her." Faith backed up and opened the door wider for him to pass and then lead Isaac towards the living room.

"Please, come in, make yourself at home. I'm just going to take a quick shower."

"I brought us some bagels and cream cheese. How 'bout I throw them in the toaster, make some coffee, and we can have a late breakfast and read the paper."

"That sounds wonderful, thank you," Faith smiled at Isaac and then tried unsuccessfully to suppress her laughter at the wrinkles in his scrubs.

"Looks like you had a bad night. I figured it had to be a zoo there when you hadn't called." Her quick laughter hid the flash of disappointment she felt because she hadn't heard his voice before she fell asleep.

"Beyond belief, but it's over now, as of about 40 minutes ago. Thank God for interns who don't ask a lot of questions! I always keep a change of clothes in my gym bag in the call room, so I figured I'd just shower here if you don't mind. If you'd like, we could head up to Hammonassett. A walk on the beach might be nice. Maybe grab lunch somewhere on Route One."

Faith was touched that Isaac remembered her love of the ocean air. She padded over to him, reached her face up to his, and with both hands on his shoulders for balance, she kissed him lightly.

"I'm so glad you're here. I'll be ready in a flash. Help yourself to whatever," she called over her shoulder as she turned to head back to her bedroom.

"Ok," he called after her. "What do you like on your bagel?"

Isaac waited for a response but received none. After a moment, Isaac walked up the hall and stood right outside her bedroom door. "Faith?"

Isaac heard the sound of running water and then the rush of a shower curtain as it was pulled closed. Isaac headed back to the kitchen, where he sliced the bagels and put them in the toaster, then filled the coffee pot and placed it in the coffee maker. He searched the kitchen for the coffee, opened cupboards and even the refrigerator, but there was nothing. He finally opened the freezer and found a bag of ground coffee with a label that read "French Vanilla" from a popular donut shop near St. Mike's.

"Oh, baby, come to Papa," Isaac said to himself. French Vanilla was his favorite, but the hospital cafeteria didn't have it, and most days were too darned busy to take even a short break to get a fresh cup. This was definitely a treat. Besides the bag of coffee, he found some fresh fruit, a couple of light yogurts, a quart of skim milk, and a wedge of sharp cheddar cheese.

"Well, that makes sense," as he realized exactly why his Faith was so slight.

"My Faith," Isaac said out loud, and he looked up the hallway toward the sound of running water, which grew louder as he walked towards her bedroom. Steam billowed out of the partially open bathroom door, and through the opacity of the shower curtain, Isaac was entranced by the flawlessness of Faith's silhouette.

He was drawn to the mysteries on the other side of the shower curtain where the answer to every question in his heart was standing. He pulled his scrub shirt up over his head and then dropped his pants in a crumpled heap on the floor. Pushing the door completely open, he walked over to the bathtub and slowly pulled the curtain back. Faith spun around in surprise, holding the facecloth up over her breasts.

Her hair hung straight down, her curls flattened by the hot water, and it trailed halfway down her back. Her eyes were wide, and she slowly lowered the facecloth, waiting for him to speak. Isaac's gaze locked on hers, and he intently studied those green, gold-flecked eyes, almost ethereal, in the face of an angel. Glistening drops of water clung to her lashes seemingly like tiny diamonds before she blinked them away.

He didn't look down at her body. He didn't have to. The woman who stood in front of him was more breathtaking than any painting he had ever seen in any museum, more perfect than any goddess ever chiseled by a sculptor's hand in the purest of ivory marble.

At that moment, Isaac wanted her more than he had ever wanted anything in his life. He wanted to join her, wanted to feel the luxurious slickness of her body as the water ran over it, wanted to know the sensation of velvet lips on his own once more. Seeking permission, he found invitation in her eyes. As he stepped over the edge of the tub and into the stinging spray of the hot shower, he closed the curtain behind him.

"I don't think I said, 'good morning,'" Isaac whispered in her ear as he pulled her into his arms and engulfed her in a kiss that levitated Faith, she was convinced, right off her feet. She wrapped her own arms around his shoulders and pressed her naked breasts against his chest, leaning into him in an attempt to get even closer. Isaac picked her up, and Faith felt as if she were weightless and floating on air.

When the kiss ended and she slid down his body, she felt his second warm "hello" rub up against her belly. Isaac pulled her close and rested his cheek on top of her head as his breath caught in his throat.

"Sorry, I..." then he stopped short, words caught in his throat, lost in the incredible sensation of her touch.

Faith lightly teased her fingertips up Isaac's back, then down from his neck to his buttocks, then back up again. She knew exactly what she was doing with electric, yet gentle, touches that made no secret of what she wanted, and as she pulled him tightly against her body, she asked in a throaty voice, "So...how do you like your coffee?"

Isaac answered her with a deep, passionate kiss that took her breath away. He teased her tongue with his own as it led hers in a seductive waltz and only stopped when he felt her knees go weak and her head fell back. He leaned back against the shower's cold tiles and smiled down at her.

This time, it was Faith who reached up and, with both hands, pulled his head down to hers. She kissed his neck and then planted soft kisses on his cheeks, his forehead, his nose, and then finally his mouth, where she pressed her own against his, likewise teasing his tongue, and sucked it gently. The sensation brought Isaac to a more heightened state of arousal, and as the kiss became more passionate, Isaac reached down and lifted her effortlessly in his hands.

Faith's legs wrapped around his waist, and Isaac turned to lean her back against the shower wall. She locked her ankles behind his back, balancing her weight so that Isaac's hands were free. He began a stream of passionate kisses followed by a trail of light butterfly flicks of his tongue down her neck, to her breasts, to her nipples, stiff and pointed with arousal. His hand took its place on her breast, and his thumb continued to lightly circle and coax, and the exquisite sensation gradually increased the intensity of heat that had begun to overtake Faith.

He used his other hand to reach down between them, and so, so softly, he caressed her. Faith tightened her arms around his shoulders as Isaac explored her body, and he quickly discovered her most sensitive and intimate places. Somehow through the loss of her friend and patient, perfection and love had found its way into her heart, and that perfection and love was Isaac Goldman. Isaac hugged her close and this time, there was no apology for the heat Faith felt.

He looked down at her, his Faith, and he found the welcome in her beautiful green eyes he had hoped to find.

Faith saw pure love shimmering in the eyes of the man who had captured her heart. With absolutely no doubt at all, she knew what filled her heart, certain that this was the same truth which now filled her soul. She held him tightly, assured of her love for this man, for far more reason than bagels and coffee and the Sunday newspaper. Faith clasped her hands behind Isaac's neck and whispered softly in his ear, "Take me to bed."

Isaac held on tightly to Faith and leaned down so she could reach the faucet and shut off the water. He stepped out of the bathtub and walked into her bedroom. Dripping wet, he turned and fell backwards onto the bed and pulled Faith down on top of him, her mouth down to his own. He reached down between them to touch her again, but she was warm and ready. Faith helped guide him to join them together as fate had meant them to be.

As if it was as natural as breathing, they moved together in a rhythm that matched their heartbeats, and Faith arched her back, drawing Isaac even more deeply inside her body. Her eyes closed and she bit her lip, and as their hearts raced, so did the intensity of their rhythm. Determined, yet so natural, with familiarity as if they had done this many times before, Isaac finally reached up to pull her down to him and held her face in his hands.

With eyes locked, simultaneously they felt their bodies shudder with waves of incredible passion that seemed timeless and unceasing. Finally, Faith rested her forehead against Isaac's, and her hands caressed his face and shoulders. Again, she kissed him and then sat up to look down at him as he lay with his eyes closed. His face was completely relaxed, almost serene. She watched as one beautiful eye opened, and he raised an eyebrow.

Isaac smiled and he whispered, "Milk, no sugar."

Smiling in return, Faith whispered, "Toasted with jelly."

Chapter 28

As she stared out over the blue waters of the ocean at Hammonasset, Faith watched the waves as they rhythmically rolled towards the beach and then crashed on the shore. She had never felt such serenity, such an amazing sense of perfection, as she did at that moment. The sound of the waves was a soul-soothing balm that healed her senses, and Faith felt herself release her worries into its magnificence. The cyclical nature of the tides coming and going with the moon reflected the ebb and flow of what Faith had experienced in her world, how it had formed her and shaped her into the person, the humanitarian, and the nurse she had become.

Isaac stood back and watched her profile as the wind blew her beautiful curls back, and he breathed in the salty smell of the ocean air, enchanted by the peaceful, gentle expression on Faith's face. He reached over and brushed a wisp of hair back behind Faith's ear. She smiled shyly and then stepped into his arms and buried her face in his chest. In a muffled voice, she said, "I don't think I've ever felt as relaxed as I do right now." She looped her arms around his back and hugged him tightly.

Isaac rested his cheek on top of her head and looked out over the water, lost in thought. Faith could not see when Isaac became pensive, his gaze focused on something beyond the horizon, off into the future. He just knew. Less than 72 hours ago, Isaac began to see life very differently and he realized how important Faith had become to him. He marveled how life could change in an instant and thanked God that it had. Seventy-two hours later, he looked with hope and promise toward a future with her by his side.

Isaac leaned away from her and clasped both of her hands, then smiled and pulled her along the beach. "Come on. Let's take a walk on the jetties."

Walking out onto the long, rocky wall that had been created a century before, they felt the cold mist from the ocean spray glaze them both, and they laughed together. Isaac commented, "I can see why you love the beach so much. It's amazing here."

Faith smiled wistfully. "My grandparents had a summer home on the south shore of Boston, in a small town called Scituate, and we used to spend a lot of time there during the summer. It was so wonderful, and I had such a happy childhood. Our whole family would go for the weekends, all the cousins and aunts and uncles. We had huge Sunday dinners at this massive dining room table, and Grammy made everything homemade."

"My Uncle Fred used to take us crabbing off a jetty just like this one. And the beach! That beach was so rocky that my Grammy had a special pair of shoes she wore only when she went swimming. She would wear them right into the water, and she always swam at low tide when the waves were small, just ripples really. That water was so darned cold, but Grammy didn't care. She'd just walk up to about her waist, splash her arms and bless herself with the water, and then she'd squat down and relax and kind of bob up and down with the waves. I called it 'Grammy bobs.'" Faith chuckled at the memory, a far-away smile on her face.

"As bitter cold as that water was, we all loved it. Actually, you couldn't get us out of it. We'd swim all summer long, every day, and by the time school started, we were all covered with freckles and our hair was all bleached out. Oh, the sunburns! We never wore sunblock. Did they even make sunblock back then? We'd wear one of Grampa's white cotton tee shirts over our suits at the beginning of the season for protection, but even so, by the end of the day our skin would feel all crispy from the salt and the sand and the sunburn." Faith grew lost in thought for a few moments, caught up in remembrances of times past.

"I haven't been back in years. Grampa died when I was twelve, and a few years later, my mother died, too. Then Grammy sold the house and tried renting other cottages for a couple of years, but it just wasn't the same anymore. I really miss it." Faith looked over to Isaac and chuckled self-consciously.

"Sorry, I tend to wax poetic about my childhood. It was a fairy tale. I was really blessed."

Isaac smiled at her tenderly and knew he would never tire of her life stories, of learning her likes and dislikes, of anything that made Faith who she was. He knew he had a lifetime of questions for her, and he hoped for a lifetime to ask them.

"Tell me about your mother. What happened to her?"

Suddenly Faith's smile disappeared, and she looked over the water with a flat, far-away gaze. "Cancer. An astrocytoma. Wicked fast. She was sick for about a year and then she died. And that was that."

Isaac stood silently, grateful that she trusted him enough not only to share even just a few intimate details of her life with him but also to allow him into her world just a little bit more. After a few minutes, Faith turned back to him.

"I'm not really good at talking about this. It still breaks my heart that we couldn't do more for her. No one should have to die like that, withering away to nothing, in so much pain. It just devastated us all, my whole family." Faith dropped her head back and took a deep breath of the salty air, comforted by the sense of déjà vu that the beach always gave her.

"I think that's why I love the beach so much. It reminds me of the happiness of a really idyllic childhood, of memories that are so sweet and precious. Just standing here, I sense her with me. I know I can always come here to find her."

Isaac struggled to find words, any words but was unable because no loss of such magnitude and significance had ever happened in his life. He absorbed all that Faith had said and tried to fathom all that she had not. He contemplated his time on Surgical Oncology and tried to wrap his head around what Faith had shared about the devastating heartbreak and tragedy in her own life. He attempted to reconcile the loss of a mother, which might have been a breaking point in another woman's life, with Faith's determination to use her personal heartache to better her patients' lives in sickness and sometimes, even in death.

Isaac knew of no book or lecture in existence that could teach him this. A true academic in mind and heart, Isaac contemplated the world with the practical, evidence-based eye of a scientist. Slowly but surely, he had come to realize that many of medicine's, and life's, most important lessons could not be learned in college.

Faith had obviously learned this valuable lesson at a very young and tender age and put it into practice daily as a nurse. Isaac knew he wanted to protect Faith, to give her the love and support she needed to sustain her through sadness and the losses of not only her mother but also her patients. He also suspected he had so much more to learn from her. He pulled her close and rested his cheek against the softness of her curls. There on the jetty, he spoke from his heart.

"Faith, I'm in love with you. I'm sure of it. In fact, I think I've always known it, ever since that first day I showed up on the unit, though I didn't realize it at the time. Honestly, I thought I was looking at an angel, your hair falling out of that barrette, and your eyes so tired. You had a gentle smile in your voice, though, and I could tell you were someone special. I think I was intimidated by you at first, but then over time, I didn't want to admit to myself that there was something there."

"And now?" Faith's eyes shone with wonder at what she was hearing from this man who had captured her heart completely, who held her gently but firmly in his heart as well as his arms.

"I'm sure of it. I know what I'm feeling. Do you?"

Faith smiled and snuggled into his chest. Isaac took her face in his hands and gazed tenderly at this woman who had shown him clearly why he was put here on earth and repeated his question. "Do you?"

Faith answered him ever so softly, "Yes, Isaac, I do."

Isaac brought her hands up to his lips and kissed them, then said, "Remember those words."

Isaac led her back down the jetty and once their feet touched sand, Isaac looked at her with a playful expression on his face. "Come on, I'm starving. Race you!"

Isaac chased her back to the car. Periodically, he picked her up and swung her around, and then finally lifted her up and threw her over his shoulder. Faith laughed hysterically all the way back to the car and pounded his back with half-hearted punches, her laughter interspersed with barely coherent demands to put her down. Finally, Faith flopped like a rag doll and gave up, and resigned herself to being carried, butt-side up, to the car. Isaac put her down on her feet and ceremoniously waved his arm in front of him in a gallant, formal bow. "Your carriage awaits, Madame."

Faith laughed at the vision of herself, upside down and totally undignified just a moment before, and took his proffered hand in her own. Prissily, she stuck her nose up in the air and affected an air so unnatural to her. Barely able to keep a straight face, she replied, "Thank you, Monsieur. Let us away!"

Chapter 29

The Clam Shack was a tiny building, just four booths and two tables, but it had the quaint charm of old New England with décor reflective of the livelihood of the many fishermen whose daily catch graced the menu. Hanging from exposed beams were colorful buoys and lobster pots, and each tabletop had accoutrements with seashells and sea glass. The wooden tabletops were scarred with the markings of thousands of customers who had eaten there over the years, and the items on the menu were the same selections the owners had served when the shack first opened decades before.

Everything was fried, homemade, delicious, and meant to satisfy the hunger of beachgoers who had the kind of appetites that only sun, sand, and salt water could bring. As they walked through the door, the jangle of bells hanging on the doorknob announced their arrival. Faith breathed deeply the aroma of hot oil, shellfish, chowder, and French fries. The familiar scents reminded her so much of the little take-out stands that dotted the coast near Grammy's summer home.

"I don't care what we get, just make sure it has extra tartar sauce," Faith exclaimed as Isaac went to the counter.

"Two fried clam platters, one with extra tartar sauce, and two iced teas." He looked over to Faith, "OK?"

"Perfect."

Faith chose a booth for them, and they sat down, clasping hands over the tabletop. They chatted comfortably and laughed at each other's jokes, and periodically Isaac would lean across the table to steal a quick kiss from Faith. Just moments later, a beaming older woman named Joanie, with a perpetual tan and more crinkles in her face than a raisin, placed a tray of hot fried clams still hissing from the fry-o-lator in front of them, along with two tall, frosty glasses of icy cold tea with fresh lemon slices.

Joanie stepped back and rested her folded hands on her ample belly. "This is the best lunch after a day at the beach, you'll love it! We make our batter homemade, and the coleslaw is my own family recipe. Now you two enjoy your lunch, and please, just wave me down if you need anything else. We aren't formal here!" Joanie's laughter filled the room as she walked back behind the counter. She left Faith and Isaac to enjoy their lunch and each other, with no interruption.

Faith dipped a fried clam in tartar sauce and popped it in her mouth. She closed her eyes and sighed, "Absolutely incredible."

Isaac ate his clam au natural and winked at Faith. "What can I say? I'm a purist."

They ate in comfortable silence and enjoyed the peaceful quietude, only pausing occasionally to smile or to reach over and squeeze the other's hand.

"I can't eat another bite," she said as she leaned back and took a sip of her tea.

Isaac looked down at her still half-full plate and helped himself to one of Faith's French fries. He winked at her and with laughter in his voice, politely asked, "Do you mind?"

"Please, help yourself." Faith pushed her plate across the table. "I haven't eaten that much since last Thanksgiving. Scott bet me I couldn't eat more mashed potatoes and gravy than he could, and like an idiot, I took the bet."

Isaac laughed again. "Tough bet, I can't believe you took it."

Faith winked at him. "You've never seen me eat mashed potatoes!"

"How many are in your family?"

"Including me, five. I'm the youngest. How 'bout you?"

"Just me. I was my mother's change of life baby, although if you ask her, I was the product of more prayers than humanly possible. She swears I was conceived in France, the night my parents visited the Louvre."

"No wonder you love art so much. I was my mother's change of life baby also, although she swore I was put on earth to give her a fighting chance in a house full of men!"

Neither wanted to leave, and both tried to prolong what had turned out to be one of the best and sweetest days ever. They sat in silence and sipped their drinks, and when Faith finally hit bottom and slurped the last few drops, she said, "Well, I guess I'm done, although I wish this day could go on forever." She smiled at Isaac and they both climbed out of the booth.

"Leaving so soon? You just got here. No dessert? How about a soft serve?" Joanie walked out to the dining area from the kitchen as she wiped her hands on her apron.

"Two love birds like you, you deserve something sweet."

Isaac tucked Faith under his arm and looked down at her. "What do you say? Want to share a cone?"

"I couldn't, but don't let that stop you. I don't mind waiting."

As Joanie made a large soft-serve cone for Isaac, she called back over her shoulder, "How long have you two been together?"

Faith and Isaac looked at each other and laughed. "Well, if you include our real first date, I guess it's been about four days now," admitted Isaac, with a soft look towards Faith. Faith's face flushed, and Isaac winked at Joanie as he looped his arm once again around her shoulders.

"Well, when you know, you know. Marty and I had been dating for only one month before we got married, and we bought this place and set up our clam shack. Two of the best decisions I ever made." As she spoke, an elderly man, slightly stooped over but with a spry step and a smile that seemed to stretch from ear to ear, walked out of the kitchen behind Joanie.

"Mother, are you talking our customers' ears off again?" He smiled at her affectionately and reached out to pat her arm, then gave her a loud smooch on her cheek. Joanie actually blushed like a love-struck schoolgirl as she giggled and swatted his hand away.

"Oh, you, get back to work. I swear! Now go and have yourselves a really great day." Isaac and Faith noticed the looks that passed between Joanie and Marty, a couple who had weathered their share of winter storms and Nor'easters and obviously still adored each other. The bells on the door jangled once more as they left, and they walked out to the parking lot.

"Isaac, you are really starting to look beat. Want to go back to my place and just hang out? Maybe put our feet up and watch a movie? I have a few oldies and a few Tom Hanks flicks."

"Tom Hanks? Why Tom Hanks? I would have thought you more, maybe, Mel Gibson or even Robert Redford."

"Nope, Tom Hanks. Not only is he the cutest thing ever in a pair of black briefs, scrubbing a big ol' ugly hound dog no less, he's one of the most incredible humanitarians ever. With all his riches and all his privileges, he remembers what it's like to be the low man, and he's never forgotten his past. He's also one of the most respectful actors in Hollywood. Do you know, after his World War II movie came out, he was being honored at a banquet, and several other actors spoke about him. That new actor on "The Green Mile" told Tom that he was the only actor who would actually sit down and go over lines with him, the new kid on the block, when some of the other actors would just act like they were above him. At the end of the program, a group of disabled veterans came out on stage to honor him. One of them was an amputee on crutches because of a war injury. You could just tell from Hanks' face how moved he was by their presence. He got right up and went on stage so he could shake these soldiers' hands and have a few private words with them alone. Men and women of that era didn't seek recognition for what they did; it was their job. To see those soldiers get some recognition for their sacrifices by someone who is led by his sense of humanity, who has an innate respect for those who served their country, it was a privilege to witness it. That's something you don't see very often, that's for sure."

Isaac was mesmerized by Faith as he learned even more about the kind of person she was, in her heart, where it really mattered. He wanted to learn more: every detail of her life, what kind of flowers she liked, and what kind of vegetables she hated. Did she have a favorite band, and did she sing in the shower? What was her first car? He could go on and on, but he'd never run out of questions to ask her.

Chapter 30

"Come on in, have a seat. I'm just going to hang these up. Would you like something to drink?" Faith waved Isaac to the couch in the living room and took his coat to hang in her hall closet.

"I'm still full from lunch, thanks. So, Tom Hanks? Or old and romantic?" Isaac sat down on the couch and stretched his legs out in front of him.

"I'm game for either." What he didn't add was, "I'd rather just watch you, if truth be told."

"Since I've seen all my movies at least a dozen times each, why don't you pick? I really don't have a preference."

What Faith didn't add was, "I couldn't care less, really, as long as you're here with me."

The big ol' ugly hound dog finally won out, and Faith popped the DVD in. She kicked her shoes off and sat down at one end of the couch, folding her feet up underneath her. Smiling at Isaac, she invited him to kick his shoes off as well.

"Do you want to stretch out? You look exhausted, and I feel bad that you couldn't take a nap today." Faith patted her lap invitingly, and Isaac did not have to be asked twice. His shoes landed right next to Faith's. He stretched out full length on the couch with his head in her lap and smiled up at Faith upside down.

"It was worth it," Isaac pulled Faith's arm around his chest and kissed her hand before clasping it firmly and hugging it to his heart.

Faith used the remote control to turn the movie on and then tightened her arm around Isaac. With her other hand she began to stroke his hair as they settled in to watch her favorite actor and the biggest, ugliest dog she had ever seen in her life.

Isaac struggled to keep his eyes open, but between the rhythmic, tranquilizing strokes of Faith's fingers through his hair and total physical exhaustion caused by far too little sleep over the past 36 hours, fatigue finally won the battle. As engrossed as she was in the movie, Faith didn't notice he had fallen into a deep slumber until she finally became aware of deep, steady breathing and an occasional little snore. She looked down and saw that Isaac's eyes were closed, his face and body totally relaxed.

"Isaac?" But there was no response from him, not the faintest flicker of muscle to indicate he was even slightly aware of her. Very gently and ever so slowly, Faith eased herself out from under his head so as not to wake him and went into the kitchen to get a drink of water. She looked at the meager pickings in the fridge and then shut the door.

Faith wondered what Isaac liked to eat and made a mental note to go grocery shopping later in the week. Tomorrow night she went back to work, and she was on for two nights, off two, then on for the weekend. She went back into the living room and shut the DVD off, then sat down in the recliner across from the couch.

Faith studied Isaac as he slept and memorized every detail of his face, mesmerized by the periodic little twitches his fingers made as if he were performing an intricate surgery in his sleep. Images of his fingers as they explored her body, memories of the shudders that had washed over her as his hands worked their magic, ran through her mind. She stretched her legs out and tipped the recliner back, and recalled the day they shared together. Faith smiled as she remembered their conversation on the jetty and reflected on how her life had taken on a whole new meaning since Isaac Goldman had shown up on her doorstep. Then she thought about how her life would change if…

If. Just thinking about "if" made her smile, but then she stopped herself. Her sense of practicality took over and she thought, really, after only a few days, could either one of them truly know with complete certainty what their feelings were for the other? She pondered the possibilities of what their future might hold and as she drifted off to sleep, her heart took over. She was certain of one thing. The feelings she had for Isaac could be nothing but love for him and for what he had brought into her life just a few days ago. For right now, she was content to have Isaac on her couch, sound asleep, and she would deal with tomorrow when it happened.

Isaac woke with a start, with absolutely no clue where he was. He was lying on a couch with an afghan covering him and as he looked around, he saw Faith in the recliner chair across from him, sound asleep and curled up kind of lop-sided with her hands folded up under her chin and her head tipped sideways. Settling back down on the couch, it was his turn to watch Faith sleep.

Periodically she would smile, and Isaac imagined it was because of him. He thought about their day together, about all they had talked about and all they had shared. He grew sad when he thought about Faith's mother. He tried to imagine how tragic that situation must have been for her at such a young age, but honestly, he knew he could never understand it. He hoped his love would be enough to shield her from pain and sadness and would keep her heart safe. He knew for certain should hurt and pain find her, he'd be there to share it with her, to carry her through it if need be.

Isaac laughed to himself. Ever the pragmatist, he would never have imagined himself falling in love so quickly and would never have believed that after so few days and two real dates (well, three dates, if he included that first night they spent together, even though for most of it, he and Faith were asleep), he would know in his soul that he had found the one who would share his life. Yet there his life was, all curled up and sound asleep in the recliner chair.

Isaac looked at his wristwatch and was shocked to find that it was 5am. He was going to be late if he didn't get moving. Tiptoeing to Faith's closet, he got his coat out and then walked back to Faith to kiss her goodbye. What he wanted to do was pick her up, bring her back to her bedroom, and make slow, sweet love to this amazing woman who loved him so perfectly. He wanted to lie in bed with her all day and find out all her secrets, and then he would make love to her again.

Realistically, though, Isaac knew he had to get to the hospital for rounds, and at the rate he was going, he didn't even have time for a shower. He knelt down in front of Faith and tried not to wake her as he leaned over to kiss her forehead gently, but in all honesty, he hoped he would. Her eyes fluttered open and did not focus at first, but when her gaze rested on Isaac, she smiled.

"I was dreaming about you." Faith closed her eyes and stretched. "We were at the beach, and it was beautiful." She yawned and sat up in the chair. "Let's go to bed so we can be more comfortable. What time is it, anyway?"

"I wish I could. It's five AM and I have to go. I'm already behind, and I don't want to be late for rounds. Dr. Simon won't overlook that twice."

"Let me walk you to the door, then. I have to work tonight; I'll see you when I get in."

At the front door, Isaac's kiss was brief, but it spoke of promise and anticipation of their future. "I'll call you later," then he ran down the steps to his car.

Chapter 31

Dr. Simon cut Isaac off and refused to meet his gaze. Her body language alone made it clear how little interest she had in his explanation for his tardiness to rounds for the second time. "Look, we've got a busy schedule today, and you are due in the OR in ten minutes for a craniotomy. Hurry up, Goldman, you're late." She turned on her heel and hurried down the hall.

Isaac stared after her as she stomped down the hall. "What's her problem?" he muttered to himself, and then he cursed under his breath, chalking her curt dismissal up to the chaos of a busy OR schedule, finishing up her fellowship, and getting ready to start her career as an attending surgeon.

Personally, he could relate. He had a true sense of urgency to complete his own residency and fellowship, now more than ever. The rest of his life could not start soon enough, as far as he was concerned. He hurried to the residents' locker room to change into scrubs and get ready to go into surgery.

The morning flew by and ever the consummate perfectionist, Isaac immersed himself in his patients and their care. He stopped on the surgical unit to grab coffee, and after gulping it down, he rushed back to the OR and forgot to grab lunch in his haste to get back for his next case. With the craniotomy completed, he had a light afternoon with an open gallbladder removal and an appendectomy, and Isaac hoped he would have time to grab dinner before he met the intern on the surgical unit for evening rounds.

He would see Faith. He smiled to himself at the image of her with her hair spread out on her pillow and imagined the softness of her skin, softer than anything he had ever experienced in his life. He remembered the sensation of her heartbeat against his chest when she was in his arms, and he was sure he had felt an angel's wings flutter against his body. The sweet perfume of lavender from those glorious curls lingered on his mind, unrestrained by the barrette he hoped would disappear and never be seen again, and he was certain Heaven smelled of that pale, aromatic bloom.

With one hand, Isaac threw his empty coffee cup in the trash outside the scrub room while with the other he grabbed a mask and donned it. He entered the mysterious world exclusive to surgeons and similarly garbed surgical personnel and stepped up to the long line of sinks. As he tore open the plastic wrap on the betadine-soaked scrub brush, he smiled to himself behind the secrecy afforded by a surgical mask.

The ten-minute scrub required prior to every surgical case gave Isaac plenty of time to relive his time with Faith in peaceful solitude. Isaac wasn't ready to share Faith, or his love for her, with anyone. He dropped the brush and held his scrubbed hands up in the classic surgeon's pose, then shouldered through the swinging doors into the OR. The scrub tech dropped a sterile towel into his outstretched arms, and Isaac promptly forgot about anything but his patient.

Towards the end of the case, Dr. Simon popped her head through the doors. "Isaac, I need to talk to you. Dr. Jacobs will finish."

Isaac looked at Rob Jacobs, a third-year resident who was more than capable of closing a belly case on his own, and put his instruments down. "I'm done; we were just closing. Rob, leave a Penrose drain in and make sure the post-op orders are written. Her family is in the waiting room."

Isaac took off his bloody gown and gloves, threw them in the trash and washed his hands in the scrub sink, and then took off his mask. As he walked down the hallway towards the doctor's lounge, he saw Dr. Simon with her hand on the doorknob, and she held it open for him. Isaac began to sense that whatever she was about to tell him, it wouldn't be good.

Isaac had never seen Dr. Simon so uncomfortable, and the feeling of dread in the pit of his stomach intensified. Finally, she established eye contact with Isaac and spoke, an emotionless, flat expression on her face.

"Your Mother called the hospital because she couldn't reach you at your place. You need to call home right away."

"What? Why? Did she say what's wrong?"

"No, but she sounded pretty upset. If you need some time off, just let me know as soon as possible so I can arrange coverage for you."

She paused for a moment, clearly out of her element, and then said quickly, "Just let me know."

Isaac couldn't even respond and sat down heavily on the vinyl couch. He started to say, "I was with Faith…" but realized Dr. Simon had already walked out of the lounge and he was alone.

He peeled the surgical cap off his head and used it to wipe the sudden glisten of sweat from his forehead, then reached for the phone. He dialed the hospital operator, and his voice cracked as he said, "Outside line please, I'd like to make a long-distance call."

Chapter 32

Rachael and Irvin Goldman had tried everything they could think of for 23 years to get pregnant, yet every month, like clockwork, Rachael would hide her heartbreak at the bottom of the trash pail in the bathroom. For two weeks after her period started, Rachael would maniacally clean her house, cook lavish meals for Irvin, and, each week, she would invite her parents and her in-laws to Seder supper. She would polish the silver candlesticks her own mother had smuggled by some miracle out of Germany until they gleamed brilliantly, as bright as her love for the family around her.

At dinner, she prayed intently over the candles, and as her hands drew the light into her soul, she covered her eyes as she whispered heartfelt thanks for their many blessings. She whispered auspicious prayers for the children who would someday surround their table, children whose happy chatter would fill their ears. She was a model wife and the perfect partner to her husband. Each month, shattered yet again, she did everything she possibly could to forget that her prayers were not answered and to pretend that, even though she wasn't a mother, she was the best wife any woman could be and that it was enough.

Two weeks to the date after her period started, in addition to the mad fury of her housekeeping efforts, she would don her lace negligee, the only piece of frippery she owned, in anticipation of the baby-making that would take place that night, actually, every night for the next week. Every night, as Irvin lay spent and exhausted, Rachael would compose herself, pillow under her buttocks, legs propped up on the headboard of the bed, dreaming of layettes and bassinettes and the beautiful sweater sets her mother would crochet. Her mother had given her the negligee as a bridal gift on her wedding day, accompanied by a hushed and solemn discussion about wifely duties, honoring her husband, and "family matters."

Rachael understood her mother's intentions immediately. She wanted grandchildren. If her plan worked out, she would have a houseful of babies by their tenth anniversary, and her mother would have grandchildren to spoil and cuddle for years to come.

Month after month, and then year after year, however, nature refused to cooperate. Dr. Schwartz could offer no answer or explanation for her inability to conceive, and he would placate her with useless, trite pieces of advice: "You have to relax."

"You worry too much."

"Give it time."

Rushing out to another patient, Dr. Schwartz would leave her sitting in the exam room, desperate for more information, wanting some bit of explanation as to why her prayers had not been answered.

With no acknowledgment of the heartbreak and gut-wrenching sadness in her eyes, Dr. Schwartz ignored Rachel's pain, and Rachael was overwhelmed by a sense of dread that nature had betrayed her. Because of her, their dreams for children would never be fulfilled. Humiliated that she was unable to provide her husband with a family, Rachel was burdened, as well, with a daughter's guilt that she was depriving her mother of the opportunity to brag and share her own stories of grandchildren with the other ladies over weekly bridge games. She began to avoid the quizzical glances her mother and mother-in-law shot each other at dinner and ignored their sympathetic yet questioning smiles that invited an explanation that Rachel could not give.

Graciously, Rachel would change the subject when the older woman hedged at questions, unwilling to share her pain or even acknowledge the subject of children. Once, when the topic of conversation hit too close to home, Rachel pushed herself back from the table and abruptly left the room. The subject was never mentioned again. By her forty-second birthday, hope vanished as her periods changed, shortening in length, showing up infrequently, and then finally, not at all. Rachael admitted defeat, and the dream of a large, happy family faded, only to become a bitterly painful and unwelcome memory.

Though quiet and outwardly stoic, Irvin prided himself on his positive and bright disposition. He handled his own disappointment the only way he knew how. He ignored it. Irvin didn't have the slightest clue as to how to change his wife's demeanor back to the cheerful, smiling wife she had always been, so he did the only thing he could think of to take her mind off a dream that would never be.

"How about we take some of our savings and go on a nice, long vacation? Wouldn't a cruise or a trip to Europe be lovely? I'd love to see Paris, wouldn't you?"

Rachael was stunned by her husband's apparent apathy to her barrenness and his lack of sensitivity to her grief. She blinked back tears. Irvin must have moved on and obviously believed family was now a non-issue. Their dreams were not only gone but also forgotten. Rachael had no idea how to respond. She refused to cry yet again in front of him about the most heartbreaking thing ever to happen to her, so she sighed and agreed that a trip might be exactly what they needed.

Irvin put his arm around her shoulders and gave her a brief squeeze. "Great, then, I'll go see the travel agent on my lunch break. I hear Paris is beautiful this time of year."

Two months later, the Goldman's strolled through the Louvre and admired in wonder the magnificent works of art that, before this vacation, they had only seen in school texts and coffee table books. Rachael marveled at the contributions these famous artists had made to the art world and the history their works would carry into eternity. She was awed by the effect they had on people all over the world. Wistfully, she imagined the impact her own child might have had not only on society but on the world in which they lived.

Her imagination ran away with her, and visions of a future president, the discoverer of vaccines which prevented life-threatening illness, the prosecutor who put dangerous and violent criminals behind bars, the painter of works of art and the author of the most beautiful prose ever written, floated through her mind. She sighed over what might have been and then tucked unanswered prayers and dreams that were not meant to be into the recesses of her mind. Rachael walked on through the gallery in wonder, awed by masterpiece after masterpiece displayed on this great museum's walls. Unconsciously, despite her best efforts to sequester her dreams away, her hand rested on her belly as if to protect the memory of the dream that, sadly, would never be.

Rachael had come home from Europe mentally refreshed and renewed, yet as weeks went by, she began to feel increasingly exhausted. She tired easily and took long naps in the afternoon before Irvin arrived home for dinner. When her fatigue was no better after a couple of months at home, despite the less-frenzied routine of housework and the relinquishment of Seder suppers to her mother and mother-in-law, Rachael began to suspect that something was very, very wrong. Irvin reassured his wife that she had picked up some kind of virus, maybe a flu that she was unable to shake, or perhaps it was a "woman thing" associated with "the change." Finally, exasperation with her frequent complaints and constant fatigue overwhelmed the normally stoic and calm Irvin. Firmly and decidedly, he convinced her to see a doctor, not only to give Rachael the peace of mind that nothing more serious was brewing but also to give Irvin peace of mind, period.

Rachael returned home that evening after her appointment with Dr. Schwartz, eyes puffy and red, evidence of fresh tears on her cheeks. She had a dazed, bewildered look on her face. Irvin stared at her blankly, dread at what she was about to tell him roiling up in his gut. He knew with certainty that whatever the doctor had told her, it was much more serious than the flu. Rachael walked solemnly to her husband and stood in front of him.

She took both his hands in hers and pressed them against the subtle swell in her belly, weight they had attributed to nightly mealtime indulgences that neither could resist on their travels around the gourmet capitals of Europe. She smiled at him and almost imperceptibly nodded, and for the first time in his adult life, the consummately stoic Irvin burst into tears.

Dr. Schwartz called the birth of Rachael and Irvin's son a miracle and attributed his conception to a "hiccup" in Rachael's ovaries that led to the release of an egg, which sometimes occurred "unexpectedly" and "without explanation" during the change of life.

"Just one of those things," Dr. Schwartz pretentiously coined it. He harrumphed and cleared his throat and then mentally slapped himself on the back for a "job well done," unable to admit he had absolutely no clue what happened. Rachael dismissed his theory as the mutterings of an idiot and called the birth of her son a gift from God and the answer to her prayers. Irvin called it the shock of a lifetime. To say the birth of Isaac Goldman was the greatest blessing they had ever received, eight months following their return from the vacation during which Rachael was supposed to "get over" her dreams of motherhood, was an understatement.

Isaac was a pensive child, and even as a baby, he spent much of his time studying the world and the people around him. With eyes wide, Isaac absorbed everything his senses experienced, and he tucked his perceptions away for future reference. He was most fascinated by the workings of a living body and how it responded to joy, sadness, or pain; how it was impacted by illness; how subtle little signs like a trembling hand, failing vision, or confusion related to a person's brain.

When other boys and girls rode their bicycles on warm spring days, when they splashed around in the public swimming pool on the sweltering days of summer, Isaac could be found in the library, studying reference books that were far beyond his years, mesmerized by research articles that described advancements in medicine and new treatments for disease.

For his twelfth birthday, Isaac was ecstatic to receive his very own microscope, complete with slides of snakeskin, human hair, granules of sugar, and other organic substances. He spent days gazing intently at a world not visible to the naked eye and dreamed of the day when he could view the architecture and substance of the subject that fascinated him most: the human body.

Rachael found great joy in her son's passion for learning, proud of the drive she witnessed in this miracle child, and hopeful for a future rich with purpose and success. She began to refer to Isaac as "my son, the doctor," and while Rachael marveled at the blessing bestowed upon her family, Isaac marveled at the wonders of a living body, at what made it tick and what lay deep within the recesses of its shell, where mere mortals were not supposed to go.

Once he understood these mysteries, he then could focus on the evil that made them go awry. So much misery was caused by things that disrupted the harmony within a body: disease, virus, bacteria, malfunction, or injury. All had the power of complete devastation and the potential for destruction. Someday, he vowed, with a maturity and insight years beyond his youth and innocence, he would understand why horrid things happened to a body. Then, he would figure out how to fix them.

Chapter 33

"Dr. Simon, I've got to leave. My father is in the hospital, and my mother is really overwhelmed. She doesn't understand what the doctors are telling her, but it sounds like a stroke."

"Is there anything I can do? "

"No, just covering my shifts is enough. I'm sorry to leave you in a lurch. I'll call when I have some idea of what's going on." Isaac turned to leave and then turned back to her. "Umm, there is one thing. I tried to call Faith, but she isn't home, and I don't want to leave this kind of news on her answering machine. Could you tell her for me? And tell her I'll call her later this evening. Please?"

"Sure. Go on, you should get going."

Isaac flew to his car and got right on the highway without going home first. His gym bag had his toothbrush, deodorant, and a clean shirt in it, and he grabbed the bag out of his locker before leaving. He still had clothes at his parents' house. Anything else, well, was just superfluous at this point. Isaac had no idea what to expect or how long he would be home, but he'd buy it if he really needed it.

"God, please don't let this be it," Isaac prayed.

He didn't know what else to say. Isaac wasn't used to family illness or, God forbid, tragedy. He had never dealt with personal crisis in his own family before this and was completely out of his element. Logic took over, and he did what he always did when confronted with potentially bad news. He became a detached clinician and ran through the list of differential diagnoses: hemorrhagic stroke from a ruptured aneurysm, ischemic stroke from a blood clot, subdural hematoma from trauma, and contra-coup injury from an accident. Did he fall? Maybe it was a grade III or IV concussion. Maybe he had a tumor that was compressing an area of his brain, choking off its blood supply. Had his father tried to protect his family from some bad news he wasn't ready to share?

That was enough to shatter his detached, clinical demeanor and Isaac stopped that train of thought abruptly before panic overtook him. He couldn't force himself to dwell on the "what if's" if he didn't even know on a basic level what was going on. Time would tell.

Isaac zipped along the freeway towards the dock where he would board a ferry to Long Island, and then he would drive directly to the hospital to see his father. Hopefully, his mother would be able to fill him in as best she could. He knew he was not prepared for whatever he might see when he got there; even more so, he knew he was ill-equipped to handle whatever tragedy might be ahead of him.

"Ah, Faith, I wish you were here." Isaac rested his head down on arms which were folded on the railing of the ferry boat, the cool spray from the bow misting his face as the boat sliced through the water.

When the ferry docked, Isaac sat in his car and drummed his fingers on the steering wheel as he waited impatiently to disembark. Once clear of the crowds of pedestrians who swarmed from the boat and into the parking lot, he sped to the hospital and cursed the stop lights on the way. He felt a panic rise in his chest that he would be too late and prayed to God that he would at least have time to say goodbye to his father, to hold his hand the way he had seen Faith do with her patients so many times before, to comfort his mother the way he knew she would need to be comforted after so great a loss.

His tires squealed as he abruptly braked in a parking spot, then he ran into Memorial Hospital and breathlessly asked the receptionist what room his father was in. The receptionist looked at him expectantly, a patient smile on her face, hands poised over the keyboard of her computer, and Isaac mentally palmed himself in the forehead.

"Sorry, Irvin Goldman," he said sheepishly, not accustomed to being the one in need of help, entirely out of his element at being on the receiving end of sad, potentially devastating news.

"Let's see…hmmm, oh, here we are. Irvin Goldman is on 3 North, room 315. Take elevator 3 up to the medical unit. Here's your pass," She handed Isaac a piece of paper with the room number written on it and again smiled that same, patient smile.

"I think there's been a mistake. He must be in the Neuro ICU, he had a stroke. My mother said it was serious. He can't be on a medical unit unless, oh my God…" Isaac turned and hurried to the elevators, then impatiently poked the "up" button as if the repetition would miraculously force the elevator car to return to the first floor more quickly.

When the elevator finally showed up, Isaac again hit the third-floor button several times as the doors slowly closed. He closed his eyes, braced one arm against the elevator wall, and tried to keep his legs from buckling underneath him. A transfer out of the Neuro ICU that quickly and then onto a medical unit could only mean one thing, one very ominous and cruel thing. Experience told him his father must be on "Comfort Measures Only," and the next few hours would be the most miserable and heartbreaking of his life as his family watched his father's life ebb away.

Before the doors had opened completely, Isaac escaped and ran to room 305. By the time he entered his father's hospital room, his tears had broken free, and his breath caught as he suppressed his sobs.

Just inside the doorway, Isaac almost knocked his Bubbe and Zayde completely off their feet. He was totally dumbfounded not only to see bright smiles on their faces but also to hear the familiar, soft sounds of his parents' laughter. He stood at the foot of his father's bed, his mouth agape, and clasped his hands on top of his head as he took a deep breath and blew it out in a rush. His eyes clamped tightly as he said a silent prayer of Thanksgiving.

"Ok, can someone please fill me in? Dad? Mom?" He looked first at his father, then at his mother, and awaited the explanation of what on earth had happened. Why on earth had the doctors led his mother to believe her husband had a stroke?

"Calm down, Son, it's ok. I'm ok. The doctor said it was some kind of mini-stroke and that everything would be fine in about a day or so."

Isaac understood the meaning behind the words his father spoke. His beloved father had not had a full-blown stroke, nor was he dying, nor was he even on the critical list in the Neuro ICU. A Transient Ischemic Attack, TIA, had temporarily weakened one side of his father's face, and to his trained eye he could still detect a subtle softening of his smile on that side. In twenty-four hours, if all remained well and his father was stable, he would be released home with his family. Neither dire nor life-threatening, it initially had frightened his mother enough that she thought he was dying.

Isaac's breath came out in a relieved rush, and he hugged his mother and then bent to kiss his father's forehead. Bubbe and Zayde, his Grandmother and Grandfather, looked on lovingly at the tender family portrait in front of them, and Bubbe began to fuss over him.

"Bubbeleh, sit down before you fall down. Your Dad is ok, he's ok. Hush, hush now and just relax. Your Zayde and I are going for coffee. You chat; we'll be back."

Chapter 34

Rachael poured Isaac a cup of coffee, then placed the coffee pot on the sideboard and joined him at the table. Isaac thoughtfully stirred milk into it as his spoon gently clinked against the delicate sides of his mother's china. He became absorbed in memories of his childhood with two loving parents, his years immersed in study, his years of post-graduate study, and now, Faith.

Unconsciously he smiled and his spoon stilled in mid-air as one particular memory filled his mind. Behind closed eyelids he relived a private memory of the softness of her skin, of the sweet sound of her voice as it whispered his name over and over while they made love, of the magic and wonderment in her eyes when he told her of his dreams about the two of them and life together. He breathed in deeply of the steaming cup under his nose, but it wasn't coffee that filled his senses.

It was lavender, the pure and fragrant essence of lavender that so gently, so subtly, enveloped Faith. He opened his eyes to find Bubbe in the doorway, her eyes filled with love for this grandson she had prayed for, for so long. On her lips was a gentle smile. Zayde stood behind her with his hands on her shoulders, and both studied Isaac quizzically.

"Who is she, Bubbeleh? Who makes you smile so?"

Isaac sipped his coffee and then placed the cup softly back into the saucer. "Is it that obvious, Bubbe? How did you know?"

Zayde held the chair for his wife, then sat down next to her and clasped her hand as she knowingly answered her grandson.

Bubbe tapped her temple with her forefinger, a soft but wise smile on her face. "I know because I know you, and I know a man in love when I see him. A woman knows these things, and Bubbe knows you like she knows the back of her own hand. So, tell me about this love in your life, Bubbeleh, tell me about this woman who has stolen your heart."

Isaac looked across the table at his grandparents from whom he had learned so much about strength and endurance and the healing, life-giving power of love. Each reached across the table to clasp one of Isaac's hands, and Isaac looked at his mother, one-half of the set of parents who had given him his first and most important example of perfect, unconditional love. Now it was Rachael who nodded her head, and it was all the encouragement Isaac needed to share this part of his heart with his family.

The next morning, breakfast was anything but relaxing as they all hurried to get ready to go pick up Irvin at the hospital. Isaac called Dr. Simon at St. Mike's and waited on hold for what seemed like an eternity before being connected, and with relief evident in his voice, he told her that yes, his father was out of the woods and yes, he would be back to work tomorrow. While Rachael gathered clean clothes and some comfortable shoes for Irvin to wear home from the hospital, Isaac next called Faith. As he dialed her number, his imagination began to wander, and he though how much he'd love to surprise her and just show up on her doorstep that evening. He hung up at the sound of footsteps and smiled as his mother came into view, car keys in one hand and a small suitcase in the other. He reached for the suitcase and quizzically looked over her shoulder.

"Are Bubbe and Zayde coming to the hospital?"

"No, your Zayde had an errand to run and Bubbe went with him, 'to put my two cents in,' as she put it. They will meet us back here later this afternoon. Let's go get your father before he starts to walk home in his hospital gown with his glory hanging out behind him!"

As Rachael and Isaac walked off the elevator on 3 North, they saw a man in a white lab coat enter Irvin's room. "That's Dr. Harbins. He's the Neurologist taking care of Irvin. I want to hear what he has to say because you know your father. He'll just brush everything off and go home and try to mow the lawn!"

They hurried into Irvin's room just in time to hear Irvin tell Dr. Harbins, "I'm sure they will be here any minute, Doctor; I know my son would like to meet you- Oh, here you are!" Irvin smiled at his wife and son, and Isaac immediately noticed that his smile was now as even as it had always been, with none of the subtle flattening his trained eye had picked up yesterday.

Isaac inwardly heaved a huge sigh of relief and extended his hand to Dr. Harbins. "Thank you so much, sir, we really appreciate all you've done for my father. Could we speak for a moment while Dad gets dressed?" Isaac stepped back to allow Dr. Harbins to leave the room first and then followed him out as Rachael began to hand Irvin his clothing.

"I didn't want to make my mother nervous, Dr. Harbins, I thought it better that we speak out here. How is my father, really? Neither of my parents grasp medical terminology that well, but I'd like to know what his tests showed and if he's really in the clear."

Dr. Harbins laughed and clapped Isaac on the shoulder. "No, no, really, it was just a TIA. All of his symptoms resolved completely, and he is back to baseline. Carotid Doppler was crystal clear, the CT scan was negative, and truthfully, we can't find any reason why this happened. Blood pressure, cholesterol, nothing on physical exam-I honestly don't know. Maybe he threw a tiny clot, but from where we have no idea. I'm sending him home on a baby aspirin just to be safe, but really, he's fine."

As Isaac wheeled his father out to the car in the obligatory wheelchair, his thoughts ran to Faith and the loss of her mother. Where did she find the strength to survive that kind of pain at such a young age? How on earth did she cope with that loss, even now years later let alone at 15 years old? He looked down at his father in the wheelchair, still as robust as ever, who held his mother's hand and kissed it as she walked along beside him. What would I do if it were my father or my mother? He had never known the loss of someone so intimately woven into the fabric of his life and had been very removed from the deaths of his mother's parents when he was very young. His father was still very much alive and well, and he was grateful that Death remained a stranger to him.

After dinner, Irvin went to the bedroom to lie down, and Rachael walked Isaac to the front door. Bubbe and Zayde walked outside to give Rachael and Isaac a moment alone.

"We'll be fine. You have work to do and lives to save." Rachael smiled gently at her only son.

"And you have someone waiting for you. Come again when you have more time to spend, maybe bring this lovely young woman who has stolen your heart so we can meet her."

Isaac knew better than to try and argue with his mother, and he sighed in resignation. "Let me talk to Faith, and as soon as we have an evening off together, we'll be back. I know you'll love her, Mom."

"I already do, how could I not love the woman who makes you smile that way? Get going, you are going to miss your ferry!"

Both laughed, and Isaac enfolded his mother in his arms and kissed her softly on her cheek. "Ok, Mom, you win, I'll call you later in the week."

Rachael's misty eyes followed Isaac as he walked out to his car, and she watched as her mother-in-law and father-in-law leaned close to speak softly to their grandson. Bubbe caressed his cheek, and Zayde clasped the back of his grandson's neck. She watched Bubbe hand Isaac a small, black box, and she felt warmth in her heart as her son wiped the tears from his eyes.

Rachael folded her hands under her chin and whispered softly, "Mazel Tov, my son. Mazel Tov."

Chapter 35

Isaac stood on the landing outside Faith's door and took a deep breath to calm himself and slow his pounding heart. He hesitated for a moment, but before he could even knock, the door swung open and there was Faith, all curls and green eyes and ratty white bathrobe, right in front of him. Isaac opened his mouth to say, "Hello," but before the words left his mouth, Faith flew into his arms and wrapped her arms around his neck. She pulled him down and gave him a welcoming kiss that cleared his head of all the worry of the past day and a half.

"I was so worried when Becky told me. Come in, what happened? Is everything ok? I wanted to come to you, but I had no idea how to find you, and I felt so horrible. I wanted to be with you, in case…." Faith's voice trailed off as she swallowed back a sob, and her eyes sparkled with tears as she searched Isaac's face for some hint of what had happened to his father.

"Shhh, everything's ok, I called you earlier to tell you, but I just thought I'd surprise you rather than leave a message. My father's fine, it was just a TIA, and all his symptoms resolved, thank God." Isaac pulled her into his arms again and closed his eyes in relief as he rested his head on top of Faith's.

"And I'm fine now. In fact, I'm perfect. I've missed you so much."

Faith led Isaac into her apartment and once the door closed, she gave him the kiss she couldn't give him out on her front step. Finally, she pulled back from him and said, "I can't believe I missed your call. I had such a headache this morning. Can I get you something to eat?" She walked into her kitchen with Isaac right behind her and opened her refrigerator, but Isaac picked her up in his arms and plopped her down on the counter.

"Yes, I'm starving; I've been craving this since I left Long Island."

Faith inhaled deeply as her head fell back against the cabinets. Isaac nibbled her ears, then her neck.

"Oh, my," she gasped, and her breath escaped her in a rush. She looped her arms around Isaac's neck and looked into eyes that reflected love straight back to her. She snuggled into his chest and sighed again.

"I'm so glad you're home."

"Home," Isaac thought to himself, how perfect that sounded. He scooped Faith up and carried her to her bedroom.

Gently, he placed Faith on the bed and then sat down on the edge by her side so he could look at her. Tenderly, Isaac brushed one straggly curl off her cheek and tucked it behind her ear. Faith studied him, and her head tilted to one side expectantly as she waited for Isaac to say something.

After another moment of silence, Faith sat up again. "Isaac? What is it?"

Isaac dropped his chin to his chest and closed his eyes briefly as he whispered a silent prayer for guidance to honor this moment with the reverence it and Faith deserved. He opened his eyes and reached into the front pocket of his pants and then handed her an aged black velvet box, its edges somewhat frayed and worn, its color grayed by antiquity. Faith held the box in her hand and looked at it in confusion. Isaac enclosed Faith's hand which grasped the box in his own, and began to tell her a love story.

"My grandparents married in Germany about a month before they were rounded up and segregated into the ghetto. Eventually, they were sent to a camp. They lost everything in that God-forsaken place, including my Bubbe's wedding ring. After liberation, they were finally able to come to the United States and when they settled down, Zayde started a dress shop. The shop did well, and when Zayde finally saved enough money, he bought my Bubbe a wedding band with two diamonds. He said the diamonds represented the two greatest gifts he had ever been given, his wife and their new life together here in America. When my father was born, Zayde added a third diamond. After my parents had me, he added one more diamond to the band, representing the fourth blessing in his life."

"While I was home with my family, I told them about a nurse I worked with, what a special and perfect person I thought she was, how I thought about her every day when I first woke up, and how I saw her face in the darkness before I went to sleep at night, how I danced with her in my dreams. I told them how she cared for her patients with love and tenderness and that just by watching her, I wanted to be a better human being. I told them how spending the rest of my life with her would be the answer to my most heartfelt prayers. I told them that, just by knowing her, my life would never be the same."

"This morning, my mother and I went to the hospital together to bring my father home, and while we were gone, Zayde and Bubbe took the ring to a jeweler and had a fifth diamond added to the band. When it was time to leave this evening, they walked me out to my car. Bubbe took the ring off her finger and placed it back in the same velvet box that held it the day Zayde first gave it to her. She handed me the box and said, 'Bubbeleh, your grandfather was the greatest gift God could have given me. This ring represents love and strength and a commitment to each other that has not wavered since we took our vows. It is my gift to your future wife that you two will be blessed with the same. May that love wrap you both safely in its embrace and bless you for the rest of your lives.'"

Faith stared at the box, still confused. "I don't understand."

"What are you doing this summer?"

"What do you mean what am I doing this summer? Isaac, what is this? I…"

Isaac stopped her words with a quick, tender kiss. "Faith, listen to me, what are you doing this summer?"

Faith shook her head slowly, "I don't know. I don't understand. Isaac?"

Isaac took the velvet box out of Faith's hand and opened it. He took the exquisite ring in one hand and Faith's left hand into the other and slid the ring onto her fourth finger. He then brought her hand to his mouth and kissed it.

"What are you doing for the rest of my life?"

Faith's eyes grew wide as her hands flew up to cover her mouth, then she extended her hand to look at the ring. "OhmyGod, OhmyGod, OhmyGod," she said over and over. Her shoulders began to shake, and quietly, she began to sob.

"Faith, what is it? I know. I know what you are going to say. It's too fast, isn't it? We should have talked first. It's ok, we can wait until-"

Faith took both of Isaac's hands and enfolded them in her own. She tucked them under her chin and looked at him with wide eyes that radiated the depth and magnitude of love she felt for this man. Despite her tears, her heart swelled with overwhelming joy.

"Ask me."

"What?"

"Ask me. Ask me now before I wake up. Because if this is a dream, I want to know if you are asking me to marry you so I can say yes before I wake up. And if this isn't a dream and I really am awake, I don't want to waste another moment not knowing whether or not I'm going to be your wife. If the rest of my life is going to have you in it, then I want the rest of my life to begin now. Ask me. Please."

This time, it was Isaac's turn to weep. He slid off the bed and dropped to one knee in front of Faith.

"When I was little, I was certain I would be a doctor. When I entered medical school, I was certain I would be a neurosurgeon. I knew in my soul this was my destiny as sure as I knew my own name, and I followed it without hesitation, confident it was the path to my future. Now, I realize that wasn't true. My journey to New Haven, to St. Mike's, and onto Surgical Oncology had nothing to do with my career. They were all steppingstones to you. Now, I have one more certainty in my life. I want to spend the rest of my life loving you. Every morning when I wake up, I want to see you lying next to me. Every night when I go to bed, I want you in my arms. Every step through life, I want the two of us to take it together."

Isaac held her hands tightly as he took a deep breath. "Faith O'Brien, may I have the privilege of being your husband? Will you do me the honor of being my wife?"

Faith answered Isaac by pulling him into her embrace. She kissed his face, his eyes, his cheeks, his nose, and finally his mouth. Faith's tongue etched all the words she wanted to say directly onto his own. She pulled Isaac along with her to lie on the bed and held the length of him firmly on top of her body as if their warmth would melt them together. Gentle kisses became more insistent, and the intensity of their passion built until they pulled away from each other and looked into each other's eyes. Faith opened the front of her robe and let it fall off her shoulders. Isaac quickly shed his clothes and allowed them to fall to the floor so that nothing could possibly come between the two of them and the love they shared for each other.

In Faith's eyes, Isaac saw love, desire, passion and want. He was overwhelmed to think all of these emotions were because of him and swore to himself that he would spend every minute until eternity trying to live up to the magnitude of this blessing.

Isaac rolled to his side and pulled Faith to face him. She gently held his face in her hands, and her thumb rubbed gently over the lips she had just kissed as her eyes looked directly into the soul that reached out to mesh with her own. Tentatively, a hand reached out to a breast, and gentle strokes brought shudders and goosebumps. Another hand reached out to pulsating heat, evidence of passion and want that indicated a need for release.

Feverishly, mouths and hands moved over flesh until Isaac broke away and began to kiss his way down Faith's body. Almost delirious, Faith was only aware of a trail of gentle kisses and the slickness of Isaac's tongue as it traced a line to the focal point of her arousal. With one hand on the back of his neck, she gently encouraged him, and her other hand reached over her head to grasp the headboard of her bed as her body trembled. Isaac conveyed her to the highest peaks of ecstasy, and Faith felt wave upon crashing wave of passion as it rippled upward and outward until every cell in her being cried out for release.

She reached down to pull Isaac back up and guided him into her, then wrapped her legs around him as if to pull him in more deeply, closer to her soul. With her hands on the small of his back, they fluidly moved together. Words were not necessary. Isaac anticipated the answer her body had already given him and with a visceral need for completion, he allowed the earth-shattering sensations which had rocked Faith only moments before to carry him away as well. Spent and satiated, lulled by the soothing whispers of deep and relaxed breathing, they slept.

Faith kissed Isaac goodbye the next morning, then went back to bed and pulled covers that still smelled of their love for each other up over her body. She bunched the sheets in her hands and buried her face in them as she relived every moment of last night. Something scratched her and she looked down at the ring Isaac had so lovingly placed on her finger, his belief in their future together evident in this piece of his family's heritage. She thought with tenderness of the love his Bubbe and Zayde shared with each other and the love with which they so obviously had embraced the rest of their family. She smiled at the thought of the love they would multiply for the family Faith and Isaac would have together.

"It's a dream, it must be a dream," Faith whispered to herself as she drifted into a sleep that embraced her as lovingly as her future husband had done throughout the night.

Chapter 36

Isaac had spent last evening in a whirlwind of emotions that sprang to life in Faith's arms. They made love-magical, sweet, pure love.

"What a trite expression," Isaac thought as he ran onto the unit, ten minutes late.

"It isn't 'making' love; it's celebrating it." Isaac chuckled to himself and felt overwhelming joy at facing a future and a life with Faith by his side. Lost in thought, he didn't pay one iota of attention to what Dr. Simon said during rounds, and he certainly didn't notice the tight-lipped look she shot to him several times.

As Isaac performed the ten-minute scrub necessary to prepare his hands, he imagined Faith's petite hands as she caressed his body. As he slipped his arms into the surgical gown the scrub nurse held out for him, he recalled the white robe slipping off Faith's shoulders. As he glanced around the OR at the shapeless forms of personnel draped in poorly fitting blue surgical gowns, his mind wandered to the softness of Faith's body, with visible perfection in every curve and bed sheets that draped her form and outlined every perfect detail.

Isaac shook his head, trying to snap his mind back to the neurosurgical case at hand. With residency drawing to a close and an intense neurosurgical fellowship about to begin, he was entrusted with more neuro cases to perform, and Isaac focused his full attention on the patient at hand. As the attending surgeon nodded to the scrub tech to pass the scalpel to him, Faith escaped his conscious thought, only to remain in a quiet recess of Isaac's mind where he could pull her back at will.

Between cases, Isaac called Faith. She picked up after three rings, and his heart skipped a beat when he heard her voice, "Hello?"

Lowering his voice so that inquiring minds could not hear him, Isaac whispered to her, "How is the love of my life today?"

Faith laughed. "Better now. I have to keep pinching myself that I'm awake, that I didn't just imagine last night. If your towel wasn't on my bed, I never would have believed it truly happened."

"Oh, sorry, bachelor life, I guess. This will take some getting used to for me." Isaac paused and they both listened to the soft sounds of their breathing in each other's ears. After a moment, Isaac spoke again, "My Mom has been hoping that I would meet a nice girl for so long now, and I know she is going to be so thrilled to meet you. My Dad, too. Wait until they realize I've met the kindest and most beautiful daughter-in-law any parent could pray for." Isaac smiled again, still incredulous at the amazing turn his life's path had taken.

"I can't wait to meet them. Do you think we can make it out to Long Island the next weekend we have off together? Or maybe we could just go see my father for one night, then go see your parents the next."

"Boston is a long drive, and I'd like to spend some time getting to know your father and your brothers. And I know you'd probably want to stay for more than just dinner," Isaac said, remembering what Becky had told him about the strength of the bond between Faith and her family.

"Let's do this. Long Island is closer and if we leave as soon as rounds are over Friday evening, we can have dinner with my parents and still make the ferry back to Bridgeport by 10 or 11 or even very first thing Saturday morning. I should warn you: my mother is going to have a thousand questions for you. My father is a man of few words, but he'll remember down to the last detail everything you say."

"So now I know where that photographic memory comes from," Faith chuckled.

"I can't wait to meet them and see what else you inherited from your parents and your grandparents, too."

"Then, we can drive up to Boston, and we can spend the rest of the day with your family. I'd also like to ask your father for his blessing."

Faith's eyes misted over at Isaac's consideration. "Daddy would love that. I know he's wondered if I would ever settle down and have a life with a husband and children. He is so proud of my career in nursing, but I know he worries about me being alone. He'll love you, and my brothers will, too.

Faith paused, and her voice trembled slightly. "I keep thinking I'm dreaming. I have to keep looking at my hand to make sure all of this is real. So much has happened so fast..."

Becky walked into the anteroom, and Isaac straightened up. "I have to run; I think I'm late for my next case. I love you. I'll call you later," and he hung up the phone.

"You were late this morning. Again," Becky hissed, anger evident in her voice and her posture.

"I'm not the only one who's pissed. Snap out of it, Dr. Goldman, your personal life had best not interfere with my OR schedule. Your phone calls can be made on your own time, not mine."

She hung her lab coat on a hook behind the door, took a scrub brush, and began to scrub so furiously that Isaac expected to see blood drip off her fingers into the sink.

"Look, I'm sorry I was late for rounds, but why the hell are you so angry all the time? You've been riding my case and snapping at me left and right. I'm sorry, ok? It won't happen again."

Becky wished she could do anything to make Isaac feel the pain she was feeling. She screamed inside her head, "You only stole my life right out from underneath me, and I never even had a chance to tell her how I felt. You aren't the only one with dreams, Goldman and mine were destroyed. By you..."

Becky threw the scrub brush into the sink and finished rinsing the iodine scrub off her hands and forearms. She took a deep breath to calm herself, to take a moment and collect her thoughts. With her hands up, she brushed right by him and started to shoulder the door to the operating room open. She paused momentarily and glared back at him but managed to keep herself collected. "Why don't you just go start the post-op checks? Find the intern and send her in here. We need another pair of hands."

Faith and Isaac sat together on the couch, arms around each other, legs entwined. Faith snuggled into his chest and yawned. Isaac gently rubbed her back, and the soothing, tender strokes lulled Faith into peaceful oblivion.

"She has been unbelievable this week, worse than usual. I know I was late, but come on, by now, she should have gotten over it. I mean, I'm never late...well, almost never." Isaac smiled sheepishly at Faith, but the smile quickly left his face. "She knows I work my ass off in that hospital. She even booted me out of a neuro case. A neuro case! Can you believe it? I need all the experience I can get before my fellowship starts. Shit." Isaac shook his head and let his breath out in an exasperated huff.

The emphatic curse woke Faith up with a startle. "Sorry, I dozed off. You were saying about Becky...?"

"She's brutal and I'm getting a little tired of being a doormat for her. As much as I hate to do this, I think we are going to have to put the visit to our parents off for a few weeks. The only thing I can think of that might get me back in her good graces is to stick around on my weekends off, maybe help out and take some of the load off of her."

Isaac looked down at Faith and noticed the glazed look in her eyes and the subtle dark circles that, for once, were not caused by traces of smudged mascara. You look exhausted, Faith, are you ok?"

Faith smiled and snuggled deep into his embrace again. "I'm fine, just a little wiped out. I get these headaches once in a while, usually when I'm really tired, and I think it just hit me a little harder today than usual. No big deal," She gave Isaac a quick kiss on the cheek and then resumed her position on his chest.

"Don't worry about telling our parents. It will be nice to have a little time to just revel in this. I still feel like I'm dreaming.

"But seriously, I'd give Becky a break, Babe, and I wouldn't take it personally. She's really a great person; you just have to get to know her. Remember that first night you came over? She was just about to tell me about this guy she is interested in, and she got interrupted by your knock on the door. I think she's having a tough time right now; it just seems like she has something on her mind, but she's so private, you know?"

Faith smiled at the memory of what followed that evening. She pulled back only slightly to look up into Isaac's face and thought what a beautiful man he was, inside and out, and then she continued, "I wonder who this guy is. I hope he deserves her, I hope he knows how lucky he is."

Isaac pulled her close and nuzzled her neck. "You mean 'she.'"

Faith pulled back and playfully punched his arm. "No, silly, where'd you get that idea? We were actually talking about you, and I asked her if there was anyone who had caught her attention. Becky has put so much time and effort into her career, and everything else has been put on the back burner. I'd love for her to find that special someone, to find what we have." She smiled softly and pulled

Isaac's head down to softly rub noses with him, then gently kissed him.

"It's funny that as close as we are, we don't talk about that subject very much. She has always kept her private life incredibly close to her chest, and she's obviously insanely busy with her professional life. I just assumed she'd meet someone eventually and begin to settle down. With her own fellowship winding down, maybe she's opening herself up to meeting someone. I honestly wouldn't expect her to tell me about anyone unless it was serious. Or maybe there's someone back home in California." Faith sighed.

"I hope she finds happiness, she's way too special to spend her life alone. Whoever he is, I pray to God he deserves her." Faith paused, thinking about her best friend, and she smiled.

"She's a good friend, Isaac, the best."

Isaac was thoughtful for a moment, not really sure how to approach the subject. "I thought you knew, Honey. Becky is gay. Everyone knows that."

Too surprised to speak, Faith dropped back against the couch, trying to absorb and make sense of what Isaac had just told her. All of a sudden, fragments of conversations rushed into her head, along with memories of many evenings spent talking for hours, with Becky joking about Faith being the perfect woman for anyone. Many nights, Becky had slept over because their conversations had dragged on into the wee hours of the morning. It dawned on her that Becky was talking about her, that the person of her dreams was Faith, and it suddenly became crystal clear that, on that fateful night, Becky was about to tell her so. It all began to make perfect sense. The surprise cups of coffee on those early mornings when she sat at the desk with her charts and the many times they had sat on her couch together with Becky holding her in her arms as Faith cried about yet another patient who had passed, the many glances Becky had flashed her way, all beautiful instances of what Faith had interpreted to be the gestures of a best friend- a very loving, very dear, best friend.

Faith, ever the consummate friend who lived day to day loving the world, living her life to make others lives better, grew sad that she had never picked up on her best friend's intentions. She sat up abruptly, afraid that, inadvertently, she might have given Becky a false impression. By innocently leading Becky on, had she given her hope for something that could never be? Faith's face fell, and her arms dropped to her side. She whispered quietly, "What have I done?"

"Oh, Faith, I'm so sorry. I thought you knew. You guys are so incredibly close. I figured she had told you. She's never really come out to any of us, but I had heard stories about her senior resident when she was an intern. Evidently that was something pretty hot and heavy going on between them. When she finished her residency, though, she pretty much left Becky in the dust. All I know is, now she just doesn't date anyone around the hospital. Self-preservation, I guess. Getting dumped is horrible, especially when it's out of left field like that." Isaac put his arm around Faith's shoulders again and pulled her close.

Faith nestled into Isaac's embrace again and became pensive. "All this time, I never figured it out. How could I have missed it?" She shook her head and closed her eyes, then reached up and squeezed the bridge of her nose.

"I'll talk to her. I love Becky. She's like the sister I never had, and I'm probably closer to her than any other woman in my life. She's incredibly special to me, and I don't want my love for you to end my friendship with her."

Isaac pulled her close and kissed Faith's forehead. She smiled up at Isaac, and again, he noted the pinched look in her expression and fatigue in her eyes. He held his hand out to her.

"Come on, let's go to bed. You need to rest and maybe that headache will go away." He smiled at her gently, his concern for her apparent in his expression.

Isaac drew the covers up to Faith's chin, then climbed in beside her and pulled her close to his body. They fit together more perfectly than spoons, and she knit her fingers with his and drew them up under her chin. They grew quiet, each lost in his and her own thoughts: Isaac of his future wife and their life together, and Faith of her future husband and their life together, along with a very special, beloved friend sharing a warm and welcoming place in her heart.

Chapter 37

The opportunity to speak with Becky eluded Faith and for the next few weeks, they played an odd game of "Cat and Mouse." Every time Becky was on the unit, she intentionally avoided Faith and would duck into patients' rooms if Faith walked towards her. If their eyes happened to meet across the desk, Becky would pick up the phone to suddenly and conveniently make a phone call or answer a page. Faith's gaze would follow Becky as she walked across the unit and out the doors and she would feel her heart break just a bit more as each day went by without even an acknowledgment of her presence. The loss, to her, felt as painful as if Becky had died, and it was unbearable.

"Let's have dinner tonight, just the two of us, maybe just a pizza or some Chinese, and talk about the weekend. Any more thoughts on how we should do things? Long Island first, then Boston? We can call my parents and your father after dinner and make definite plans."

Faith sat in her usual spot at the end of the desk as she worked on the never-ending charts. She blew her hair off her forehead and tried unsuccessfully to tuck some stray curls that had fallen out of her barrette back behind her ears. She rubbed her temples to chase away the dull headache that started after one of her patients had to be transferred to the Coronary Care Unit. During transport, the cardiac monitor alarmed as soon as the elevator doors closed, and his heart stopped beating. Faith had climbed directly onto the bed with the patient and performed forceful compressions on his chest in the hot, claustrophobic confines of the elevator and continued them all the way into the CCU. By the time she finished giving report to the unit nurse, she was hot, sweaty, and nauseous from the exertion of trying to keep her patient alive.

"Fantastic. I have a quick errand to do this morning. I just want to pick up a few things at the grocery store, and then I'm going to take a nice long nap." Faith stifled a yawn and brushed back another curl that had fallen onto her cheek.

Isaac looked a little more closely at Faith and frowned. "Are you feeling ok?"

"I'm fine. I just have a little headache, probably from the code." Faith smiled, but it fell short of her eyes. She shrugged and admitted, "It's been a long shift."

"I'll see you tonight, then. Get some rest." Isaac looked around and, with no one in sight, leaned over and kissed Faith on the top of her head before he hurried off the unit.

First stop grocery store, Faith immediately went to the coffee aisle to grab a bag of French Vanilla coffee from her favorite donut shop. She was grateful to know that it was available there so she could avoid an extra stop. As exhausted as she was, she continued to fill her basket with milk, bread, eggs, bacon, and everything she loved to have for breakfast at her father's house. She smiled at the thought that Isaac, as well, shared a love for the very same. On to the snack aisle where she found cookies, little chocolate snack cakes, and barbecued corn chips. She crinkled her nose at the last item.

"Ok, maybe we won't share those," she thought as she picked up the cheese poofs she preferred and tossed them into her basket.

Faith walked back up to the cash registers and as she stood in line, she glanced cursorily at the magazine rack. A bridal magazine caught her attention, and she took the magazine out of the rack and then absent-mindedly leafed through it. A full length shot of an obviously ecstatic bride in a flowing white gown, with a filmy lace veil framing her face, smiled up at her from the cover. She thought back over the past couple of months with Isaac in her life and the five years since that fateful morning in the Surgical Unit when they first had met.

She scanned the layouts of elaborately layered dresses with beaded bodices, flowing trains, and elegant veils that framed the brides' lovely faces and trailed down their backs. Many were detailed with the addition of crystal and pearl-covered combs and jewelry that added to the splendor of the occasion. Her eyes grew soft at black tuxes, complete with cummerbund and bow ties, and she imagined Isaac standing at the altar, waiting for her father to place her hand in his.

Turning another page, Faith smiled at a photographic spread of children dressed in flower girl gowns and tiny tuxes, miniaturized versions of the bride and groom. In their hands, they carried baskets full of rose petals and small satin cushions with shining gold bands fastened securely by white silk ribbons.

Faith looked at the last page thoughtfully and then slowly slid the magazine back into its holder. Her hand rested briefly on the magazine cover as she contemplated her soon-to-be-created union, and then she turned her cart around to get one last item: a pre-wedding gift for her husband-to-be.

Faith opened her front door to find Isaac with a bag containing her favorite General Tso's chicken in one hand and a bottle of Pinot Grigio in the other. "I wasn't sure what wine went best with Chinese, so I played it safe and stuck with white." Faith smiled and held the door open for him, then rose up on tiptoe to give him a kiss.

"That smells great. Here, let me help you." Faith took the bag from Isaac's arms, and he followed her into the kitchen. She took plates from the cabinet and silverware out of a drawer as Isaac got some wine glasses and the corkscrew.

He deftly removed the cork with no shred of it ending up in the wine, and Faith laughed. "How many times have I had to pour my wine through a coffee filter to get rid of those nasty bits of cork?"

Isaac laughed as he filled one glass and then started on the second. Faith held her hand up, "None for me, thanks." She smiled and Isaac noticed the circles under her eyes again, not smudged like this morning, but puffy, nonetheless.

"Still exhausted? How's your headache? Maybe you are coming down with something." Isaac felt her forehead with the back of his hand and then leaned forward to place a soft and gentle kiss where his hand had been.

Faith closed her eyes as Isaac's lips brushed her forehead and thought to herself what a phenomenal cure love was for most of life's ills. "I'm fine. My nap really helped."

Isaac held Faith securely under one arm and re-corked the bottle with the other. "Why don't we just save this for another time when we both can stay awake long enough to enjoy it?" He then shooed her toward the living room.

"I'll make us both a plate. Why don't you go get comfortable?"

Placing the laden plates on the coffee table, Isaac dropped down beside Faith and pulled her into his arms for the kiss he had dreamt about all day, and not just on her forehead. He reveled in the smell of her hair yet again, thinking he would never be able to get enough of the gentle scent of lavender. The kiss grew deeper until Faith finally pulled away. Then, she gave him one last quick kiss before she smiled into eyes that reflected a peaceful warmth right back to her.

"Tell me about your day." Faith took a bite of her chicken and listened thoughtfully to Isaac as he began to speak.

"No, let's talk about the weekend. Any idea what you'd like to do first? Long Island? Boston?"

Faith put her fork down and wiped her lips. "Well, I have a better idea. Why don't we have your parents and my father here for a late lunch, get to know each other a bit, and we can tell them all at the same time? I think it will be fun, and I know my father will be thrilled to meet your parents. I'd really like to have both our families hear our news together."

"I love it. Think your brothers will want to come as well?"

"We'll have to see, they are all so busy with their own lives and it's a rare opportunity that we are all able to connect on the same day. Let's finish dinner, and then we'll call them and see what will work for everyone."

Faith and Isaac carried their now empty plates into the kitchen where Isaac piled them in the dishpan and turned on the hot water. He added some liquid dish soap as he said to Faith, "This will take me two minutes, go sit down and I'll be right in."

"Honestly, I'm in awe. Perfect surgeon, perfect husband-to-be, and now you're the perfect housewife! How did I get to be so lucky?" Faith smiled over her shoulder and then she disappeared into her bedroom only to return several minutes later with her hands clasping something behind her back. Isaac had already finished with the dishes and was seated on the living room couch.

"Before we call anyone, I have a little something for you. Now shut your eyes and hold out your hand."

Isaac playfully did as she asked and closed his eyes, one hand outstretched in front of him. He smiled as his fingers closed around a long rectangular box, and when he opened his eyes, he saw a jewelers' logo embossed in gold ink on its white cover. He studied it for a moment and then slowly slipped the top of the box off and removed the layer of soft cotton batting cushioning its precious contents.

He looked down at the treasure inside the box with a slight uplifting of one corner of his mouth, and Faith reached to wipe away a solitary tear that began to roll down his cheek. Isaac looked up at Faith with an unspoken question in his eyes and she nodded ever so slightly. He reached to clasp her hands which rested gently on her still flat belly, her fingers folded protectively over her most precious wedding gift for her husband-to-be. There, within the rectangular cardboard box, nestled safely on its soft bedding of cotton, lay a white cylinder of plastic that bore two pink lines in its window. Within Faith's belly, snuggled under a heart that beat with pure love for their new family-to-be, lay a tiny babe nourished and protected by the warmth and love of its mother.

Chapter 38

Faith and Isaac were nose to nose in bed, and their bodies touched in all the right places. Faith giggled out loud and teased Isaac, "Honey, I'm probably about five minutes pregnant right now. Trust me; making love is not going to hurt the baby." With an innocent but playful smile on her face, Faith reached down to gently stroke Isaac and he struggled, unsuccessfully, to resist her invitation.

Isaac groaned but pulled Faith even closer. "I know, I know. Rationally, I should know that. I'm a doctor, for Pete's sake. But this isn't a textbook case, this is my child," Isaac said, and he reached down protectively to cover Faith's belly with the palm of his hand.

Faith groaned, "Well, this is going to be a very long pregnancy then…."

Isaac closed his eyes and sighed as Faith allowed her hands to roam freely over his body. He tried to control his passion, which grew by the second with Faith's gentle but insistent touch, then pulled her onto his chest to lie back on the pillows.

"I remember in medical school, all of us students would wait in the delivery suite for a woman in labor to get close to delivering the baby, and then we'd go in with the obstetrician and watch. If we were lucky, we'd be able to assist with the actual delivery. It looks so easy on television, but I'll tell you something. Those babies are as slippery as eels when they come out. The one baby I was allowed to deliver myself, I almost dropped him. I thought the husband was going to reach right over his wife and punch my lights out. I was scared to death, but it was also one of my most exhilarating moments as a student. I helped introduce a new life to his parents, imagine that." Isaac gazed off Faith's shoulder, and the memory of the moment took his breath away again as he shook his head in wonder.

"Really, it was such a sacred moment. I almost felt as though we needed to be silent just so we could absorb the significance of it all. Then the Attending said he had to get home for dinner and he ran off, and that was that. That was my only delivery, but wow. Imagine how it will be with our own baby."

Faith felt her heart warmed by his story and was thrilled to learn he was as enchanted by childbirth as she was. "When I was in my Maternal/Infant Health rotation during junior year, we did a one week stretch in the OR to observe C-sections. In the very first case, I started to get really dizzy after the first incision was made, and by the time the baby was out, I was close to passing out. This happened several times, but I never said anything to anyone about it because I didn't want to be known as the weak student in our class who couldn't handle the sight of blood.

"One time, though, I actually did pass out cold. I woke up to find my instructor holding my knees up while another nurse held a cold cloth on my forehead. My instructor wanted to pull me from that part of the rotation. The reality of it was I wasn't put off by the sight of blood at all. Without even realizing what I was doing, I was holding my breath until I heard the baby cry.

"Once the baby cried, and I knew for sure it was breathing on its own, then I could breathe, too. Once I figured it all out, I just concentrated on taking deep, slow breaths as soon as the OB picked up the scalpel and the problem was solved." Faith smiled at the memory, at how silly it all seemed once she figured it out.

This time it was Isaac who very tenderly allowed his hand to wander over Faith's body. He leaned forward to kiss her and then to nuzzle her neck. As his lips trailed down to her shoulder, in between featherweight kisses, he mumbled softly, "So what about this weekend?"

This time it was Faith who put a halt to Isaac's attempts at arousal, and she laughed out loud as she pulled him back up to face her. "Isaac Goldman, I absolutely will not talk about our parents while you are doing that! Honestly!"

"Ok, ok!" Isaac laughed as well and hugged his bride-to-be.

"Look, I know how you must feel about a real wedding with a real white dress and a veil and your father walking you down the aisle. But especially now, I just don't want to wait for 'You may now kiss the bride.'"

He held Faith's face in his hands as he asked her, "Why don't we just do it? No pomp and circumstance, just us with our families, and maybe the hospital chaplain from St. Mike's could officiate."

Faith listened to Isaac's words and slowly nodded her head.

Isaac continued, "I remember what you told me when we were on the jetties at Hammonasset, how you feel so close to your mother at the beach. Why don't we have our ceremony right there, by the jetties?"

Faith looked up at Isaac, and a fleeting look of sadness flashed in her eyes, quickly replaced again by a peaceful look of certainty. "My mother would have loved you, Isaac. She'd have loved you like one of her own sons. And she would have loved our baby…"

Her words were cut off by a sob that escaped her, and tears flowed not only for the overwhelming happiness that had been handed to them both but also for the heartbreaking loss she felt once again. Since the age of fifteen, she had mourned the loss of her precious mother. Now, she grieved for the loss of a loving mother-in-law to her husband and a beloved Grammy to their child.

Isaac cradled Faith against him and whispered, "Our day will be all about us and about the start of our family. It will be perfect…"

Gradually, Faith's tears slowed. All of a sudden, she laughed out loud. "I have a great idea. Having our marriage ceremony at the beach is a fantastic idea, and I love it. I think it's only fitting that we go to the Clam Shack afterward, the whole group of us, for dinner. What do you think?"

Isaac brushed her lips gently with his own and then said, "I think it's a great idea, and I can't imagine a more perfect celebration."

He paused for a minute and then asked Faith, "Are you sure you are ok with this, with not having the whole she-bang? You won't regret not having a real church wedding with flowers and a limo or a reception with a cake and a band and dancing?"

Faith paused, lost in thought, and then answered him. "Sincerely, no, I won't regret not having any of that. I guess the only thing I've ever really thought about since my mother died is having my father walk me down the aisle. That will still happen, just in a different venue. I looked at a bridal magazine this morning and got an idea of how much planning would be involved in a big ceremony and reception, with all the little details and everything that goes into a wedding. It looks daunting and I'd be doing it all without my mother's help," Faith's eyes began to mist again, but only for a moment.

"Isaac, I've seen some of the most perfect couples in the world, with the most love-filled, blessed marriages ever. I'll bet none of them cared one iota about how they got married or where they had the party afterward when they were lying on their deathbeds. They truly honored and cherished their love for each other 'til death do us part. That's all I want for us. It's the only thing I'll ever want."

Chapter 39

Becky Simon was living the professional life she had dreamt of since she first decided to go to medical school. She had an operative schedule chock full of surgeries that would send any surgeon just shy of completing her fellowship straight into nirvana.

Attending surgeons routinely would go into the operating room long enough to watch her make the first incision, then leave the patient in Becky's capable hands and go have coffee. In the time it once took her to close a surgical wound from the inside out, she could now complete an entire surgery. Becky had more than mastered the surgical techniques that would serve her patients well in her own practice. Now that her goal was literally within her grasp, she was in glory.

Once the morning cases were completed and all notes and orders written, she returned to her office to find an envelope on her desk, with the return address of a prestigious surgical practice located on the West Coast in the upper left-hand corner. Her hands shook with excitement as she read her formal acceptance to the practice of her dreams and a request for notification of her start date.

As foreign as tears were to her, Becky began to cry. The practice was affiliated with an incredibly busy hospital in a rapidly growing community, and Becky knew she would have a full caseload in no time. Her feet would certainly hit the ground running.

Finally, she had arrived. For the first time in her life, Becky uncharacteristically imagined herself floating on air. And float she did, through an entire day in the operating room and through post-op rounds, until later that evening when Isaac Goldman walked into the Surgical Unit.

From her first glance, Becky somehow knew. The soft smile on his face, the expression of pure joy in his eyes, the confidence readily apparent in his posture, and the purpose in his step could only mean one thing. Isaac hadn't looked this relaxed since she first met him, and Becky felt as though she had been kicked right in the stomach.

Since the night Isaac had shown up on Faith's doorstep, she had evaded every attempt her friend had made to tell her about their blossoming relationship and then just avoided any contact with her, period. In her own analytical way, Becky diagnosed her response to her friend's happiness as avoidance or perhaps even denial; either way, if she didn't have to hear the words directly, then it couldn't be true. With her head down, she stuffed her stethoscope in her lab coat pocket and turned to leave the nurses' station before Isaac saw her, intent on avoiding the truth just a bit longer.

As difficult as it would be to see her, Becky wanted to hear the truth from Faith and did not want Isaac Goldman around to witness her pain. She would wait until morning rounds when the time was limited with a busy OR schedule as a convenient excuse when she could say good-bye and then disappear. It was better that way, really.

Faith sensed rather than heard someone behind her and turned her head to see Becky, but unlike previous mornings on the unit, Becky's eyes did not light up when she saw Faith. Her face remained neutral. Becky's shoulders seemed to slump a little bit as she walked over to stand by Faith, her hands stiffly jammed in the pockets of her lab coat. She did not move, did not say anything, she just looked at her. Faith felt a lump in her throat, and her eyes grew moist with the sad realization that she was the cause of her friend's pain. She reached out to place her hand on Becky's arm.

"Becky, I'm so sorry," she whispered, and her tears threatened to spill down her cheeks.

Once again, Becky felt the unfamiliar threat of tears in her eyes, but this time, they were not tears of joy. These were the tears of a shattered heart, the type of tears she hadn't shed since the end of her intern year, the type of tears she had prayed she would never shed again.

Becky struggled to keep her voice steady, "I know, Faith, and it's not your fault. I know you and Isaac will be happy, and eventually I am sure I'll be happy for you, as well. But…" Becky stopped abruptly to inhale a huge breath of air in an effort to buy herself some time to regain her composure and avoid choking on words she did not want to speak.

"I just wanted to let you know that I'll be leaving this weekend. I've joined a practice back home, and they want me to start as soon as possible. And well, I figured, why not? There really isn't anything here in New Haven for me…"

Becky's voice trailed off and she dropped her head before looking away. Faith stood up and pulled Becky toward the Bubble. She shut the door to afford them some degree of privacy.

"Becky, please, I had no idea how you felt, I guess I always just assumed we were friends, really good friends, and I don't want anything to ever change that. Please come over tonight, I can change my plans with Isaac. You can't leave like this. I can't just let you leave and pretend that our friendship never existed."

Becky shook her head, then lifted her eyes to Faith's and squared her shoulders. "I'm sorry, Faith, I can't. I really have to get things organized. The movers are going to come Friday, and I'll be flying out first thing Saturday morning."

Faith's voice shook with desperation. "Becky, please, just one more day? We are going to get married on Saturday, and I want you there with me, with us. Honestly, you are more than just my best friend, you are my sister. I love you like a sister. Can't you just…"

Faith's voice trailed off as her head dropped, and unconsciously, she clasped her hands low over her belly.

With her eyes closed, she whispered, "Please, Becky, I need you."

With a brilliant mind as well as keen intuition, all of a sudden Becky understood. Her worst nightmare played out before her, and it wasn't just Faith's upcoming marriage. A pained expression crossed Becky's face as she steeled herself against the truth.

"Faith, seriously, do you think this is easy for me? I had wished it would be me standing at the altar with you, that we would start our life and have a family and grow old together. Oh, realistically, I guess I knew it could never happen, I know you don't share those feelings for me. But still…"

As hard as she tried, Becky could not suppress the sob that rose up as her heart shattered. She paused with her eyes closed and tried to buy a few moments of time to compose herself and then let it out in a rush as her eyes focused on a spot over Faith's head.

"I know you aren't gay, but that doesn't make it any easier for me. I wish you the best. I wish you both the best, truthfully. Leaving, though, is the right thing to do for my career." She finally allowed her eyes to meet Faith's.

"It's the right thing to do for me."

Becky leaned over to give Faith a quick hug. Faith clung to her best friend, desperate for the right words to say to keep the sister of her heart here and was very reluctant to let her go. Ever so quietly, Becky whispered very softly, so softly that Faith had to struggle to hear her.

"Be happy, my Love, and have a beautiful life with your husband. I will never forget you."

Chapter 40

Faith closed her eyes and breathed deeply. The familiar and comforting smell of salt air filled her senses and immersed her in a cloud of tranquility and peace. She was dressed in a long, strapless white sundress with tiny blooms of lavender and sprigs of green ivy embroidered on the hem and bodice. Her hair curled naturally on her shoulders, restrained only by simple pearl combs that swept the sides up and beautifully framed her face. It was a far cry from the lace and bustles and crystals that adorned a formal, more traditional wedding gown, but no bride had ever looked lovelier in the simplicity of her surroundings.

Faith felt a subtle suggestion of her mother's arms encircling her, and she sensed more than she heard her voice whisper, "I'm here with you, precious daughter, I'm here."

Faith looked up at her father, her cheeks pink from the warmth of this perfect day which filled the blue sky with fluffy white clouds and sent a whisper of a breeze that softly blew her curls into a gentle caress against her cheeks. She smiled at the very first man to ever steal her heart, who along with her mother had taught her the meaning of unconditional love.

"Are you ready, Daddy?"

Her father paused for a moment in wonderment to study the beautiful woman who stood before him. He remembered the sweetest face he had ever seen on a tiny, newborn angel baby, who had grasped his pinky finger the first time he held her immediately after her birth. He marveled at visions of her growing years which flashed before his eyes: her strength and character which had shone through during her mother's illness, her glory and accomplishment upon graduation from nursing school, her passion for the career in which she was able to lessen the pain and suffering of her patients in ways she hadn't been able to for her own mother.

He sighed as he thought of Faith's blessed mother, physically absent from what would be the happiest day of their daughter's life. He wondered how on earth all that time had gone by in what seemed like a blink of an eye.

He reached into the front pocket of his trousers and closed his fingers around the treasure he had placed there just that morning. He extended that hand out to Faith, palm up, and opened his fingers to reveal a set of crystal beads that were spaced in a familiar pattern throughout the length of silver chain.

A simple, unadorned crucifix dangled from the end. Each bead represented a whispered prayer offered up to Heaven by his wife for the health and happiness of her family every day. When Grace had become too weak to even pass the beads through her fingers, he took over. His fingers moved over the beads in the same way hers had for so many years, as he whispered the very same prayers his wife had said for their family, the focal point of her, of their, life. He allowed the beautiful beads to hang from his fingers, and Faith reached up with one hand to cover her mouth as her eyes grew wide. Her other hand hesitantly reached out, and her father gently draped the treasure across her palm.

The beautiful crystals sparkled in the sunlight and dazzling prisms of color splashed across the front of Faith's dress as he tenderly closed her fingers around her mother's Rosary.

"I bought this for your mother on our honeymoon in Ireland, from a little gift shop near a beautiful, old Cathedral where we attended Mass. I knew as soon as I saw it that I had to buy it for her. She cherished it. Every day she would sit at the kitchen table and say her Rosary with her morning cup of tea, praying that you children would be safe and healthy, always protected from harm, and most importantly, happy. She always finished her prayers with a smile on her face as she kissed the crucifix and blessed herself with it."

"I had a feeling that this day was going to involve more than just meeting your new boyfriend and having dinner with his family. I'm not sure how, really. When I called your brothers to tell them about today, I didn't even have to ask twice. We were all pretty quiet on the ride down; it was so strange how we all just knew. I want you to have these, Baby, to carry as you say your vows. Grace would want you to have them. She loved you so much, Faith, and I know that love will bless you and your husband for the rest of your lives together. May the love she and I shared fill your hearts and bless your own family as well."

He held his arm out to Faith and said, "Now I'm ready. Are you, Baby?"

"More than you know, Daddy, more than you know."

As both whispered a silent prayer, Faith heard her mother's voice once more, "Be happy, my darling Faith, I love you." She clasped her father's arm, and they headed across the sand.

Faith and Isaac faced each other on the sand near the jetties, and their families gathered around them in a semi-circle. They listened intently as Reverend Boyle spoke. "Isaac, do you take Faith to be your partner through life, to love in good times and bad, to care for in sickness and health, to celebrate together in times of great joy and to support each other through times of sadness, for as long as you shall live?" As he bit his lip to keep tears at bay, Isaac could only nod.

"And Faith, do you take Isaac to be your partner through life, to love in good times and bad, to care for in sickness and health, to celebrate together in times of great joy and to support each other through times of sadness, for as long as you shall live?"

Faith turned for just a moment to smile at her father, who stood behind her with her brothers, each with his arms around the shoulders of the others, and they nodded their heads in encouragement. She turned back to Isaac, her mother's rosary clasped in her hands, and she rubbed the crucifix between her forefinger and thumb. She looked into Isaac's eyes and her own misted over as well. Faith spoke clearly over the crash of waves on the beach.

"Yes. Yes, I will."

"You have chosen each other as husband and wife and have spoken your vows here before God and in the presence of your families. May the love you feel today follow you both all the days of your lives. It is now my honor to pronounce you husband and wife. As a sign of your love and commitment to each other, you may seal your vows for eternity with a kiss."

Chapter 41

The door opened wide, and Joanie and Marty stepped out to greet the very first wedding party they had hosted in all their years at the Clam Shack. "Welcome, welcome, congratulations and best wishes to you both! Come in!" Joanie smiled widely and began to dole out hugs and handshakes to all her guests while Marty did the same.

"This is such a beautiful day, a perfect day for a celebration!"

Faith could not believe this was the same Clam Shack she and Isaac had visited not even three months ago. The entire dining room had been scrubbed, and tables had been rearranged in close proximity throughout the room. Beautiful white tablecloths covered their surfaces with simple glass pitchers of beach grass and hydrangea blossoms as their only adornment. In the air hung the wonderful smell of freshly cooked seafood, and the bride and groom clasped each other's hands and smiled. Faith hugged Joanie tightly and whispered in her ear, "This is just beautiful, Joanie, so beautiful. Thank you!"

Marty clasped Isaac on the shoulder and pumped his hand. "This is the perfect way to start a marriage! We are so glad you asked us to share your day with you."

Joanie and Marty beckoned a gracious welcome to the wedding party and encouraged them all into the dining room with an invitation to take a seat. "The buffet is against the wall. Please, everyone, help yourself. There is plenty, so don't be shy. It's amazing how the salt air just gets your appetite going, so eat up! We have doggie bags, too, so you can bring dinner home with you. Don't forget to leave room for cake!"

Faith and Isaac went first. Isaac piled his plate with clam bellies, fresh corn on the cob, cole slaw, fresh boiled shrimp and cocktail sauce and then topped it off with a large lobster claw. He gazed longingly at the rest of the seafood on the buffet. Faith laughed as she scooped much smaller portions of the same on her own plate.

As tiny as the dining room was, the families fit quite comfortably, and the tables were close enough that conversations sprang up immediately.

"Well, I'm a surgeon, neurosurgery is my specialty…"

"I'm not sure what I'll do, but I'll never stop nursing…"

"This is Bubbe's ring…"

"She's the picture of her mother…"

"I'm fine. It was just a mini stroke…"

"Isaac, he's my miracle baby…"

"Four sons in our family and Faith…"

The conversation wound down and gradually the guests began to sit back. Some rubbed their bellies and swore they would not be able to eat again for at least a week. All proclaimed it, without a doubt, to be the best seafood they had ever eaten. Joanie and Marty cleared off the tables and buffet, and soon the smell of freshly brewed coffee began to waft out of the kitchen. The kitchen door swung open again and Joanie and Marty walked out with a two-tiered wedding cake on a large platter.

As they placed it in the middle of the buffet table, the group gathered around and simultaneously, everyone began to laugh. Perched on top of the cake were the typical bride and groom, with an added flair: the bride, a nurse with curly hair and a stethoscope around her neck, and the groom, a doctor with a white lab coat and a head lamp on his head. Beside the cake was a silver knife that had a shiny white satin bow embellished with tiny seashells tied around its handle. Faith picked the knife up and with her hand covered by Isaac's, they cut their first slice. Together they fed each other their first bite of cake and shared a sweet, frosting embellished kiss. Then Joanie took over and served the cake to all their guests.

Back at their seats, Isaac and Faith remained on their feet and asked for everyone's attention. They held hands as Isaac began to speak, "Thank you, everyone, for coming on such short notice to share this day with us. We thought we were going to surprise everyone, but my Bubbe had this all figured out before I had even proposed to Faith. And, well, it sounds like Faith's family had a pretty strong suspicion as well!" He smiled down at Faith and kissed her hand.

"I can't help but believe that Faith and I, our marriage, our life, was planned out a millennium ago, and we just had to wait for our paths to cross, for us to find each other. And here we are."

Faith smiled back at Isaac and then she began to speak. "I always knew nursing was my life and would always be part of my world, but I hadn't expected it to lead me straight to my future. I thought that 'future' started when Isaac and I realized we wanted to spend the rest of our lives together, but really, we just learned the true meaning of 'future' last week." Faith's eyes softened as she looked to Isaac for strength and encouragement.

Isaac lifted her hand to his lips and kissed it again, then had to hold back a sob of emotion which threatened to overwhelm him. Once he regained his composure, he finished what Faith had started to tell their families only moments before.

"We are so incredibly happy to share the news that Faith and I are expecting our first child."

The dining room was completely silent, but only for a second. Bubbe and Rachel burst into tears, and then Irvin began to chant, "Mazel Tov, Mazel Tov!" Faith's family joined in as well as they clapped along with the Goldmans, and they all encircled the ecstatic couple.

Faith immediately sought out the comfort of her father's arms and whispered in his ear, "Congratulations, Grandpa."

This time, it was her father's turn to burst into tears.

Chapter 42

Pregnancy was the most heavenly, magical, ethereal experience Faith had ever known, and the wonderment of every single moment exceeded any notion of what she had expected carrying her child to be. She found a website that plotted out, week by week, the development of a zygote, then an embryo, then a fetus, and then finally, a recognizable baby. She first thought of their child as a growing lima bean: small, oblong, with no real indication of the tiny being it would eventually become. It started to bear resemblance to a tadpole when finally small fins started to form, and Faith laughingly began to refer to the baby as a pollywog.

Shortly thereafter, the fins elongated, and little buds formed which would eventually become tiny fingers and toes. When Faith noted the tiny black orbs enlarging into recognizable shapes which indicated the formation of her baby's eyes, the windows to its soul, she realized that yes, as a matter of fact, her child was the most beautiful thing she had ever seen. Faith began to glow with a constant radiant smile on her face and the beautiful, dreamy expression of a woman who was living a fairy tale in real life, with her own little secret tucked safely under her heart.

At night, Faith would climb into bed early just to lie down with her hands on her belly. She waited impatiently for the sensation of their baby making its presence known, anxious for some small movement, even a tiny whisper of a flutter, to let her know that her child was saying hello. Isaac often climbed into bed with her and lay on his stomach, his head near Faith's belly so he could talk to his child and anxiously await that first kick against his palm. Faith's hands would skim her flat belly gently as if her baby could absorb the heat of her hands and become familiar with her gentle, soft touch. As her belly slowly but surely began to increase in size with their growing baby, her heart began to swell with joy and even more love than she had ever thought possible.

"Everything looks perfect, Faith. The baby is developing nicely; everything is right on schedule. Just keep taking your prenatal vitamins, eat healthy, four glasses of milk every day, and get a walk in at least four or five times per week. Are you still working night shift? I want you to make sure to get enough rest. Don't forget, if you are tired, then so is your baby. He needs as much rest as you do."

Faith nodded her head and smiled. "Sure thing, Dr. Richman, healthy diet, exercise, rest, and vitamins make a healthy baby. And yes, I'm still on night shift and so far it hasn't bothered me one bit. In fact, I think night shift is why I didn't have any morning sickness my first trimester. I'm always busy, and as soon as I get home, I go right to sleep. Even if I did have morning sickness, I either slept through it or was too busy to notice. It was a pretty pleasant three months, I have to say, and this trimester seems to be pretty much the same."

"Well, let's keep it that way. The first sign that those crazy shifts are wearing you out, you have to go to a normal schedule that won't wreak havoc with either you or your pregnancy. Now, is there anything else?" Dr. Richman put his head down in Faith's chart and began to record his observations and evaluation of her status.

"The only thing is these darned headaches. I've had them all my life, but they seem to be coming more frequently now. My mother died from a form of brain cancer, and I'm worried that I may have a tumor or something…"

"Now, now, Faith, just because you hear gallops, don't picture a zebra where a horse must be. I guarantee you, as soon as you deliver, they'll either go away or go back to your usual pattern. Just take some Tylenol, lie down with a cool cloth on your forehead, you'll be fine. And think about getting off night shift, ok? That will help." Dr. Richman smiled at her with poorly veiled condescension, and his hand on the doorknob indicated that, at least according to him, the visit was over. He rushed out the door and left Faith to chew on the inside of her lip, a worried expression still on her face.

"Oh, I wouldn't worry about it, Faith. If he was really concerned about the headaches, he would have told you. Honestly, between your hormones and the increase in blood volume brought about by the pregnancy, it's a wonder all pregnant women don't have headaches," Isaac commented after Faith told him about her visit with the obstetrician.

"You're right, I know." Faith sighed and snuggled up closer to Isaac who was engrossed in yet another journal of neurosurgery.

"I just get nervous, you know, because of my mother."

Isaac put his book down with a sigh and reached to hold Faith's hand. "Honey, even if he wanted to do a CT scan, he wouldn't because of the radiation and the risk to the baby. Just try to relax, this is a passing thing. I'll bet stress has a lot to do with it. Why don't you see if you can go to day shift; maybe that will help ease the headaches or maybe even stop them."

Isaac let go of Faith's hand and once again picked up the journal. "If you've had them all your life, I don't think you should be surprised that they are getting worse now." Isaac turned back to his reading, once again lost in the mysterious world of the human brain.

Faith tried a different tact and changed the subject. She lowered her voice to a throaty pitch and whispered in Isaac's ear, "Shall we go play some newlywed games?" She nibbled on his earlobe and then seductively kissed his neck.

Isaac remained head down, preoccupied with an abstract and challenging procedure he was unfamiliar with but needed to commit to memory, and absentmindedly said, "I'll be in in a little while to tuck you in, Honey. You go ahead."

Faith sat up with a surprised look on her face which Isaac did not notice. His distance and inattention were foreign to her and it shocked her even more that he would rebuff her blatant invitation to lovemaking. She tried to shrug the episode off as the result of a very busy, incredibly exhausting and miserably stressful fellowship.

"OK, well, goodnight then." Faith waited for his response but Isaac didn't reply. His eyes were closed, and his lips moved soundlessly as he repeated to himself in precise detail everything he had just read. He immediately stored it away for future reference.

Once settled in bed, Faith picked up the phone and dialed the familiar number of the one person who, besides her husband, could always make her smile. By the third ring, she heard a familiar voice, "Hello?"

"Hi, Daddy, how are you doing?"

"Baby, this is a surprise! I didn't expect to talk to you until Sunday! Is Isaac at the hospital tonight?"

"No, believe it or not, he's studying. I honestly thought he had learned everything his brain could have absorbed during medical school and residency. I didn't think there was anything left that he didn't know! He's amazing, though, commits it to memory the first time he reads it. Just unbelievable, I wish I had a memory like that."

"Don't sell yourself short, Faith, there is nothing wrong with your memory." Faith could hear her father shake his head as he remembered the many times Faith told him in intricate detail about the lives and circumstances of her patients. "You can still tell me about the very first patient you ever had, your very first clinical day in nursing school. Mrs. Desmond? She had something wrong with her leg…"

Faith giggled, "Her name was Mrs. DeSimone, and she had a diabetic foot ulcer. I swear, Daddy, every nurse remembers her first patient. That's nothing."

"And the codes. And the emergencies. And the families. You amaze me, Baby, you always have."

"That's different, Daddy, I remember them all because they took a little piece of my heart with them when they left and blessed me with a piece of theirs in return. Isaac, well, this is almost like an indelible stamp on his brain. I just can't figure out where he has an unused speck of gray matter left to store any new information.

This time, it was Faith who shook her head, and then she sighed. "Oh, Daddy…"

"What is it, Baby? I know you didn't call to talk about Isaac's brain. What's going on? Is it the baby? You've had a lot of changes in your life recently; I can only imagine how overwhelmed you must be. To top it all off, your brand-new husband is up to his neck in an intensely fierce fellowship."

He paused for a moment. "Is everything ok with the baby I mean?"

"Oh, the baby's fine. Dr. Richman says the baby's healthy as a horse, and so am I." Faith fussed with a thread on the bedspread and chewed the inside of her lip while her father waited patiently for her to continue.

"Daddy, can I ask you a question?"

"Of course you can, what is it?"

"When Mommy was pregnant with us, did she ever have headaches?"

"Headaches? Hmm, I'm not really sure; I guess maybe an occasional one. Nothing really stands out in my mind, though. Why?"

"Well, it's probably nothing, but I've been having headaches, and I seem to be the only one worried about them."

Faith's father laughed out loud. "Honey, you've had headaches all your life. Your mother was convinced something was really wrong with you when you were thirteen, remember? And your monthly started shortly after that. Your hormones have got to be wreaking havoc with your system. Do you think your crazy hours might be making them worse? They certainly can't be helping matters."

"Oh, Daddy, you're the third one now to mention that. I just don't see how, after all these years of working night shift, they'd be getting worse. Well, you are probably right. It makes sense that these are just 'hormonal headaches.'" Her Dad heard the very familiar lilt of laughter in Faith's voice.

"Remember my patient, Mr. Savino? He told me once about his 'hurricane headaches,' how he could always tell when a storm was coming because he'd get a throbbing headache right behind his eyes. You wouldn't believe what he told me. He said, 'as the barometer drops, the pressure starts to suck your brains right out of your nose, and you get this horrible pain' and he'd use two fingers on one hand to point right at his eyes." Faith chuckled again and nestled down under the covers as she relaxed.

"OK, 'hormonal headaches' it is, then. You always know just what to say to make me feel better. What would I ever do without you?"

"With God's good graces, you won't have to figure that out for a long, long time, Baby. Now put my grandchild to bed, and I'll talk to you on Sunday, OK? I love you, sleep well."

"Good night, Daddy, I love you, too." Faith hung up the phone and sat quietly for a moment, then reached over to her bedside table. Opening the drawer, she reached in and pulled out her mother's beautiful crystal Rosary and blessed herself with the silver crucifix. Holding the first crystal bead between her fingers, she rested her hands on her belly, closed her eyes and bowed her head as she had seen her mother do so many times over the years at the breakfast table.

"Our Father, who art in Heaven…."

Chapter 43

"Faith, I promise you, when the baby comes, I'm going to take a month off to be home with you two. The Department Chair already approved it, and even if we can't give him notice, it's alright." Isaac put his arms around Faith and rubbed her back reassuringly, then kissed the top of her head. As the familiar scent of lavender soaked into his senses, it calmed and soothed him. He realized that it had been a while since he had been close enough to Faith to notice it, and he sighed with regret.

"Honey, I am so sorry. I know I've been really distant, but it's just this darn program and trying to get ready to take the boards. I am beyond overwhelmed, but I shouldn't have let that affect you. I know it has been going on for too long. I'm going to try to back off a bit so we can spend more time together. It's only going to be the two of us for a little while longer, so I better take advantage of it, right?"

Isaac noticed tears on her cheeks and felt his heart drop because while he had seen his wife cry before, he had never been the cause of her pain. Isaac used his fingers to comb Faith's hair back from her face, then gently held her face in his hands and used his thumbs to wipe away the wetness. He leaned in for another kiss, but this time, he took his time and pulled her more closely into his embrace.

He felt Faith's hands leave his back slowly and then encircle his neck as she leaned more deeply into him, and the shame of remorse diffused as he was again overcome with passion for his wife. She drew strength from his apology, and in return the fervor of his passion was buoyed by reassurance of her forgiveness.

Effortlessly, Isaac scooped her up in his arms. Even in her third trimester, with much, much more than a little "bump" for a belly, she was still as light as a feather. He carried her into the bedroom and gently laid her on their bed as he remembered the first time they had made love and was determined to recapture the intensity of those moments again. Isaac lifted Faith's nightgown, and she arched her back so he could pull it over her belly and then her head. He dropped his own clothes in a heap by the bed and climbed in with her.

His eyes never left her face as his hands so carefully and so lightly teased her skin, and his featherweight touch raised goose flesh all over her body. Faith enjoyed every second of her body's response to her husband and felt the desperate need for release quickly intensify. She rolled onto her side and Isaac lay behind her, his hand heightening her passion as he softly stroked her, and then he slid inside the velvety warmth of her body. He moved slowly at first, giving Faith time to crest the waves that suddenly brought her senses to indescribable heights.

As he felt her body shudder as she climaxed, he moved more quickly and then rapidly reached his own pinnacle as a fine sheen of sweat broke out over both their bodies.

They lay quietly, each lost in his or her own thoughts. Isaac curled one arm under his head and the other around Faith's belly. Faith, likewise, lay with one arm cushioning her own head and the fingers of her other hand intertwined with his. All of a sudden, she felt Isaac's hand freeze and then abruptly flatten against her stomach.

Startled, he sat up in bed and Faith turned her head to look back at him. She laughed at the blatant anxiety and concern she saw on his face. "Braxton Hicks. Remember those from medical school, my-oh-so-brilliant-surgeon/husband-with-the-photographic-memory?"

Isaac blew his breath out in a rush and his head dropped down in sheer humiliation, mortified once more that he had neglected his own wife. "Faith, I've been such a shit, and I'm so sorry. I don't know where the past months have gone. I can barely remember anything but the dozens of books and journal articles I've read. I knew this fellowship was going to be hell, but I never expected it to take over my life the way it has. As soon as it is over, I promise you, we are going to be all about family and each other."

Isaac leaned down to kiss Faith's belly and then rested his cheek where his lips had just been. He felt a nudge against his cheek, then a more insistent kick.

"I think she's saying, 'Hi, Daddy, what's up?'" Faith smiled as she ran her fingers through Isaac's hair.

"Then again, it could be 'he', you know." When Faith didn't respond, Isaac looked up at her.

"How do you know it's a 'she?'"

Faith shrugged her shoulders, a small yet thoughtful smile on her face. "After the wedding, I started saying my Mother's Rosary before I went to sleep, and as my belly grew, I would rest my hands on it while I said my prayers. It was almost like my mother's hands were feeling the kicks and sending love through her Rosary beads. And then I had a dream one night, I was talking to my mother on the phone, but I also could see her in the distance and she had a baby in her arms. I was telling her about the pregnancy and the baby and how worried I was about the headaches. I could see her smile from so far away, and she looked right into my eyes and then told me not to worry anymore and that she would take care of her granddaughter until it was time." Faith smiled as Isaac kissed her belly once again and they lay in silence, momentarily lost in the magical dreams of their child-to-be.

"Honey, I think I'd like to name our daughter Grace. I know for certain my mother has had her granddaughter in her arms every second of this pregnancy, and I just feel so peaceful knowing what an amazing Guardian Angel our baby has."

"I think Grace is a perfect name, but seriously Honey, shouldn't we have a boy's name picked out, just in case? I mean, really, you can't be one hundred percent sure about this."

Faith just smiled as she stroked her husband's hair but remained silent. She would let Isaac pick out a boy's name, but she would tuck it away for another baby at another time. This baby's name was Grace, the daughter she had always dreamed of, the youngest member of the family that Fate had led her and Isaac to create.

Chapter 44

The alarm clock buzzed at 4:30am, and after turning it off, Isaac rolled over to pull his sleeping wife into his arms. He buried his nose in her curls and breathed deeply of the life-giving essence that was so uniquely Faith. He clasped his hands around her and rested them on her belly. Suddenly, her belly grew taut under his hands. He heard Faith breathe very deeply, in and out, in a concentrated and determined effort to relax and control the pain she felt. When the contraction ended, Faith turned onto her back and smiled at Isaac.

"Phew, I'm glad your alarm finally went off. I was getting pretty close to waking you anyway." She took Isaac's hand in her own and kissed it, then placed her cheek in the palm of his hand and cradled it. She noticed the shock still apparent on his face and giggled.

"Honey, what's wrong?"

"Faith, what on earth do you mean, 'what's wrong?' That was a contraction, and a strong one by the feel of it. Why didn't you wake me up? Shit, we have to get going...." Isaac's voice trailed behind him as he flew out of bed and began to pull on the first clothing he could find- dirty scrubs from the laundry basket.

Faith slowly sat up in bed. "Honey, slow down, the doctor said it could be hours, and the contractions are still about five or six minutes apart. Take those filthy scrubs off; in fact, why don't you get in the shower with me, and we both can do this the right way. Ok?" Faith smiled gently at Isaac, and he relaxed just a little.

Isaac sat down on the bed again and placed his hand on Faith's forehead. "You're sweating. Those contractions must be getting tough, huh?" He reached for her hand and kissed the back of it, then turned it over to kiss her palm.

He noticed the pinched expression on her face and said, "Are they getting pretty intense? Why don't we just get to the hospital and see if you can get an epidural now. You should rest before you have to push."

"I'm fine, Isaac, really. The pain is bearable. I don't need an epidural yet." Faith shut her eyes for a moment and then opened them as she tried to smile at Isaac. Immediately, her eyes slammed shut again and her lips compressed into a flat, strained line. Isaac frowned.

"Faith-"

Isaac had no time to finish as Faith quickly turned over on her side again and this time, the controlled breaths intensified and came quicker. Faith began to pant, and she arched her back and clasped her hands at the sides of her head. Isaac knelt behind her and rubbed her lower back as he attempted to encourage her with soft words and soothing noises.

When the contraction was over, Faith pushed herself up on one elbow and slowly swung her legs over the side to sit on the edge of the bed. "OK, I think you are right, I think it is time for that epidural. Honey, can you hand me my robe?"

Isaac helped her slip into it one sleeve at a time. He held her arm to keep her steady as Faith stood up, and Isaac immediately stepped back as a sudden gush of fluid fell from Faith's body and splashed on the floor.

A panicked look crossed Faith's face and she grimaced again as she sagged against Isaac. "My head, oh my God, help me, it hurts, Isaac…"

The tone of her voice changed, and Isaac's name came out like a shrill, high-pitched scream. Slammed by yet another contraction which took Faith's breath completely away, torrential tears coupled with a drenching sweat soaked both of them as she moaned in agony.

"Hospital, Isaac, get me to the hospital."

His years of medical training had prepared him well and the clinician in Isaac took over as he went into emergency mode and scooped Faith up in his arms. Isaac jammed his feet into his surgical clogs and prayed he had left his keys right by the front door so he wouldn't have to waste precious time scrambling to find them. Then he ran for the car.

Isaac pulled into the ER directly in front of the sliding doors and jumped out of the car. He threw his keys at the Security Guard who immediately hurried over to him.

"You can't park here, Buddy; you'll have to move your car."

"This is an emergency, get me a gurney stat!"

The Security Guard immediately recognized Doctor Goldman and gaped as he watched him attempt to pull his very pregnant wife out of the passenger's side of the car. Isaac screamed at him again, the urgency obvious in his voice, "Move!"

Isaac cradled his wife in his arms as she whimpered, her eyes clamped tightly shut against the blinding pain, her hands pressed against her temples as if to keep her skull from shattering. Isaac hurried towards the doors which lead into the ER just as the Security Guard and two nurses pushed a gurney out the door. He carefully placed Faith on the stretcher, snapped the side rails up, and began to run with one hand on the stretcher. With the other he clasped his wife's hand.

"Hang on, Faith, just hang on. Everything is going to be OK."

As they swung the gurney into the trauma room, one of the nurses yelled for the Obstetrics resident on call while another called for the Neonatologist who would take over the newborn's care once it was delivered. Isaac stepped back, out of the way, as the emergency personnel started to work.

Faith groaned again and slowly tossed her head from side to side. With her eyes closed, she whispered, "Why does it hurt so badly? Isaac, make it go away, make it go-"

She was cut off by the nurse who yelled to the OB resident as she rushed into the room, "Her BP is 230/140!"

The resident began to snap on gloves as she called out orders, "Get some hydralazine. Push some magnesium IV, hurry up, she's going to seize! Get the crash cart in here and where the hell is that infant warmer? Get Respiratory, they should have been here already. Hurry up, people, move!"

Isaac moved to the head of the gurney and tried to stay out of the way of the team which worked frantically to help his wife and save his child, yet close enough to give her the support and reassurance he knew she needed to hear. Not used to being a bystander, the doctor in Isaac tried to recall everything he had ever learned in medical school about pregnancy-induced hypertension. He watched as the resident pushed on her feet and looked for the tap-tap-tap of clonus; four beats in succession indicated a seizure was imminent, and Isaac knew if a C-section didn't take place, and quickly, he could lose both his wife and his child.

The resident performed an internal vaginal exam on Faith and Isaac heard her whimper softly, "Push, please, I have to push."

The resident nodded her head and looked up at Isaac, "She's at ten centimeters and I can't wait for Dr. Richman to get here." She turned to the nurse and asked her to check another blood pressure as she put on a sterile gown and fresh gloves.

"OK, she's down to 140/90, I think we're safe. We've got the delivery cart and the incubator. The Neonatologist should be down here at any minute. He's just finishing up with a crash C section in Labor and Delivery."

"Dr. Goldman, get behind your wife and hold her shoulders up so she can get some leverage. OK, Faith, let's get this baby out. Are you ready? Hold her legs up, let's go!"

The nurses, skilled at emergency deliveries, knew exactly what to do. As one readied a table with blankets, radiant warmer and resuscitative equipment in case the newborn exhibited signs of respiratory distress, the other two pulled up Faith's legs and supported them in the classic position for delivery.

Isaac held his wife up and encouraged her to push. "Push, Faith, the baby's almost here. I can see hair, Honey, the head's crowning. You're almost there, now push!"

The resident watched the baby's head advance and then retreat, advance and then retreat, with every push. As Faith's pushes grew weaker, she asked the nurse to get a vacuum extractor and applied it to the baby's head.

"OK, Faith, this time give it all you've got. I know it hurts, but push through that ring of fire and your baby will be here."

Faith's eyes were glazed and unfocused. Her forehead dripped with sweat and her eyes with tears. "Oh my God," Faith whispered, "My head…the baby…Isaac…"

She took a deep breath and with what little strength she had left, she pushed. A progressively deepening rubor spread across her face and chest as she held her breath and bore down, and the baby's head emerged followed quickly by the rest of its body. Her breath let out in a rush and her body went limp. Isaac hugged Faith close and kissed her on the lips.

"You did it, Honey, she's here. Baby Grace is here. She's so beautiful, Faith, look at her!"

The resident placed their newborn on Faith's chest, and a nurse immediately began to dry the slickness off her tiny body.

Another pulled on a stockinet cap. Isaac couldn't take his eyes off his baby girl, his Grace, and whispered to Faith, "She's so beautiful, Faith, just like you. She looks just like you."

Isaac looked down at Faith and froze. Her head fell backwards as Isaac pulled his arm out from behind her, her eyes unfocused and partially closed, her mouth slack. He tried to rouse her, "Faith, can you hear me? Faith... Faith!"

At the sound of urgency in Isaac's voice, everyone in the room froze, then immediately sprang into motion to execute the familiar sequence of steps learned by harsh repetition in the very manic, often cold, life and death world of the Emergency Room.

"Stand back, Dr. Goldman, let me help her."

The resident stared at the heart monitor, willing it to reveal the normal sinus rhythm of a beating, living heart.

"Agonal rhythm, no pulse. Start compressions."

An ER technician began CPR and compressed Faith's breastbone until Isaac was sure it would snap. A Respiratory Therapist placed an ambu bag over Faith's nose and mouth and began to squeeze it in a slow but steady rhythm. The breaths caused Faith's chest to rise and fall in sync with the pattern of compressions. As the team worked, Dr. Richman burst into the room and sought out the resident.

"What the fuck happened?"

"Sir, she came in fully dilated and complaining of a severe headache. Her BP was 240/130 so I gave magnesium and hydralazine, and her pressure finally came down to where she could safely push. As soon as the baby was out, she went unresponsive and then flat-lined. We're doing compressions and have pushed a round of ACLS drugs, but nothing…"

Dr. Richman walked over to Isaac and assumed the air of a physician used to being in charge. "Isaac, it appears that Faith has had some complications of Pregnancy Induced Hypertension. We are doing all we can for her. Maybe it would be best for you to step out to the waiting room while the team works on your wife."

Isaac abruptly shrugged Dr. Richman's hand off his arm and grabbed him by the collar. He backed him up until he was flat against the wall. "Where the hell have you been? And where were you during this pregnancy when Faith kept coming to you with the headaches? I'll tell you where you were, you egomaniacal son of a bitch, you were blowing her off because you couldn't be bothered with a neurotic first time mother! This is your fault, and I suggest you get out of here before I throw you out myself." Isaac let him go as several staff members tried to pull him off of Dr. Richman.

He stepped back and held both palms up, and then calmly informed the room, "I'm fine. But anyone who tries to remove me from my wife's bedside will have to get the Security Guards to do it. I'm not leaving, period!"

"OK, we have a rhythm. Check another blood pressure and call Radiology. We're heading to CAT scan."

Not ten minutes later, Isaac stood in the control room and watched his wife as the table on which she lay slid into the scanner. He stood back and watched the screen, and as images of Faith's brain came into view, he drew in a sharp breath and his shoulders slumped. He squeezed his eyes shut as if to block out the horrific images on the screen, similar to those which had taunted him time and again in the past, of other demons lurking in other patients' brains.

Monster-like, the images scoffed at the neurosurgeon in him. They mocked his expertise and dared him to try to do something, anything, to fix the damage. A sinister, black apparition filled one side of Faith's brain and spread menacingly over toward the other side. It shifted healthy brain tissue over and compressed it against the inside of her skull, and when it could be compressed no more, it forced the brain tissue downward. Isaac stared at a massive intracranial bleed which had already progressed beyond the point of repair at the hand of any great surgeon. It was only a matter of time before the base of the brain was affected. Known as brain stem herniation, it was a fatal complication of an unchecked bleed of this magnitude.

Dr. Goldman, the neurosurgeon, understood the death sentence something like this imposed on a patient. Isaac, the husband, vomited on the floor. The entire room went silent, and the technicians somberly finished up their tasks and then went to take Faith out of the scanner.

Chapter 45

In the span of about fifteen minutes, Isaac Goldman's idyllic world abruptly collapsed, and the Heaven he had been living with Faith no longer existed. Becky bore witness to this from the doorway of Faith's hospital room.

"Momma Sue," Faith's trusted colleague in ICU, had assumed the heartbreaking task of nursing her dear friend who would never again awaken. She cared for her as any mother would care for her child, and provided the only real medicine that would make any difference at all in the scenario now playing out in front of her. With warm and gentle touches, soft words and comforting smiles, Susan selflessly loved and cared for her patient, and also her patient's husband. As soon as Faith had been admitted to the ICU, as soon as Susan had received report from the ER nurse, she had called Becky in California and explained briefly the tragic events that had led to her admission. Going immediately into the mode of a highly educated clinician, Becky had begun to ask questions in rapid fire succession. Susan had gently cut her off. "It's time to come back, Dr. Simon. And hurry."

Fate often demonstrates neither rhyme nor reason when it chooses its next victim, and this time, it had chosen to annihilate an entire family through the cruelty of an unforeseen enemy. Becky watched her former student study his wife and could imagine his analytical mind as it weighed the implications of all that his critical eye noted in this patient who lay in the bed before him. A moment later, she saw pain and torment take possession of a husband who silently prayed to God to be merciful and spare his wife, to allow her to come back to him and to their newborn daughter whom she had never met, had never held close to the heart that had watched over her for nine months. She watched as Isaac tenderly brushed the hair back from Faith's forehead.

Becky felt like an intruder, and she turned her head away from the intimacy displayed before her but then was drawn back to Isaac as he kissed her hand, then her lips, and tried to smile through his tears at a wife who was unaware of the love he so desperately prayed would rouse her from her dark, terminal slumber.

Becky understood his need to dissociate the professional from the personal self and found herself doing the very same. She braced herself against the shock of what she knew she would see and then turned her gaze to Faith, her best friend, her soul mate. As her heart beat in a sharp staccato rhythm against her breastbone, Becky composed herself and swallowed. She allowed the clinical Becky to come forth to save her from the turmoil of confronting a myriad of emotions which hovered very close to the surface and threatened to drop her to her knees.

Becky observed the patient lying in the hospital bed, not moving. Her chest rose and fell steadily as the ventilator actively forced air into her chest and then passively allowed it to escape again with a soft "whoosh." Intravenous bags which hung from poles behind the head of the bed dripped life-sustaining hydration and electrolytes into her veins. On the cardiac monitor's screen traced the normal sinus rhythm of a healthy, young heart, which belied the neurological devastation of this patient who, not a week before, had been a vibrant, breathing, loving human being. Now, the woman who lay before her was being kept alive artificially in a non-seeing, non-feeling, never-again-to-awaken state by cold, soul-less, emotion-less machines.

Becky dug her nails into the palms of her hands and stifled back the sob that threatened to escape, and then silently approached Isaac. She gently placed her hand on his shoulder, unable to offer him any words that might ease not only his pain but hers as well.

Isaac sensed her intent before she said a word and spoke, "I know what you are going to say, Becky. I know it because it's what I would say to any family in this position. But I can't give up on her yet. I'm not ready. What if she is one of the less than one percent who wakes up? How can I know for certain that she won't? I won't be able to live with myself if I have to spend the rest of my life wondering if I did the right thing. What if removing the breathing tube denies her the time she needs to heal and recover enough to breathe on her own? I could be killing her by prematurely taking her off life support. She's so strong and determined. What if right now she can hear everything I'm saying but just can't show it? What if she is screaming inside her head for me not to give up on her? I can't be sure, and I can't live being haunted by that scream in my own head."

Isaac covered his face with his hands and scrubbed it briskly as he tried to rid himself of the haze that fogged his mind and the physical exhaustion brought about by the watchful vigil he kept at his wife's bedside.

"Isaac, don't make this a power struggle between life and death. You won't win this one. Faith is gone, Isaac. She's gone, and nothing you can do will change that. Be her husband now, not a doctor. You know what Faith would want. Honor her, Isaac. Honor her life. Give her this gift, if not for yourself, then for the daughter you have together. They are both relying on you to make the right decision now, for both of them."

Isaac set his jaw and with more façade than bravery, he said, "I can't. I'm not ready." He closed his eyes briefly and took a deep breath, then glared at Becky with grim determination. "I won't."

In the next breath, he broke down and allowed his own emotions to give way to the anguish that, finally, had built to an immeasurable and uncontrollable level.

"I don't know if I can go on, I don't think I can. I should have known. I should have seen this coming. Faith had been having headaches and told me she'd had them all her life. I just figured they were migraines, maybe hormonal. I should have known, Becky, I should have ordered the fucking scans myself. How could I have missed this? Why didn't I listen? What have I done?" A loud, hiccoughing sob broke loose, and it took several deep breaths before he was able to speak again.

"I've lost her, and I know I'll never love another woman ever, as long as I live. Not like my Faith. Oh my God, what am I going to do? What about our daughter? How can I make a decision that will force Grace to grow up without a mother? How can I subject her to the heartache my own wife has had to live with since the age of 15? Faith told me once it was life-altering, the grief and the emptiness she felt at the times a woman needs her mother the most. At least she had brothers to share her pain and help her move on. What is Grace going to do?"

Becky struggled against her own emotions which threatened to bubble over and then took a deep and steadying breath. "Isaac, Grace is going to look to you to show her what to do. She's going to need you to be strong for her, to be her support and her guide as she goes through life. You'll be her father, and in Faith's stead you'll be her mother, as well. You can do this, Isaac. You can do this because deep inside, you are trying to bury the reality that's lying right in front of you, trying to keep it separate from your heart. You know it is the right thing to do. Faith is gone. Her soul left this world as soon as Grace's soul entered it, and nothing could have prevented it. You didn't know the aneurysm was there, you have to stop blaming yourself. And honestly, even if Faith had known about it, she wouldn't have done anything differently, not if it meant jeopardizing her pregnancy. Grace is her final gift to you. Your daughter is your wife's legacy and her promise that life, both yours and Grace's, will go on."

"It's time to give Faith permission to go. This isn't life. She wouldn't want to live this way, and I know you wouldn't want her to, either. It contradicts everything she ever stood for, everything she represented in her life and the lives of those who love her. Think of Grace, think of how much she needs you to do the right thing for her mother."

Isaac sat with his head in his hands, seemingly oblivious to all that Becky had just said, but Becky knew in her heart that Isaac had heard every single word of it. She was equally certain that he knew it all to be true in his own heart and that it was time to let his heart override his head. She walked over to Isaac and kissed him on top of his head, then squeezed his shoulder.

She walked to Faith's bedside and looked down on the most beautiful woman she had ever known, not only on the outside but also inside, where her soul and her humanity were nourished and sustained by a heart that beat with the purest of love for the world around her, and for everyone in it. In her own lifetime, Becky had never known love like that, and though Faith had never loved her the way she loved Isaac, just the presence of her friend's perfection in her own world was almost enough. She leaned over and kissed her friend on the forehead.

Then, she rested her head on Faith's chest and absorbed into her soul the first and last time she would hear and feel the love of her life's precious heartbeat. She left the room to give Isaac the crucial time he needed to make the most difficult decision he would ever make for his family.

Chapter 46

Isaac sat with his eyes closed and tried to wipe all the fears borne of years of training, as well as many hours of witnessing many patients in this exact situation, out of his mind. He was numb, unable to grasp what had happened to his wife, unwilling to recognize the worst-case scenario which now played out before him. He rubbed his eyes, then folded his hands under his chin and rested on them, his elbows on his knees, his shoulders hunched.

He quieted himself and calmed his breathing and focused on a vision of Faith the very first time he saw her sitting at the nurses' desk, charting, black smudges under her eyes, that spectacular hair of hers escaping the confines of her barrette and curling in little wisps around that angelic face. He pictured those curls which had relaxed gradually because of pregnancy hormones that had coursed through her bloodstream.

Isaac saw in his mind the image of her tiny frame rounded with the gentle swell of early pregnancy and smiled as he pictured her bulging belly last week hanging over her feet and blocking the scale's numbers from view. Faith had finally resorted to using a hand mirror to view the numbers and then shrugged as she self-consciously patted her swollen belly. He had looped his arms around her and pulled her backward into his embrace, and they both smiled at the tender picture of an expectant Mother and Father reflecting back at them in the mirror over the sink. With overwhelming joy on their faces, their eyes met in the mirror as they locked their hands together over their baby's safe, warm nest for the next few weeks to come.

Isaac stared at the shell of the woman who used to be his Faith, his beautiful and enchanting wife. Their daughter lay in a bassinet by his side. "Baby Goldman" was written in black magic marker on a card also printed with flowery pink script which bore the joyful words, "It's a girl!" Propped at the end of the bassinette was a small white Teddy bear with a pink satin ribbon around its neck, a thoughtful gift from "Momma Sue." Though a few days old, Grace bore a striking resemblance to her mother, who was not three feet away from her.

Isaac looked over very briefly at his daughter. He had kept a desperate vigil at Faith's bedside. He had willed her awake, desperate for any sign of activity that might remain. He silently pleaded for something, anything, which might indicate life, even a subtle flicker of her eyelids or a twitch of a finger.

Periodically, he would squeeze her hand and say to her, "Wake up, Faith, open your eyes and look at me. I love you, Faith, please open your eyes." He would kiss her and hoped that by love alone, she would defy the odds and awaken from this maddening nightmare.

The faintest whisper of hope remained in his heart, and over and over he whispered a desperate prayer, "Please, God, pleasepleaseplease...."

In his mind, though, Isaac knew. He knew that love alone couldn't save his wife, and he knew the incomprehensible horror of what lay ahead of him. Once again, he tried to shrug the defeat off his shoulders and the pain from his face. Even though Faith would never see his face again, he did not want her soul to bear witness to his cowardice and his inability to show the same strength his wife had demonstrated every day of her life.

"Had." Isaac groaned and dropped his head in his hands. All hope for a future with his wife or for his daughter's future with a mother who had spent every day of the past nine months living only for her tiny angel vanished. His shoulders wilted even more under the burden of a decision he had prayed he would never be forced to make, and he sighed through tears which now flowed freely down his face.

Isaac picked up his daughter, snuggled her close under his chin and gently swayed with her. He supported her tiny head in one hand, and with the other he cradled her body, still curled in the innocent repose of a babe nestled snuggly within her mother's womb. A vise of tragic hopelessness constricted his chest and prevented Isaac from taking a deep breath. It squeezed more and more tightly until finally, he felt his heart shatter under the suffocating pressure of reality, not only for his loss but also for their daughter's. Isaac summoned whatever bit of strength he had left to prevent his knees from buckling and took the last few steps to his wife's bedside.

"Help me make the right decision for you and for our Grace. Here she is, Faith, this is Grace. This is our daughter. She looks like you, see?"

Isaac gently lowered Grace to an enface position with her mother. "She has green eyes with tiny little flecks of gold, and the fuzz of her head already has a hint of your coloring. When she sleeps, she holds her little fists curled right under her chin, just like you do. And when she lets out her little sighs, she reminds me of all the times I've heard you sigh in contentment for whatever joy you were finding in your life at that particular moment.

"I promise you, I will keep your memory alive for her every day, and she will know you. She will know of the love you had for her long before you ever felt her move in your belly. Grace loves you, and so do I."

Isaac removed the blanket which swaddled Grace and opened the soft flannel tee shirt that kept her warm and snug. He leaned over his wife and taking Grace's tiny fist in his hand, he ever so gently stroked Faith's face, allowing their daughter a moment to know the feel of her mother's skin. Grace's gentle touch, in its innocence, blessed Faith with the first and last touch of a daughter who would only know of her mother's love through stories and photos that would never quite capture the truth and magic that was Faith.

Isaac gently placed Grace in the crook of Faith's arm and curved it around her daughter. He reached over to the ventilator that had kept his wife alive during these interminable, cruel, hateful hours and days of diminishing hope, destroyed today by the final realization that she was never coming back to him, never coming home to a life with their new family. With one last prayer, he flipped the switch to the "off" position and the ventilator went silent.

For the last time, Isaac climbed into bed beside his wife. He encircled his family with arms he naively believed would always protect them from any harm which dared to threaten their perfect world and cursed himself that he hadn't been able to prevent this.

Isaac kissed his wife tenderly on her forehead, on her nose, and on both cheeks. He leaned over Faith's body and tenderly kissed the top of his daughter's head. He listened to the "beep, beep, beep" of the heart monitor, and the harsh staccato of beats grew farther and farther apart as Faith's heart rate slowed. He waited for the dreaded, shrill alarm which would sound at her life's last moment when Faith's heart would cease beating forever. Isaac leaned over to bury his face in her hair and breathed in for the last time the faintest whisper of lavender scent that miraculously still lingered in her curls. He then hugged Faith's other arm closer and drew baby Grace more tightly into the family circle to allow his daughter the chance to be embraced by the warmth of both her parents' love for her for the first and final time. Then Isaac waited for his wife to die.

Chapter 47

Disoriented and half-asleep, Isaac groped for the buzzing pager on his nightstand. He fumbled to silence it and read the message: male patient, status post fall, probable intracranial bleed. He didn't bother with the rest of the message. Its urgency was implied, "Get here stat," or something to that effect.

Isaac hesitated only momentarily as he looked back over his shoulder at Faith to tell her he had an emergency at the hospital, to promise her a continuation of the passion that so filled his being he could barely breathe for want of her. Isaac was shocked to find the other side of the bed empty. The covers were smooth and unruffled, and the pillow remained puffed and unmarred by the imprint on her head. No familiar ratty bathrobe was draped carefully over the end of their bed.

Isaac was confused at first by Faith's absence and started to call out for her, but then wakefulness slammed him with a stinging, cruel slap of reality, and the memory of the horror that had destroyed his family and blackened his soul rushed back. He stumbled to the bathroom and splashed some cold water on his face and stared in shock at the stranger who glared back at him in the mirror. He barely recognized the gaunt contours of the face which had been aged drastically by grief, and he was momentarily taken aback by the deep and dark craters with red-rimmed eyes that peered out from their depths.

Swallowed whole by agonizing pain and misery, Isaac had yet to heal from the trauma of indescribable loss, even at this point in what should have been the healing process. Grief refuses to follow a set timeline. There exists no hard and fast rule to indicate the sharp line of demarcation between immobilization by anguish and moving on with the heart's permission and encouragement. Isaac had been dubbed with the title of widower with obscene prematurity. He stared himself down and vowed to win the battle with this macabre stranger in the mirror, then his shoulders slumped in defeat. Isaac epitomized a man who had been victimized by unimaginable circumstances, and he was scarred visibly and permanently by the injustice and heartbreak of the situation.

Isaac hastily brushed his teeth and then threw on a pair of wrinkled scrubs which had been thrown haphazardly onto the floor next to the laundry basket. He ran out of his bedroom, his shirt half-tucked in and then slid his bare feet into once-green surgical clogs, now bronzed with years of iodine and blood stains. He allowed himself just a brief moment to remember the loving hands that had tried so hard to scrub off evidence of the many hours he had spent in the operating room and the gentle laughter in her eyes as she ignored his arguments that nothing could possibly scrub those stains away. Isaac paused just long enough to jot a quick note on the pad of paper in the kitchen for Meredith, the live-in housekeeper and nanny for Grace, and then he flew out the door.

Mr. Johnson had been brought into the emergency room by paramedics who had responded to a frantic phone call from his wife of 60 years. Nightly, Mr. Johnson's dreams had been interrupted by familiar burning pressure in his bladder which signaled the need for yet another one of nature's calls to the bathroom. The result of a swollen prostate gland that was the bane of many an older man's existence, Mr. Johnson answered the call more and more frequently, and he hadn't had a restful night's sleep in months.

Exhausted beyond belief, he had climbed out of bed with his eyes half-closed and tripped over an old leather slipper he had carelessly kicked off at the foot of the bed and mistakenly left in his path to the bathroom. It happened so quickly he was unable to throw his hands up in an attempt to protect himself, and he cracked his head on the sharp corner of the marble-topped bureau as he crashed down to the floor.

His wife was startled from sleep by a loud thud as her husband slammed to the floor, and she had to struggle to get out of bed. Arthritis, which had stiffened her knees and hips to a fraction of the mobility she enjoyed in her younger years now hindered her progress, and she had to fight against horrendous pain that took her breath away. She willed her body to bend as she walked to the end of the bed and haltingly lowered herself to the floor. As Mrs. Johnson knelt at her husband's side, her mouth hung open in a silent scream as she watched a dark maroon puddle spread out from under his head. She cursed her uncooperative joints as she struggled to her feet and desperately fought against the agony that threatened to halt her in her tracks as she hobbled to the phone.

Isaac closed his eyes and took a deep breath. He concentrated on the pale circle of shaved skin shrouded in blue drapes that covered the face of this elderly man who was his patient this late night. He held his folded hands tightly against his belly so he wouldn't contaminate his sterile gloves and stepped back from the table. A circulating nurse familiar with Dr. Goldman's demand for expediency had hurriedly obtained the CAT scans and hung them on the bank of lights on the wall. He studied the film which revealed a darkened area of bleeding over the surface of the left temporal region, inwardly extending and invading the temporal lobe of the brain.

Readily apparent to his trained eye, the film was all the more concerning to him because the area of bleeding had continued to increase in size, extending more deeply into the brain and compressing more healthy tissue in its path. A memory struggled to reach the surface of conscious thought of a similar yet more sinister bleed, and he consciously pushed it away, determined not to let anything interrupt or interfere with his determination to do for this patient what he had been unable to do for his wife.

If the bleed was left unchecked, the end result would be disastrous. If Isaac could not control the bleeding quickly, the hematoma would expand, and the brain would swell. Inevitably, Mr. Johnson's chances of successful outcome would become nil. The brain literally would suffocate for lack of life-sustaining oxygen and life, as this patient once knew it, would cease to be. Death would follow, and quickly.

An all too familiar scenario to Isaac, it was up to him to perform the emergency surgery that would save this man's life. Isaac did not voice his concern that the bleeding had quickly and dramatically increased due to the blood thinning medication Mr. Johnson took for his heart disease, but the entire surgical team from scrub tech to intern sensed his tension, and they all performed their own tasks quickly and with precision. The medication had certainly done its job, but paradoxically, it was now working against this man because his blood was very slow to clot.

The anesthetist had taken the necessary steps to reverse the medication, even though these measures potentially could allow a fatal clot to form in other parts of his body. Without it, however, more blood was going to ooze into the brain tissue and that was disastrous. Time was of the essence in order to get a clamp on the ruptured artery and stop the bleeding. With his residency and fellowship complete, Isaac now had clinical expertise and technical skill to correct this situation. He knew he had the ability to spare Mrs. Johnson the agony of making the decision he had been forced to make for his wife.

"Ten blade," Isaac quietly said as he extended his hand, palm down, fingers curved into position and ready to grasp the scalpel. He sensed, rather than felt, the cold metal scalpel passed cautiously from the scrub tech's experienced hand into his own. His fingers reflexively closed around the handle of the shiny instrument, so sharp it could split a human hair, let alone slice through human flesh. He refused to see anything human before him, only white scalp which glared up at him through a small, round window in the blue drapes which hid from view any evidence of the living being beneath them.

This time, clinical detachment and complete dissociation from the humanity on the table in front of him was an absolute necessity; otherwise, he would be unable to cut through the living, feeling tissue in front of him, or to perform the invasive surgery necessary to save this patient's life.

As Isaac pulled the scalpel across the scalp, blood welled up in its wake, and the intern quickly blotted it away to give Isaac a clear view of his operative field. He continued on through layers of tissue and then reached down to peel back the scalp and revealed pie skull which glistened up at him. He would have to saw through solid bone to expose the organ that ruled all living beings and governed thought, emotion, movement- all things that make each human being the unique individual he or she is. The CAT scan glared at Isaac from the bank of lights, and the shadows of the massive bleed taunted him and dared him to try to intervene. Unless the pressure of all that blood was relieved soon, Mr. Johnson would be catching an express train to the hereafter.

Isaac's beloved Zayde had told him once when he was a very young child that the purity of a person's soul would guarantee his place in heaven. Since Zayde could never be more specific as to the soul's location in the body, Isaac envisioned it to lay deep within the brain, inaccessible to the world, unlikely to escape with a routine appendectomy, or to be dislodged by a sneeze. Now years later, as he performed surgeries and assumed the role of miracle worker, he half expected a beam of pure white light or a puff of silver smoke as the soul freed itself and floated upward, the sure sign of a well-earned ticket to Heaven. He felt a brief but distinct flash of relief at its absence, as if maybe it meant it wasn't this patient's "time."

Without a word, Isaac handed the scalpel back to the scrub tech. A brief acknowledgment of the fact that he, a mere mortal, could wipe out years of violin lessons, conscious recollection of a lover's touch or the memory of the taste of a freshly baked apple pie with one false move flashed through his mind. Isaac then felt the scrub tech place the bone saw in his hands and he handed it over to the intern who began the laborious task of sawing through the skull.

He watched the intern lean into the task as the saw cut through the skull with a high-pitched shriek, then it halted abruptly as the resistance of bone gave way to the tense layer of Dura mater below, now stretched tautly by the hemorrhage below the gray membrane. Isaac picked up his scalpel again and gently cut through the tough layer which was meant to protect the brain from invasion. Fresh, bright red blood gushed uncontrollably into the surgical field and obliterated his view. The level of tension in the operating room skyrocketed to an almost palpable level.

"Get that blood pressure down, I can't see a damn thing," he stated calmly to the anesthetist and then waited for quickly administered intravenous medication to decrease the patient's blood pressure and slow the gush of blood into the operative field.

Although no one in the operating room saw evidence of the panic that raced through Isaac's body at that moment, his own heart pounded so hard he could hear the blood rush in his ears. He stuffed the gaping hole he had just created with more gauze and waited for the medication to work.

As the bleeding slowed to a slight trickle, another vision of Faith lying in the ICU filled his mind. Isaac whispered a silent prayer, "Please Faith, please help me help this man. Don't let me condemn his wife to the life I've been living."

He allowed his memories just one more brief moment in consciousness but then pushed them farther and farther away until Faith slipped from awareness. Isaac enlarged the incision and probed more deeply as he continued his quest for the small weak-walled bleb which had formed on the walls of the artery and then had burst.

Meticulously and painstakingly slowly, Isaac dissected through the gelatinous, gray matter of the brain. He avoided some blood vessels and cauterized others. At one point, a circulating nurse stood behind Isaac and whispered to him, then stepped back so Isaac could extend his arms to the scrub nurse who wrapped a sterile towel around his gloved hands. Then, he turned back to the circulator and took a few steps away from the table. She pushed his mask aside and then held a glass of orange juice with a straw up to his mouth so that he could gulp the ice-cold liquid. Isaac remained in place for another quick moment while she mopped the perspiration from his face before she replaced the mask.

Isaac didn't have to ask when he resumed his position at the head of the table. Focused solely on his patient, he held his hand out and the scrub nurse handed him his surgical instruments. He bent his head and got back to work.

After what seemed like an eternity, Isaac paused, and the intern leaned forward to peer into the wound. "See that pulsation? That's it, that's the source of bleeding. He must have some clot sealing off the rupture, so let's get a clamp on it before it blows again."

As Isaac began to ease the clamp around the vessel, he meticulously avoided any unnecessary movement that might jar the aneurysm and break the clot free. The intern abruptly yelled, "Oh, shit," and a spurt of blood showered the front of his gown.

The torrent of blood was too heavy, too fast, and it obliterated Isaac's view. The intern packed gauze sponges into the wound as Isaac requested more fresh frozen plasma and a unit of packed red blood cells.

Isaac looked up at the clock, shocked to see that he had been operating for over five hours and then focused once again on his patient's enemy. This elusive menace had lurked deep within Faith's brain and brutally, it had murdered her. He was confronting the enemy head-on now, and he would be damned if it would murder again.

Chapter 48

"Alright, folks, thanks for your efforts, we're done here." Isaac stepped back from the surgical table and arched his back, then rolled his head side to side with a long and very deep sigh.

He was exhausted and physically drained by the stress of a long, tedious, anxiety-ridden surgery. All he wanted to do at this point was go home, go to bed, and pull the covers over his head. The outcomes of emergent surgeries such as this were rarely positive. Patients frequently were left paralyzed, speechless, or comatose; many died during surgery if they even survived the ambulance ride to the hospital. He snapped off his bloody gloves and vigorously rubbed his face as he unsuccessfully attempted to scrub away the stressors and exhaustion of this surgery. The intern stopped Isaac before he could leave the main OR and stood in front of him as he shifted from foot to foot.

"If you'd like, Dr. Goldman, I can go talk to the family."

Isaac sighed and looked at the intern with a small smile that did not reach his eyes. "No, I'll go. This was a long case, and I'm used to this. You aren't. Go get some sleep."

Relief flooded the intern's face as Isaac walked into the locker room. He changed out of his scrubs and into clean clothing and shoes that were not spattered with his patient's blood. He was determined to spare Mr. Johnson's family one more moment of the interminable wait he had lived through while waiting for any sign that would determine Faith's fate, and he hurried to find them.

Good news or bad, no textbook, no journal articles, no medical school lecture could ever prepare a doctor to comprehend what people suffer during the illness of a loved one.

"I'll never understand how you did it, Faith," Isaac thought to himself as he walked the long corridor to the Surgical Waiting Room. He stepped into a room that was eerily silent despite the number of people who awaited news of their loved ones. Isaac noted the pairs of anxious, hopeful eyes that turned towards him as they looked for the familiar face of their loved one's surgeon and anticipated with hope the good news of a surgery successfully completed and a full recovery soon to follow. Others sat with hollow eyes and clenched hands, fingers white-knuckled as nails dug into palms, as their hearts threatened to break from the harsh news they prayed not to hear.

In one corner of the room sat a lone, elderly woman. One wrinkled hand nervously clutched the collar of her coat around her neck. Her other hand gripped a simple plastic Rosary given to her by a hospital chaplain who had stopped by to offer prayer and consolation. She held it tightly between fingers that moved from bead to bead as her soundless, white lips whispered desperate prayers and pleaded for mercy. She looked up at Isaac with heavy-lidded eyes and froze, mid-prayer. Isaac recognized her expression all too well because a similar facade had stared back at him from the bathroom mirror every morning since Faith had died.

Memories crashed back and a tsunami of profound sadness washed over him. He remembered the endless hours at Faith's bedside as he whispered the prayers of a desperate husband who begged for his wife to be spared, for her to come home to him and their newborn daughter. Once again he felt the weight of isolation, desolation, and ultimately devastation as it pressed down on his shoulders and threatened to drop him to his knees.

Isaac's eyes met Mrs. Johnson's, and he saw himself. For the first time in his life, he understood. A wave of compassion washed over him, and all of a sudden, he understood exactly what had moved Faith to allow patients into her world because who better than she could understand the fear of what the future might hold? Now it was he who completely comprehended the agonizing emotional turmoil that Mrs. Johnson experienced because he had lived the same way and had felt it with his heart. Medical school had not prepared him for this, but Faith had. Slowly, the misery that had constricted his own emotions tightly into a hard-shelled knot blessedly fell away, and the Isaac he had allowed only Faith to see stepped forward.

The many days of speech rehearsals in the mirror, his ego, and many dreams of awards and accolades came forward out of the recesses of distant memory and conceded to Faith's humanity. Isaac allowed himself to embrace fully everything that had driven Faith, with warmth and support, to do everything in her power to make her patients' and their families' lives just a bit better. Faith had grasped onto that concept much sooner in life than most and subsequently, she had lived her life determined to spare other families as much of the agony she had endured as possible. Isaac had been shielded and protected from that anguish by a life completely free of sorrow, and he had been spared from ever having to beg for merciful relief from heartache and loss. Now, it was he who understood what it felt like to be crushed under the weight of heartbreak, to be broken by almost inconceivable grief. He was determined to spare Mrs. Johnson as much of that crushing heartache and agony as possible.

Isaac held his hand out to Mrs. Johnson. She grasped it tightly as she struggled to stand but then failed as her stiff knees buckled under the weight of the unknown. Her eyes searched his face, her thin lips clamped into a tremulous line of panic. Her other hand reached up to cover her mouth, physically holding back the sobs that threatened to break free. She knew her worst nightmare was about to come true, that she would live out the rest of her days alone, without her loving husband by her side. She braced herself against the devastating news she was about to hear and squeezed Isaac's hand until his fingers blanched as white as her own.

"What?" she whispered. "Please tell me, what?"

Isaac was momentarily unsure of how to begin, but then he sensed Faith so close to him, by his side, in his heart and in his soul. He heard her whisper, "I'm here, Isaac. Just tell her. It's OK."

Isaac eased himself into the chair beside Mrs. Johnson and smiled gently at her. Reassured that love would guide his words, he began to speak. "He's fine, Mrs. Johnson. Your husband is just fine. It took a little longer than we first anticipated, but we were able to clamp the artery and stop the bleeding. Everything we are seeing right now is very encouraging. Come with me; let's go see your husband."

Isaac walked with Mrs. Johnson hugged to his side and felt a warm and familiar rush of peace he hadn't felt in months, even as he felt the subtle whisper of Faith slip away. Isaac gave her memory a long and lingering hug, and then he tucked her away in his heart where she belonged. He released his pain and loss and replaced them with love and hope, for his and for Grace's future, in their place.

About The Author

Teresa Little Smith is a Nurse Practitioner, wife, and mother of two, and is thrilled to publish her debut novel, DNR: Love's Final Gift. Like her protagonist Faith, Teresa's mother died when she was 15. This life-changing event, plus witnessing her father's care for her mother throughout her illness, inspired her to become a nurse to care for people during the most trying times of their lives. Teresa spent many years in Critical Care and is now in Advanced Practice as a Palliative Care Nurse Practitioner. She educates her patients to live their best lives and stay out of the acute care arena and brings her care to them in their home. Teresa believes that a "Do Not Resuscitate" order is the most significant and heart-felt gift families can provide to their loved ones, and she strives to support them as they make that heartbreaking and final decision. Teresa lives in Connecticut with her husband and their two children, as well as a stubborn Corgi named Tzushi, and two cats who believe they rule the roost.